cold mercy
an avril dahl thriller
book three

L.T. Ryan

with
Biba Pearce

Copyright © 2025 by L.T. Ryan, Liquid Mind Media, LLC, & Biba Pearce. All rights reserved. No part of this publication may be copied, reproduced in any format, by any means, electronic or otherwise, without prior consent from the copyright owner and publisher of this book. This is a work of fiction. All characters, names, places and events are the product of the author's imagination or used fictitiously.

For information contact:

contact@ltryan.com

http://LTRyan.com

https://www.facebook.com/JackNobleBooks

avril dahl series

Cold Reckoning
Cold Legacy
Cold Mercy
Cold Witness

chapter
one

THE SUN HADN'T YET CLEARED THE RIDGE WHEN OLAV Bergvall stepped onto the ice.

The light was the color of pewter, dull and heavy, without warmth. A thin wind hissed across the frozen lake, skimming loose snow over the surface in whispering sheets. It looked like drifting ash, swept out here by some far away inferno.

Olav pulled his woolen cap lower over his ears and shifted the weight of the auger on his shoulder. He had been coming to Frostsjön every winter since he was a boy, when his father would bring him out at dawn with a thermos of coffee and a tin of cinnamon buns. His father's voice would rise above the wind, gruff but warm, telling him to keep the auger straight, to respect the ice, to listen for its moods. These days, Olav came alone. His father was gone, the bun tin long since rusted at the hinges, but the ritual had stuck.

The ice groaned under his boots as he walked, the deep, whale-low sound of water locked beneath, shifting restlessly underneath him. It never worried him. He knew this lake's moods, its safe routes, the way the wind scoured some patches bare while piling snow high in others. Frostsjön could be dangerous, yes, but not for him.

About fifty meters from the northern shore, he stopped. The spot felt right. Sheltered enough from the wind by a rise in the ice, but far from any tracks that might spook the fish. He knelt, set down his gear, and positioned the auger.

The first turn bit into the ice with a satisfying crunch. Olav worked steadily, arms pumping, boots braced. The rhythm was hypnotic: press, twist, pull. Ice shavings curled up in pale ribbons. The wind picked up, flattening them against his parka.

Halfway down, the auger caught. It couldn't be a rock. This part of the lake was flat-bottomed, composed of silt and sand. He adjusted his grip and tried again, forcing the blade, but it wouldn't give.

A frown creased his weathered face. He leaned over, peering into the half-drilled hole. At first, all he saw was cloudy ice, striated with air bubbles. Then, something... a blur beneath the surface.

He scraped at the edge with his glove, widening the opening as the wind burned his cheeks raw. His breath misted, then froze white in his beard. The shape resolved slowly, as if reluctant to be revealed, Pale, mottled flesh pressed against the underside of the ice. A lock of hair, darkened by water, drifting in frozen strands. And a scarf, frozen stiff, its ends splayed like brittle seaweed caught in a tide.

His stomach lurched.

He jerked back, sat hard on the ice. For a long moment, he could only stare at the hole, unable to force breath past the tightness in his chest. He had pulled strange things from Frostsjön before—a rusted bicycle, a deer carcass tangled in weeds, once even an outboard motor—but never this.

His pulse hammered in his throat.

He forced himself forward again, peering down through the milky ice.

The woman's face was turned away, but the curve of her cheek, the fragile arch of her ear, were clear enough. Frost had built up along her skin, the same hoarfrost that rimed the lake, blurring the line between human and frozen water. She looked less like a person than a figure carved from the ice itself.

For a long moment, the only sound was the wind and the distant groan of the ice shifting. With clumsy fingers, he fumbled for his phone. It took two tries to get it out of his pocket, his gloves too thick, his hands shaking too badly. He dialed 112.

The operator's voice came through, flat and precise, the Swedish vowels clipped.

"Emergency services. What is your location?"

"Frostsjön," he said, his voice raw. "Outside Hälsingland. On the ice... near the north shore. I–" He stopped, swallowing hard. "I've found... a body. Under the ice. A woman."

There was a pause, the faint scratch of keys. "Is she alive?"

Olav's eyes lingered on the pale cheek beneath the ice. The stillness there was absolute.

"No. She's long gone."

"Stay where you are," the operator instructed. "Polisen are on their way. Do not attempt to retrieve the body yourself."

As if he would.

He slid the phone back into his pocket but didn't move. The urge to retreat was strong, to flee back across the groaning lake to the safety of the tree line, but he couldn't leave her alone, out here in the middle of the icy lake.

The wind shifted, colder now, cutting through him. Olav shuddered, but he knew it wasn't entirely from the cold. He tugged his coat tighter around him and took a steadying breath, the frigid air burning his lungs.

He straightened, eyes scanning the shore. No one else was out here. No one to witness what he had found. The snow hissed over the ice, erasing his tracks almost as soon as they were made.

Somewhere beyond the trees, the rescue crews would be mobilizing, pulling on boots, readying snowmobiles. They would be here soon.

But until they arrived, it was just him, the lake, and the woman in the ice—suspended between worlds, waiting to be claimed.

chapter
two

Three weeks earlier...

THE NEWSROOM WAS ALMOST SILENT. Only the faint hum of the radiators and the occasional groan of the old building carried through the empty floor.

Lara Berglund sat hunched over her keyboard, a pool of lamplight casting everything beyond into shadow. Her desk looked chaotic, but only by design. If anyone came snooping, they'd see a collage of clippings. Regional headlines, train timetables, census figures, even a flyer for a youth job fair. To her editor, it would look like she was dutifully pulling together her "Youth Exodus" feature.

The truth sat in her leather-bound notebook, hidden in plain sight among the rest.

On the surface, her assignment was routine. A thousand words on why Norrdal's twenty-somethings fled for Stockholm and Gothenburg. The reasons were obvious. Lack of jobs, lack of nightlife, lack of anything. The statistics spelled it out. This was an aging town, full of retirees and young families.

At twenty-six, Lara was the exception. She wouldn't be here either if the *Chronicle* hadn't given her a job as their Features Reporter. Fresh out of college, it afforded her the opportunity to gain experience as an investigative reporter. That was her goal, after all. Not that there was very much to investigate.

But that all changed when Freya disappeared.

Lara studied the photograph in her hand. It was of Freya and herself, taken a couple of years earlier. They'd gone up to the lake for a weekend. They both enjoyed hiking, and the area was so beautiful at that time of year. Her eyes stung as she stared at it. They looked so happy. So carefree. Summer flowers adorned the grassy banks, and the sky was cobalt blue above them.

Freya, with her laughing smile and wild, copper hair. Freya, who had vanished last winter without saying goodbye.

The official story was that she had left town. Packed her suitcase, written a short note, and caught the train out of Norrdal to start over somewhere new. That was the story her parents were told, the line the Polisen had accepted.

But Lara had her doubts.

She pulled the folded sheet from her notebook, flattening it carefully on her desk. Sighing, she read it for the hundredth time, even though she knew the words backwards.

DEAR *MAMMA*,

I've had enough of Norrdal so I'm leaving. I've met someone, and I'm going to live with him in Stockholm. I'm sure you won't miss me that much.

Freya

IT WAS FREYA'S HANDWRITING. She recognized the looping letters, the careless slant. But the words didn't sound like her.

Freya had never been close to her parents. Not to her mother, and certainly not to her stepfather. Her real father had died when she was still a baby, and by the time her mother remarried almost ten years later, there were two new children in the house. Freya had always felt like she'd been an afterthought, an accessory to the family. During their school years, she had practically lived at Lara's, escaping the constant reminder that she didn't belong.

They'd drifted apart at college, each caught up in their own lives. Yet somehow, both had found their way back to Norrdal in their twenties. Freya, because she never seemed to find her footing anywhere else. Lara, because the Chronicle had offered her a job.

Lara pressed her fingers to her temples. How many times had she gone over the same ground? The bars Freya had favored. The friends she sometimes saw. The men she'd dated. None of it led anywhere. On paper, it still looked as though Freya had simply boarded a train and left town.

Behind her, the newsroom clock ticked half past six. Most of her colleagues had left at five. Only the newspaper's editor, Eva, and Fred, one of the graphic designers, were still here.

Eva Strömberg strolled over on her way out. Lara hastily closed her notebook.

"Don't stay too late, Lara."

"I won't."

She paused at her desk. "How's the Exodus article coming on?"

"Nearly done," Lara lied, forcing a smile.

A nod of approval. "Send me the 1,000 words as soon as it's finished."

She gave a tense nod. "Will do." She'd have to pick this up later.

The graphic designer packed up and left soon after.

"You do know we don't get paid overtime," he joked as he walked past her desk.

Very funny. She pulled a face and got back to work.

There was no point in going home. She was meeting a source tonight. Nothing to do with Freya's disappearance. It was for one of the other articles she was writing—a feature-length piece on a municipal contract scandal. It was more in line with the type of investigative work she thrived on.

Still, she couldn't shift her focus away from Freya's disappearance. She reached for her phone, the screen lighting her tired face. At the top of her messages was the one she never deleted. A year old now, but she opened it every night like a ritual.

. . .

Cold Mercy

Meet me later. Svartälgen. 10 p.m.

Freya's last message before she'd disappeared, asking to meet at Svartälgen—the Black Elk—a local bar in town.

Lara set the phone down, staring at it as if the words might rearrange themselves and reveal some hidden truth she had missed. The wind rattled the frosted windows, and for a moment, the whole building seemed to shiver.

She pulled her scarf off the back of her chair and wrapped it around her shoulders, fighting a sudden chill. Her mind drifted back to that night. What had she missed? What had Freya wanted to tell her?

She'd arrived at the bar, but her friend hadn't been there. The barman said she hadn't been in at all, which was strange. Freya worked at a nearby restaurant, so they often met at the popular bar for a drink in the evenings. It was a chance to catch up and gossip about what was happening in their small town.

Confused, Lara had walked the two blocks to Freya's apartment. She'd lived above a bottle store, which could be rowdy at night, but the rent was cheap. When nobody had answered the door, she'd gotten worried.

It was when her mother had said she hadn't heard from her either that Lara had become alarmed. The Polisen wouldn't do anything until the following day. As nice as Polisassistent Erik Lundgren was, he was a stickler for protocol. Still new to the Norrdal Polisstation, he'd been terrified of making a mistake, and with his Kommissarie away for the weekend, he wasn't going to budge. Two whole days passed before Freya's mother finally reported her daughter missing on Monday morning.

Lara closed her eyes, feeling the familiar frustration build. Precious time wasted.

She checked her watch. An hour until she was due to meet her contact. Just enough time to rattle off a rough 1,000 words. She could fine-tune them tomorrow, before Eva got in.

At seven o'clock, Lara packed up and left the office. Outside, Norrdal lay in icy silence, the snow-packed streets glowing faintly under the streetlamps. She trudged the few blocks home, freshened up, then left to meet her source. As per their agreement, she didn't take her phone or notebook. He would only speak to her off the record, and that meant no recording devices—not even the pen-and-paper kind.

That was fine with her. Normally, she wouldn't meet a stranger without her phone, but this was at a crowded bar, at nine o'clock at night, and very close to home. The barman, Igor, was her friend, and she usually knew more than a handful of punters.

She was quite safe.

She opened the door and stepped inside. The bar was full—not bad for a weeknight. Lara scanned the crowd, her gaze falling on a man sitting at a table at the back. He wore a black shirt, jeans, and worn, leather boots. His coat was draped over the back of his chair. Even with his back to her, she recognized him.

Walking over, she took a deep breath before slipping into the vacant chair opposite him.

"Thank you for meeting me."

chapter
three

THE SERIOUS CRIMES DIVISION WAS BASED ON THE THIRD floor of the Stockholm Police Headquarters building. Despite the gravitas of the title, it was a small space, crammed with desks, printers, telephones, and the overriding smell of coffee.

The windows were closed, and the heating was on low. Because of the dimness outside, every light on the floor was on. Being mid-winter, the sun only rose for a few hours each day, and even then, it sat low on the horizon, as if reluctant to raise its head. Maybe it was afraid of what it might see.

At least she had her own desk now. She couldn't believe it had been almost a year since she'd quit her job with the FBI and returned to Stockholm. After the Terra Nova case had ended, she'd taken some personal time and gone back to America, packed up her apartment, and given it to a real estate agent to rent out. There was no point in leaving it standing empty, especially since she had no plans to go back there anytime soon. That chapter of her life was closed—for now.

After returning to Stockholm, she'd done some much-needed renovations to her father's—now her—house in Täby, a municipality located northeast of Stockholm. Krister had helped her. She glanced up as he beckoned her over.

Krister Jansson. Her colleague, childhood friend, and next-door neighbor. In reality, he was much more than that, but she'd avoided analyzing that further. Strong emotions were not something she was particularly good at. It was like her brain shut down when anything got too intense.

It made her a great detective, but a lousy partner. Why Krister put up with her, she had no idea. She was just pleased that he did.

"What's up?" she asked.

He shoved his phone back into his pocket and nodded toward the back of the office. "Sundström wants to see us."

"What about?" She didn't like surprises. In her experience, nothing good came out of a visit to the *Kriminalkommissarie's* office.

He shrugged. "Let's go find out."

Sundström's door was open, and he beckoned them in as soon as he saw them. They stepped inside and stood in front of his desk.

"Sit." He motioned to the two chairs facing him.

This room made Avril feel like she was at school, being reprimanded in the principal's office. Maybe it was the certificates on the walls, the austere, uncluttered desk, or their boss's stiff expression, but the whole room seemed to vibrate with tension.

"How's that gang-related shooting progressing?" he asked Krister. Avril frowned. Sundström received the weekly case briefs. He knew full well where things stood with the indictment preparation.

"We're good," Krister answered anyway, as she'd known he would. "We've filed the supplementary witness statements, the forensics are processed, and the prosecutor's office has the ballistics report. We're just pinning down the timeline."

"Good." Sundström leaned back, but his gaze moved to Avril. "Which means you won't mind if I release Dahl for a few weeks."

Krister opened his mouth to ask why, but Sundström held up his hand.

"Something's come up in Norrdal. They've got a dead girl in the ice. Murdered. And they need our help."

"Norrdal?" Avril frowned, wracking her brain, but she'd been away too long.

"Five hours north," Krister supplied, his brow creasing. "Middle of nowhere. Västerbotten, isn't it?"

"Jämtland," Sundström corrected. "They've got a police station with three staff. The officer in charge is Kommissarie Hans Bergqvist, and there are two *polisassistenter*. One's barely out of training, the other's a research assistant who covers admin. They don't have the manpower or experience to run a homicide properly."

Krister exhaled while Avril studied Sundström. "When was the body found?"

"Yesterday. A fisherman spotted it under the ice at Frostsjön. They aren't sure how long she'd been in the water, and there was no ID on her. Her body has been transferred to the regional mortuary in Östersund. The autopsy is scheduled for Friday."

Avril knew the first forty-eight hours of a murder investigation were crucial. Every day that slipped by would make it more difficult to find witnesses, evidence that hadn't been compromised, footage of the victim, and so on.

She exchanged a glance with Krister.

He cleared his throat. "Do you think it's wise that Avril goes by herself? I mean, Odin is still out there somewhere."

Odin. The mysterious leader of Terra Nova, and the man who'd escaped her—and the Swedish police—vanishing into thin air after diving into a canal near the Stockholm International Convention Center earlier this year. His final words still haunted her.

I'll be seeing you, Avril.

"If Odin hasn't come to exact his revenge by now, I doubt he's going to," Sundström said, arching his bushy eyebrows. "At any rate, he'll never find her up there. We won't tell anyone where she's gone, and Norrdal is almost too small to find on a map."

Great. She felt like she was being sent to the North Pole.

"I suggest you get up there as soon as possible," Sundström said gruffly. He too knew how important it was that they didn't waste any more time.

Beside her, Krister sighed, already resigned. Avril saw there was no getting out of this. One of the main reasons she'd agreed to stay in Stockholm was to work with Krister. Instead, she'd spent several weeks undercover, then summer in the States, and now she was being sent to a tiny speck on the map five hours north of Stockholm.

Still, she supposed a homicide investigation was more exciting than a gang shooting they'd already tied up. Krister and his team could handle the rest without her. Her time would be better spent helping solve this poor girl's murder.

"Okay," she said, standing up. Krister glanced up at her, the muscle in his jaw tensing.

"I'll drive up there today."

Sundström gave a pleased nod. "Good. I'll let them know when they can expect you."

chapter
four

THE ROAD NARROWED THE FARTHER NORTH SHE DROVE. FOR hours, the E4 had stretched out ahead of her in a long, monotonous ribbon of tarmac, bordered by skeletal birch trees and endless dark forest. Now, as she followed the smaller county road toward Norrdal, even that sense of connection to the world fell away.

Snow pressed in on both sides, banks piled high from weeks of plowing. The forest rose close and dark, spruce trees bowed beneath layers of white. Occasionally, a break in the forest revealed frozen marshland or a glazed lake, its surface scoured by wind.

The sky was the color of slate—flat and impenetrable. In Stockholm, winter skies had at least been tinged with light. Here, five hours north, it was as if the sun didn't bother at all. The light never grew warm. It stayed cold and metallic, reflecting off the snow until everything blurred into shades of gray and white.

Her windshield wipers squeaked against the glass, fighting the powder the wind whipped across the road.

Avril tightened her grip on the wheel, shoulders aching from the long drive. She'd stopped once for coffee and fuel in a town she couldn't remember the name of. Beyond that, there'd been nothing but road, trees, and the steady ache of silence.

This was the kind of silence she remembered from her childhood, before she'd ever considered joining the Swedish police, let alone Quantico. A silence that pressed in on you, that made your own breathing sound too loud. She'd tried the radio, but had grown sick of it 90 miles back.

Finally, a hand-painted sign loomed out of the snowdrift. *Norrdal 5 km.* She exhaled, leaning forward as though the extra inches might get her there faster.

The road wound downhill into a valley, the forest breaking apart into clusters of timber houses and barns, their roofs heavy with snow. Smoke rose in thin plumes from chimneys. The dim lights of the town glowed in the half-light, scattered along the frozen river that cut a dark line through the white.

SHE PULLED up outside the Norrdal Police Station, a squat brick building half-buried in snowdrifts. Its windows glowed yellow against the deepening darkness around her. A battered sign out front bore the word *Polis*, its blue paint faded from exposure to the elements.

Avril killed the engine and sat for a moment, stretching her neck. Finally, she was here. Leaving her service weapon, which was locked in the safe box in the trunk, her suitcase and purse in the vehicle—there'd be time to take them to the guesthouse later—she climbed out into the biting air.

Her core temperature plummeted as soon as she was out of the warm interior. Holy crap, it was cold. It had to be close to zero out here.

She took off her glasses and rubbed her eyes, gritty and dry from the long drive. Then, slipping them back on, she gazed around at the starkness of the town.

Norrdal was exactly what she'd expected. A scattering of shops lined the main street, their interiors dark at this hour. She spotted a grocery store, a petrol station, and a pharmacy that still had their lights on.

Across the square, a café's faded neon sign flickered in the gloom, its windows steamed from within. Beyond that, little else. The place had the hollowed-out feel of an insular community that kept to itself, particularly this time of year.

Taking a deep breath, she climbed the salt-streaked steps of the police station. A pair of municipal snowplows were parked haphazardly to the side. Drawing her oversized coat tighter around herself, she exhaled, braced, and strode toward the entrance.

Avril pushed open the door and stepped into the harsh, fluorescent light of the station. A blast of hot air hit her, making her eyes water. Blinking, she peered through her misted-up glasses. A reception desk sat just to the side of the door. The slim blonde woman sitting there glanced up as she entered.

"Can I help you?"

Opposite the entrance was a line of plastic chairs for visitors, above which hung a corkboard with community notices pinned to it—a photograph of a lost pet, a church bake sale. There was also a *Missing* poster of a young woman with blue eyes and a pensive smile.

The victim?

Avril turned to the young woman. The name card on her desk said *Polisassistent* Maja Ekström.

"Er, yes. I'm Avril Dahl from the Swedish Police Authority in Stockholm. Is Kommissarie Bergqvist here?"

The young woman's eyes grew wide, and she jumped out of her chair. "Of course. Sorry. I'll just go and get him."

Avril didn't know what the woman was sorry for, but the polisassistent left her standing at the reception desk and hurried to a door situated at the back of the bullpen.

The main bullpen area held three desks pushed against opposite walls, each piled with case files, maps, and outdated desktop PCs. There were two windows, but they were streaked with ice and impossible to see out of.

Ekström knocked, then—when a deep voice answered—poked her head around the door and whispered something like, *"That FBI agent from Stockholm is here."*

There was a curt reply and the sound of a chair scraping against the wooden floor. Ekström hurried back, a polite smile covering obvious nerves. Avril supposed a new face—especially one from Stockholm's Serious Crimes Division—was bound to unsettle them.

Sundström had said there were three officers stationed here, but she couldn't see the third. Maybe he was out or had left for the day. It was after five o'clock in the evening. Except, with a recent murder, she would have expected them all to be on duty, working the case.

"He says to go through." Ekström nodded toward the open door.

As Avril walked toward the Kommissarie's office, her gaze fell on a whiteboard on the wall containing several photographs. A frozen lake, a hole cut through the ice, and the pale profile of a young woman, hair fanned out around her. Squinting, she tried to get a better look, but there was no time. Bergqvist was waiting.

Avril pushed open his office door and stepped inside. Bergqvist was on his feet, expecting her. A head taller than her—around 6'1"—he looked like he kept himself in shape. Broad shoulders, trim waist, blond hair with touches of gray at the temples. Late forties, maybe.

He strode around the desk, arm extended. "Special Agent Dahl, it's good to meet you."

His hand was cool, his grip firm.

Was it?

She wasn't sure. His deep-set brown eyes lacked warmth, even though he was smiling.

"Avril, please. I'm not with the FBI anymore."

Her gaze flicked around the room as he nodded. The office was orderly, but not neat. A stack of case files on the desk, a pot of pencils beside the phone, a coffee mug on a coaster.

On the wall hung a glass case of brightly colored fishing flies, their barbed hooks arranged in neat rows like tiny works of art. On the shelf were several framed photographs: a commendation, a photograph of Bergqvist shaking hands with someone Avril didn't recognize, and a picture of him in waders by a lake, holding up a large pike for the camera.

He didn't offer up his first name, even though she knew it to be Hans. She'd managed a quick look at his bio before she'd left. It was important to know who she was dealing with.

Kommissarie Hans Bergqvist had been in charge of the Norrdal Polisstation for twelve years, but he'd been working here for eighteen. He'd started as a polisassistent, then been promoted to Kommissarie six years later. By all accounts, he was a capable leader—with no marks on his service record, no internal investigations, no complaints.

"Welcome to Norrdal. Have you checked in at your guesthouse yet?" This town didn't have hotels. Not much need for them.

"I prefer to get started," she said, more sharply than she intended. "Have you ID'd the victim yet?"

He studied her for a moment, then walked around his desk. "We have. Come with me and I will brief you on what we know so far."

Avril followed him out of the office and back to the whiteboard. Another officer had appeared in the meantime, seated at one of the desks—a young man with earnest eyes set in a boyish face, still carrying the unease of someone new to the job. Very blond, with tentative stubble on his chin. Avril guessed he had to be in his mid-twenties, but he could have passed for eighteen.

"This is Polisassistent Lundgren," Bergqvist said, pointing. "And you've met Ekström." While Ekström gave her a wide smile, Lundgren offered a quick nod and went back to what he was doing.

Avril wondered if he had a problem with her being there. She turned back to the board. "What have you got?"

Bergqvist cleared his throat. "The victim is Lara Berglund. She went missing a week ago after meeting someone at a local bar. We don't know who. She was reported missing by her boyfriend, Tarek Khalil."

Avril nodded, noting that the boyfriend's name wasn't Swedish. In a rural village this size, that was surprising, but she didn't comment. There would be time to dig into the victim's friends and family later. Right now, she just needed the basic details.

"Who found her?"

"An ice fisherman." Bergqvist frowned and shook his head.

She studied his reaction over her glasses. "What?"

He gave a soft snort. "What are the chances? The guy drills one hole—maybe twenty or thirty centimeters wide. He could've picked anywhere on that frozen lake, but of all the spots, he happened to bore down exactly where she was trapped beneath." He nodded toward the photograph on the board.

Avril frowned. It was a startling coincidence. "Have you checked out the fisherman?"

"Ja. He was the one who called emergency services. I spoke to him myself—he was shocked by the discovery. I doubt he had anything to do with it. He lives in Hälsingland, close to Frostsjön. Retired forestry worker. Been fishing that lake all his life. Said he didn't even know the victim."

In that case, it was unlikely he was involved. As Bergqvist said, just a bizarre coincidence. "Do we know how long she'd been in the water?"

Bergqvist shook his head. "Not yet. The crime-scene techs secured what they could, but there's no local pathology unit. We had to transfer her down to Östersund. Autopsy is booked for Friday morning."

Avril knew that too—she'd just been wondering if there'd been a preliminary report by a duty doctor or anyone who'd taken a look at the body. Obviously not. Things didn't work the same way in rural environments like Norrdal.

Unfortunately, in cases like this—as Avril knew only too well—the victim was killed soon after being abducted, but Avril wasn't about to assume anything. Grimacing in frustration, she studied the photograph of the pale face, strands of frozen hair, and the red scarf. The victim's eyes were closed, making her appear peaceful. The freezing temperatures had preserved her body, so there was very little decomposition and no obvious swelling or discoloration.

"Do we know how she died, at least?"

"The crew that pulled her out of the water said it looked like she'd been strangled. There were deep bruises on her neck. That has not been confirmed, however."

"Got it." At least that was something to go on. "Do we have a photograph?"

Lundgren cleared his throat. "They're all on the drive, Special Agent Dahl."

"It's Avril. And could you print out one of the markings on her neck and pin it to the board?" She'd get access to the drive in due course.

The polisassistent glanced at Bergqvist, who gave a slight nod. Avril realized she probably should have cleared it with him first, but she wasn't known for her tact. The officer had done the right thing by deferring to his superior.

Lundgren turned back to his computer. "Of course."

While they waited, Avril went through the basic questions. "Have you spoken to the boyfriend?"

"Ja. He came in this morning. Wanted to know if the body found at the lake was Lara's. He identified her through the photographs." Bergqvist gestured toward the board.

"Poor man was devastated," Ekström added, and Bergqvist glanced up, as if surprised she'd spoken.

"I'll have to re-interview him," Avril said, then realized how that might come across. "For my own benefit."

Bergqvist didn't object.

"What about her family? Parents, siblings?"

"Not yet." He frowned. "We only identified her this morning."

"Of course." That would have been top of her list. She would have expected a police officer of Bergqvist's pedigree to be more proactive. Or maybe they'd been waiting for her to arrive.

"Any friends? In a small town like this, everyone must know everyone else's business."

"She worked at a local newspaper," Ekström provided helpfully. It seemed she'd finally found her voice. "The *Norrdal Chronicle*."

Avril turned to her. "Good. We can go there and talk to her colleagues. They might know who she was meeting." She turned back to Bergqvist. "How did you know she went to meet someone?"

"Boyfriend told us," he replied.

Avril frowned. "Does he know where? Or who she was meeting?"

"No, although we haven't officially interviewed him yet."

"Okay, that's something we need to do first thing tomorrow. I'll spend the evening reading the case notes. Can you print me out a copy?"

Bergqvist nodded to Ekström.

The woman hurried back to her desk, eager to please. Not a bad thing, but she needed to develop a bit of a backbone to survive this job.

"One last thing," Avril said, as Lundgren got up to fetch a color printout of the picture. "Was she sexually assaulted?"

Bergqvist shrugged. "We don't know yet. We'll have to wait for—"

Yeah, she got it. "The autopsy on Friday," she finished.

Bergqvist grunted.

Lundgren pinned the photograph on the board. Avril studied it, her gaze dropping to the purple bruises around the victim's neck. The markings were wide apart and large. A man's hands.

She drew in a breath, summoning up what they knew. Lara Berglund had gone to meet an unknown person at a bar, during which —or after which—she'd been kidnapped. A short time later, he—and she was pretty sure it was a *he*—had strangled her and disposed of her body in a lake several miles north of here. What was it called again? Frostsjön. *Frosty Lake.* How appropriate.

Lara worked at a newspaper, lived with her boyfriend, and her family was in town. Someone must know something. Tomorrow, she'd interview everyone who knew Lara and start piecing together to the final moments before her disappearance.

chapter
five

THE *NORRDAL CHRONICLE* WAS EASY ENOUGH TO FIND. The newspaper's offices occupied the ground floor of a squat brick building at the end of the main street, wedged between a bakery and a shuttered electronics shop. A faded brass plaque on the wall beside the door read *Norrdalsbladet*.

The sun hadn't even come up by the time Avril got there, so when she pulled the door open and stepped inside, the warmth hit her immediately. The dry, slightly stale air smelled of ink, old coffee, and paper. There was no real reception desk or anyone to greet her, so she stood inside the doorway and scanned the interior.

The newsroom stretched out in front of her. It was open plan, although not large. A dozen desks formed uneven rows, each piled with printouts, marked-up drafts, and coffee mugs. The rattle of an aging printer echoed somewhere in the background.

On one wall, pinned pages of the current week's edition had been laid out for review, headlines circled in red marker. A whiteboard stood nearby, crammed with scrawled story ideas and deadlines. She glanced at some of the topics: council budget vote, school closures, road accident on Route 84.

The atmosphere was tense and industrious. It wasn't yet nine o'clock but there were four reporters hunched over keyboards, the rhythmic tapping of their fingers filling the space. A phone rang but went unanswered. No one looked up at her right away, and she guessed it wasn't the sort of office that got many visitors.

Avril adjusted her scarf and took a step forward. Several eyes turned to her. Curious, cautious. She was a stranger in their world, an outsider—and they all knew it.

She spotted the editor's office at the far end. It was a glass-fronted room with Venetian blinds tilted half-closed, the light inside a little brighter than the rest of the newsroom. Before anyone could say anything, she marched through the rows of desks and knocked on the editor's door.

A female voice said, "Come."

Avril felt the gazes of the staff reporters on her back, but she ignored them, and opened the door.

Eva Strömberg was a slim, middle-aged woman with curious eyes, high cheekbones and shoulder-length dark hair streaked with silver. She wore it loose, which Avril thought made her look bohemian.

"We were wondering when you'd show up," she said, pushing her tall frame out of her desk chair.

Avril paused. "Excuse me?"

"Polisen. You're not from here, are you?"

"No." She moved forward and extended her hand. "Avril Dahl, from Stockholm's Serious Crimes Division."

"Ah." She gave a knowing nod. "How does Hans feel about you muscling in on his turf?"

"I, er—I don't know." Why did it matter? She was here. He needed her.

Eva gestured to the vacant chair opposite her. "Sit, please."

Avril sank down, admiring the woman's attire. She wore a dark gray poncho-style turtleneck with black, wide-legged trousers. It looked sophisticated, yet casual.

Avril was the first to admit she had no dress sense. She didn't have the time or inclination to read fashion magazines and had no interest in shopping. Her days at the FBI had been spent in dark skirt suits and white blouses, and in her downtime, she wore jeans and a jumper. Easy. Functional. Didn't require thinking about.

"I'm here to talk about—"

"Lara Berglund. Her body was discovered yesterday at Frostsjön, outside Hälsingland. Yes, we heard." She bit her lip, and Avril could tell she was holding back her emotions.

"I'm sorry for your loss," she said automatically.

"Thank you. She was a valued member of our team."

Avril looked around the office, at the photographs on the wall, a couple of framed certificates, a statuette on a shelf. "What was it Lara did for you?"

"She was our Features Writer. Lara came to us fresh out of college. She wanted to be an investigative reporter. I think she had big dreams of working for *The Guardian* in London, or *The New York Times*." She glanced down at her hands, her voice dropping. "Such a tragic loss."

Avril wasn't here to talk about Lara's hopes and dreams. She wanted to know who'd killed her.

"Was she working on anything in particular?" she asked.

"Lara had several projects she was working on," Eva said, pulling herself together. "Three that I know of. Those were the only ones with deadlines, anyway."

"Could you run me through them?" Avril took out her phone. "Do you mind if I record our conversation?"

Eva shook her head. "Go ahead."

Avril pressed record and set the device on the desk, while Eva bent down, opened a drawer and took out a stack of papers. "These files were on Lara's desk."

Avril frowned. She had hoped to go through Lara's desk herself, but Eva had pre-empted her.

"Okay." Avril sat back to listen.

Eva straightened the papers and spoke in a measured voice.

"The first was a piece on municipal contracts. She'd been digging into some irregularities in the council's procurement process. Road maintenance, waste collection, snow clearance, things like that. Lara thought there was favoritism in the awarding of contracts. She even mentioned kickbacks."

Avril filed the detail away. Small-town corruption was hardly unusual, but it could provoke strong reactions if exposed.

"The second," Eva continued, "was a logging company operating just outside town. There were claims of chemical run-off into the river system. Lara was looking into whether they'd falsified environmental reports to keep their license. She was tenacious about it. I know she requested records, interviewed locals, and tried to speak to insiders at the company."

"What about the third?" Avril asked.

"A human-interest piece. More of a feature than exposé. She was writing about the youth leaving Norrdal. Graduates heading to Stockholm, Uppsala, anywhere but here. It was personal for her, I think. She had a good friend who left to go live in the city just last year."

Avril leaned forward. "I'll need copies of all of her notes."

Eva stiffened. "These are *Chronicle* property. I can't just hand them over."

Avril kept her voice even. "Would it help if I got a warrant? If her work got her killed, these notes could be valuable evidence. You want us to follow every lead, don't you? Find out who killed Lara?"

Eva studied her, eyes narrowed. Eventually, she said, "I'll hand over Lara's notes, if you promise me an exclusive. Lara was a valued employee, as I said, and we'd like to be the ones to inform the public of the outcome of the investigation."

That sounded fair. Avril could get a warrant and take them anyway, but she didn't want to give Eva time to alter or destroy the notes.

"Okay, that's a deal. I will inform you myself once this case is concluded."

"Will you give me updates along the way?"

Avril shook her head. "You know I can't talk about an active investigation."

Eva sighed but slid the files across her desk to Avril. "It was worth a shot."

"Thank you." Avril left them where they were. She wasn't done yet. "Was Lara distracted at all in the days leading up to her disappearance? Did she appear anxious or uptight?"

Eva frowned. "Not that I noticed. You might want to speak to Frederick, the staff photographer. He knew her better than the rest of us. They worked closely together."

"Is he here? Could you ask him to join us?"

She nodded, picked up her cell phone and typed a message. Less than a minute later, the door opened and a young man with a shock of dark hair and at least a couple of days' worth of stubble stepped in. He had tired eyes behind a pair of heavy glasses and was dressed in a pale blue sweatshirt emblazoned with a wide-eyed anime fox.

"Fred, this is Kriminalinspektör Dahl from the Swedish Police. She wants to ask you some questions about Lara."

Fred shuffled closer and dug his hands into his pocket. "I saw her that night, before I left," he said, solemnly. "She was working late. She often worked late. I joked with her, told her we didn't get paid overtime."

"Did she say where she was going?"

He shook his head. "No, but then she wouldn't have. Lara kept her work close to her chest, you know? She wouldn't have told me if she was going to meet a source."

Avril bit back her frustration. Nothing was ever that easy. "Did she say anything about where she was going? Or why she was working late?"

"No, but I didn't talk to her for long. I teased her as I walked past her desk, then went out the door. I wish I had now." He glanced down at his shoes.

"How did she seem to you?" Avril asked. "Was she nervous at all? Worried? Concerned?"

"I—I don't think so. Like I said, we didn't talk for long, but she didn't seem any different than normal. She pulled a face at me before I left."

Avril scratched her head, frowning. That didn't sound like she was anxious or upset. She glanced at the stack of notes on the desk. Maybe the answer lay in those. If she'd left to meet a source, hopefully she'd documented it. They needed a lead. Something, no matter how tenuous.

"Okay, thank you, Fred," Avril said, and the man left his editor's office. Avril glanced up at Eva. "Do you mind if I go through Lara's desk?"

"No, but there isn't much there."

"Still, I'd like to check."

Eva got up. "I'll show you where it is."

Avril followed her out into the newsroom. Lara's desk was situated by a window that overlooked the street. It was misted up now, but in the summer months, it would have a bird's-eye view of what went on outside.

With Eva watching, she went through the desk. The drawers were neat, the surface bare. Nothing of value remained. She closed the last drawer and stood.

"I'll send someone over to collect her work hard drive," Avril told Eva.

Eva shook her head. "Lara didn't use our machines. She worked on her laptop, like many of our staff reporters. They're more mobile that way."

Avril glanced around. "Where is it now?"

Eva spread her hands. "Not here. She would have taken it with her when she left. Lara always had her laptop on her."

Avril glanced at the clock on the wall. Nearly a quarter to ten. She wanted to talk to Lara's boyfriend, but Bergqvist would be wondering what had happened to her. She hadn't told him she was heading here before work.

She ought to fill him in on what she'd discovered, before she went to question the boyfriend. This was his case, after all. She was just assisting.

Avril thanked Eva, and holding the notes tightly in her hand, walked back out into the brittle morning.

chapter six

"You went without consulting me?"

Bergqvist's voice was low but tight, the words clipped. He put his hands on his hips, and she could see the muscles in his jaw flexing. He was furious but trying to control it, conscious of the two younger officers watching from the side.

"I wanted to get a head start."

"This is still our investigation," he went on. "You can't just head off on your own and not tell me. We need to work as a team."

The silence that followed pressed down on her. The others were eyeing her, waiting for her response.

She wanted to say she was only doing what he should have done yesterday, but she bit her tongue. There was no point in causing any more animosity. She almost heard Krister's voice in her ear telling her to apologize. Smooth it over.

"I'm sorry." She forced herself to meet his gaze. "You're right. I should have checked in. At the very least, I should have told you where I was going."

Bergqvist's nostrils flared as he breathed out slowly, letting the anger drain. He gave a short nod. "I know you probably do things differently in Stockholm, but we work as a team here. What matters is we keep each other in the loop from here on."

She'd give him this one. It was his police station, after all.

"Agreed."

His posture eased. "Good. So, since you've already made the trip, why don't you update us on what you found?"

Avril gave a relieved nod. The tension had passed. They were still on the same side. Krister would be proud.

"Of course." She walked over to Ekström's desk and set the stack of documents down. The junior officer stared up at her with huge, gray-blue eyes. "These are the cases Lara Berglund was working on when she disappeared," Avril said, her finger still hovering over the top one. "Can you make copies of them?"

"You're thinking it might have been something she was working on that got her killed?" Bergqvist asked.

"We have to consider it. Lara Berglund was an investigative journalist. Her specialty was writing feature articles and exposés. Her editor told me she was working on some municipal scandal, as well as a potential environmental cover-up. Both the kind of stories that could rattle the wrong people."

"Do it," Bergqvist said to Ekström. "Make two sets and then scan them and store them on the drive."

She nodded, picked up the papers, and hurried over to the photocopier.

Avril looked at Bergqvist. "I would like to question Lara's boyfriend, Tarek Khalil. Do you want to come?"

He nodded. "Ja. Definitely. Lundgren, you're in charge till I get back."

"Yes, sir." He gave a pleased nod.

"Let's take the squad car," Bergqvist said, touching his pocket to feel for the keys. "I'll drive."

Avril nodded. He was desperate to assert some control over the investigation, no matter how small. It didn't matter to her who drove, as long as she got to talk to Tarek Khalil.

"If Lara's laptop is at her house, we need to take it into evidence," she pointed out. "Her editor said she took it with her when she left the office on the night she disappeared. It may contain information on her cases. Names of sources, that kind of thing."

"I've got evidence bags in the car," he said, heading for the door.

Cold Mercy

Avril followed him out into the frigid mid-morning air. The sky hadn't brightened much in the last hour. A pale grey glow fanned out in the east where the sun skimmed the horizon, but the streetlamps still burned, joined by the glow of shopfronts and flickering neon signs. Cars slid past on the wet road, their headlights casting long orange beams through the dimness.

Lara's house was tucked away on a narrow side street just off the town center, only a few minutes' walk from the *Chronicle*. The neighborhood was a cluster of older wooden houses, built close together, with sagging fences and small front gardens now hidden under a crust of snow. Lara's place was one of the more modest ones, painted pale yellow, though the color was fading.

Bergqvist went up the short path, boots crunching over the ice, and knocked on the door. Three firm raps, evenly paced.

After a brief pause, it opened and a slender man stood in the doorway, his face drawn with fatigue, short, black afro mussed, and eyes sunken from too little sleep.

"Sorry to disturb you, Tarek," Bergqvist said. "But we need to ask you some questions about Lara. Do you mind if we come in?"

Tarek's eyes drifted to Avril.

"Excuse me," Bergqvist said. "This is Avril Dahl from Stockholm's Serious Crimes Division. She's assisting us with the investigation."

Avril bet he added that part just so there was no mistake.

"I'm sorry for your loss," she said softly.

He lifted his gaze to hers. "Thank you."

Tarek wore sweatpants and a faded hoodie, his bare feet braced against the cold tiles just inside. She noticed his eyes were reddened, like he'd been crying.

He held the door open. "Come in. Please excuse the mess, I haven't felt like cleaning."

"Don't worry," Bergqvist said with a wave of his hand. "We understand."

Tarek gestured to a dining table in the living area and they all sat down. Avril didn't want to wait for Bergqvist to take the lead, so she got straight to it. "Tarek, did you see Lara the night she disappeared?"

Bergqvist's lips thinned, but he didn't comment.

He shook his head. "No, I wasn't here when she came home."

Avril frowned. "So she did come home?"

"Yeah, her backpack was dumped in the hall and she'd changed her clothes."

She leaned forward. "Does that mean you have her laptop?"

"It should still be in her backpack."

"We're going to need to take it with us," Bergqvist said.

Tarek gave a little shrug.

"Do you know where she went?" Avril asked.

Another dismal shake of his head.

Avril studied him, but she couldn't discern anything suspicious. He just looked sad. "She didn't tell you she was going out?"

"She told me that morning, yeah, but not where."

"Is that unusual?" Avril asked.

"Not if she was meeting a source. Lara was ethical like that. She never divulged a source."

Bergqvist's eyebrows shot up. "Then, she was meeting a source?"

He nodded. "That's what I assumed, anyway. That's why she left her phone behind. Some sources would only speak to her off the record, you know?"

Avril adjusted her glasses. "Wait. She didn't take her cellphone with her?"

"No. I found it in her backpack when I tried to call her later that night... when she didn't come home." He stifled a sob.

"We'll need that too," Bergqvist added.

Avril thought for a moment. There weren't many places in town to go. "Did she usually frequent a particular place when she met a source?"

"The Svartälgen, maybe. Or Centralen. Sometimes she met them at the Stag Brewery, a microbrewery on the road leading out of town, but if she didn't take her phone, I don't think she would have gone there. It's too remote. She wasn't stupid."

They'd have to check them all anyway. Maybe someone would recognize Lara and could tell them who she met, or left with.

"So within walking distance?" Avril said.

Tarek nodded.

"Was Lara acting strangely in the days leading up to her disappearance?" she asked, keeping to the standard line of questioning. "Anxious, out of sorts?"

He shook his head. "No, she was fine. Same as always."

Avril took a deep breath. That's what her colleague at the office had said. It seemed that this was a standard meeting with a source. Nothing untoward or anyone she was scared of or nervous to meet.

Did that help?

Avril wasn't sure.

It did mean Lara must have been taken by surprise, then. She hadn't taken her phone or any type of protection, so she clearly hadn't been expecting trouble.

Tarek sat with his shoulders stooped, head lolling. He was barely holding back tears. "How'd you and Lara meet?" Avril asked.

Bergqvist glanced at her in surprise.

"We met at college, about five years ago," Tarek said, his voice tight. "We shared a mixed media class, and then ended up in the same tutor group. I studied videography, while she did journalism." He grunted. "Which I'm sure you already know."

He gripped his hands together in his lap.

"What made you decide to settle here, in Norrdal?" Avril asked. There must have been a hundred other, better options.

"Lara got offered a job here," he said bitterly. "At the *Chronicle*. Features Editor. We'd talked about moving to Stockholm, maybe even London for a while, but she thought this would give her career the boost it needed. She wanted to be an investigative reporter."

Avril gave an understanding nod. "Not much work here for videographers."

He let out a short, humorless laugh. "You can say that again. Most of what I do is freelance—nature films, short documentary pieces, the odd commercial job. I've shot wildlife for Svensk Natur and Outdoor Scandinavia. Sometimes companies hire me to do promo videos for the ski resorts or the national parks."

"Where have you been?" She deliberately kept her tone light. It was good to keep him talking, help him relax.

"Oh, all over. Fulufjället, Sonfjället, the bird reserves by Lake Tåkern... even as far north as Abisko. A lot of overnight trips, early mornings, waiting for the right light. And when I wasn't in the reserves, I picked up small jobs in the neighboring towns. Weddings, local businesses needing something for their websites. Whatever paid the bills."

Bergqvist was listening intently, his head tilted to one side. "So you know Hälsingland?"

"Yeah, been there once or twice."

Then his eyes widened. "Hey, isn't that where—? Oh, my God! You're not suggesting I had anything to do with Lara's death, are you?"

"We're just covering all bases," Avril said, smoothly.

"Do you have an alibi for that night?" Bergqvist asked. Avril glanced at him. So this was how it was going to go. She would be Good Cop to his Bad Cop.

"Um, yeah. I was doing a shoot at... for a local brand. It went on quite late, so I only got home around ten o'clock. There are at least four or five other people who can vouch for me."

"We'll need their names," Bergqvist said.

Tarek turned to Avril. "It wasn't me. I loved Lara. We had plans to leave this place. Get away from here. Go to Stockholm and start over."

Avril gave a sympathetic nod. She didn't think Tarek was involved, but they had to rule him out. "Was there anyone else who'd want to harm Lara?" she asked, changing tack again. "That you know of."

His eyes widened. "God, no. Why would anybody want to harm her?"

"I don't know. She hadn't fallen out with any friends or family members?" Avril asked, studying him. He ran a hand through his messy hair; she noticed he was trembling. Shock, lack of sleep, low blood sugar. It could be any number of things.

"No. I mean she didn't get on with her family, but they wouldn't have hurt her."

"What do you mean?" Bergqvist asked.

"Lara's father is a pastor at St. Augustine's. Her upbringing was very... conservative. She wasn't allowed to do much of anything, from what she told me. Apart from being involved in the church, which really wasn't her thing."

Avril glanced at Bergqvist and raised an eyebrow. An intrepid investigative journalist couldn't have been a welcome career for the daughter of a pastor.

"Did they fall out?" Avril asked.

He snorted. "You could say that. Lara left as soon as she could and went to college in Umeå. Anything to get away. She became involved in local activism, particularly environmental issues and social equality. Sometimes I wondered if it was to spite him."

Avril pursed her lips. "Have you met her family?"

He nodded. "Once. It was a disaster."

Bergqvist frowned. "How so?"

"A Black man from Gothenburg with African roots. How'd you think he reacted?"

Bergqvist grunted.

"I'm sorry, but the guy was a racist prick. He accused her of turning her back on God's plan for her." He smirked. "She told him she didn't believe in God. You can imagine how well that went down. We left after that. I don't think she ever spoke to her father again."

It was a lot to take in. After they'd finished talking, a gloved Bergqvist took custody of Lara's laptop and cellphone, encasing each item in a plastic evidence bag. They locked them in the trunk of his squad car and drove back to the station.

"I think we should interview her father next," Avril said, as they drove the short distance back to the station. They'd log the items into evidence to prevent the chain of custody from being broken and then head out to Lara's family home.

Bergqvist navigated the icy roads with ease. "Agreed. Sounds like they weren't on very good terms."

"Do you know Pastor Berglund?" she asked.

He gave a gruff nod. "Henrik is a force to be reckoned with. Does a lot for his town, though. He may not have liked what his daughter had become, but he's more the God-fearing rather than the murdering type."

A devout pastor. A daughter who brought shame on her family. Avril decided to reserve judgment on that one.

chapter seven

THE DRIVE OUT TO PASTOR HENRIK BERGLUND'S HOUSE WAS a short one, just a few minutes from the center of Norrdal. Hans kept his eyes on the road, the squad car's heater humming, the wipers squeaking back and forth against a fresh flurry of snow. Avril sat in silence, watching the town slip by. The compact square, the shuttered shops, the old church rising above it all like a dark sentinel.

Henrik's house stood just beyond the churchyard, a solid timber-built home with steep gables and narrow windows glowing with yellow light against the pale afternoon. It looked both welcoming and austere. The front path was shoveled, the snow piled in disciplined ridges along the sides.

Hans pulled up at the gate, killed the engine, and sat for a moment, staring at it. Neither of them spoke. The house carried a quiet gravity that Avril felt before she even stepped out of the car.

When they did, the cold struck them at once. Avril tugged her scarf higher, boots crunching on the icy gravel. She glanced toward the church, the bell tower silhouetted against a dim, pewter sky, before following Hans up the path to the door.

He knocked firmly, the sound sharp in the silence. It didn't take long. The door opened, and there stood Pastor Henrik Berglund.

The man filling the doorway was tall and slender, his presence commanding even before he spoke. His thinning hair was swept neatly back, his clerical collar straight against a black sweater. His blue eyes, pale as a winter sky, fixed on Hans first, then flicked to Avril.

"Kommissarie," Henrik said, his voice low, clipped. "How can I help you?"

"This is Avril Dahl from the Serious Crimes Division. She's helping us with the investigation into your daughter's murder. We'd like to ask you a few questions, if that's okay?"

Avril was surprised at Bergqvist's deference.

If that's okay?

What was he playing at? This was a murder enquiry. She didn't care how respected the local pastor was, he was a person of interest like everyone else and should get the same treatment.

Henrik's jaw tightened. Then, with a slow step, he pulled the door open wider. "Come in."

The hallway smelled faintly of wood polish and musty hymnals. A crucifix hung on the wall, judgmental in its quiet reverence. Family photographs were arranged on a sideboard. Avril noted a wedding portrait, something that looked like a confirmation ceremony, and a pair of smiling younger children. She couldn't see a single picture of Lara.

They followed Henrick into a living room that was so neat and tidy, it looked staged. Heavy curtains were pulled back and tied with tasseled cords. Lamps glowed softly in each corner. The furniture was solid oak, arranged around a large Bible that rested open on the coffee table.

Henrik motioned for them to sit, but remained standing himself, arms folded across his chest. Bergqvist was about to lower himself onto an armchair, but when he realized Avril was still standing, he straightened up again.

"When last did you see your daughter?" Avril asked.

"I haven't recently," he retorted, gaze hardening. "Not for months."

"Can you recall the last time?" she adjusted, noting he hadn't answered her question.

"No, it was too long ago. You'll have to ask my wife."

"Does your wife see her more regularly?" Avril enquired.

"She does not." He sighed. "Lara chose her path a long time ago. Drinking, lying, abandoning her faith. She brought shame to this house. We lost her years before she vanished." His voice carried a preacher's resonance, honed by years at the pulpit. He gave a tight shake of his head. "And that man she lived with. An outsider, not even Swedish. It was another sign of how far she had strayed."

Avril had been expecting grief, not this stoic bluntness. She wondered what his wife was like.

"Do you know of anyone who would want to harm your daughter?" she asked.

His lips pressed into a thin line. "No, but I'm not surprised it came to this."

"Excuse me?" Avril stared at him. Beside her, Bergqvist stood with his arms folded across his chest, mimicking the behavior of the pastor.

"A life of sin. This is what happens," Henrik said flatly, his voice carrying the weight of scripture. *"For the wages of sin is death."*

The words were so stark, so merciless. She wondered what it was like for a girl like Lara to grow up in this environment. Stifling, she imagined. Bergqvist's expression remained steady, though she noticed him stiffen.

"Where were you on the night she disappeared?" Avril asked, the tension giving her voice a higher pitch than usual. This man didn't deserve their sympathy. He was a proud, stubborn, and unforgiving man. But was he capable of murder?

"In my study," Henrik replied without hesitation. "I was preparing my sermon for Saturday service. Ingrid was with me most of the evening."

As if summoned, a woman's footsteps padded softly into the room. Enter Ingrid Berglund, neat in a cardigan and long skirt, her hair pinned back, her face drawn with strain. She offered them a fragile smile.

"Yes," she said quickly. "Henrik was here, at home. He never left." Her eyes darted to her husband as though checking she'd answered correctly.

Avril felt sorry for her. Softening her tone, she said, "Mrs. Berglund, did you speak with Lara in the days before she disappeared?"

For a moment, Ingrid hesitated, wringing her hands in front of her. "No. It's like Henrik said, we hadn't seen her in months."

Avril wasn't sure she believed her. Then again, Ingrid wouldn't admit it in front of her husband, even if she had seen Lara. The repercussions would be severe. Avril resolved to get her alone at some point.

Ingrid's eyes glistened. "Do you have any idea who did this?"

Bergqvist spoke now, his voice kind. "We're working on it. Rest assured, we will do our best to find out who it was."

Ingrid nodded, while her husband just glared at them. "I don't see how we can be of any help to you, Kommissarie."

Ingrid flinched. Her gaze met Avril's. It was brief, but she saw the unspoken grief, the apology for her husband's cruelty.

Henrik cleared his throat. "If you are finished..."

Bergqvist gave a short nod. "That's all for now. Thank you for your time."

Avril turned her cold gaze on Henrik. "We may return with further questions." Then she nodded at Ingrid. "Goodbye, Mrs. Berglund."

Back outside, the cold hit like a slap in the face. Avril tugged her scarf tighter and turned to Bergqvist. "He's definitely a person of interest. His wife is his only alibi, and she could be lying to protect him. He could have met Lara, taken her somewhere and killed her, then dumped her body in the lake. We can't rule him out."

Bergqvist glanced at her. "You think he'd kill his own daughter?"

She shivered. "It's been known to happen."

Bergqvist gave a grave nod, but his expression was conflicted. "I don't like to think Pastor Henrik is capable of that. Also, in a town this small, we have to tread carefully. Henrik has influence here. If he feels attacked, the whole community will rally around him."

Avril glanced back at the looming church tower, its cross stark against the gray sky. "I don't care how much influence he has. If he's hiding something, we need to find out what it is. I think we should bring Ingrid in. Alone."

Bergqvist's eyes widened. "We can't do that. Everyone will know."

Avril slanted her gaze. "This is a police investigation. Who cares if people know?"

He sighed, as he unlocked the squad car. They got in. Once belted up, Bergqvist turned to her. "One thing you have to understand is that in a place like Norrdal, everyone knows everyone. There are no secrets. Not for long. If we drag Ingrid into the station, the whole town will know within the hour. And once that happens, good luck getting anyone else to talk to us. They'll close ranks."

The heater ticked as the car warmed, blowing dry air across the windshield.

Avril frowned. "So we just... let him dictate how we run this investigation? Because he's a pastor in a small town?"

"It's not about him. It's about the community," Bergqvist replied firmly. "These people don't trust outsiders. They barely trust me, and I've been here nearly twenty years. The minute we're seen to be causing trouble—targeting someone respected, even if he does deserve it—we'll lose any cooperation we might have had. Witnesses won't come forward. Tips will dry up. Doors will close in our faces."

Avril crossed her arms, unsatisfied. "That sounds like walking on eggshells. If Henrik's hiding something, Ingrid may be the only one who knows it. She looked terrified in there."

"I saw it too," Bergqvist admitted. "But if you want her to open up, it can't be in an interrogation room. It has to be somewhere quiet. Discreet. Where no one can accuse us of harassing the pastor's wife."

She was beginning to understand. He wasn't saying they couldn't interview her. The rules of the game were just different out here. She'd forgotten how insular these small communities were. How reliant on local leaders like pastors or local businessmen.

The church loomed over the town. "I'll find another way to talk to her."

He gave a relieved nod and turned back to face the front. Avril watched the snow drift past the windshield. She'd play nice, for now, but if Henrik Berglund thought his pulpit could shield him from scrutiny, he was wrong. In her book, he had just become their prime suspect.

chapter
eight

Back at the office, Bergqvist assigned Avril the only free desk, positioned against the far wall. It was midafternoon but felt later. The impatient sun had already set, its short journey complete for another day, evident by the streetlamps outside that had flickered to life.

The squad room burned with the bright, fluorescent glow synonymous with police stations all over the world. It was no different in Stockholm or D.C.

The first thing she did was google Pastor Henrik Berglund. Turned out he was born and raised in a nearby town, the son of a schoolteacher and a forestry worker. He studied theology at Uppsala University, then returned to serve the rural communities.

Like Bergqvist had said, he was well respected, and by all accounts, did a lot for church groups and charities. His congregation was large by today's standards, and the church website was modern and up to date, despite the copy being slightly old fashioned. Avril bet Ingrid took care of that.

Lara was their only child. That would make her desertion hit even harder. In some ways, it would make Henrik look like a fool. On the one hand, he preached compassion and humility, but his own daughter was estranged. That couldn't be good for his image or his standing in the community.

Avril scanned the website for information she could use. Church volunteering hours. Weekdays from two to four in the afternoon. She checked her watch. Perfect. Maybe she could corner Ingrid there, away from her husband's controlling glare.

She glanced at the stack of files Eva Strömberg had given her. Although she was dying to jump into them, this had to take priority. Ingrid had been afraid of her husband, Avril had seen it in her eyes. She wanted to understand why.

Was it just because he was a stern, unforgiving man? Or was there more to it?

She got up and pulled on her coat. "I'll be back soon," she told Ekström. "If the Kommissarie asks where I am, tell him I've gone to interview Ingrid Berglund at the church."

"You're going to walk there?" Ekström asked, glancing out the window.

"No, I'll take my rental. It's out back."

Ekström glanced at Bergqvist's office, but the door remained closed. Avril didn't wait for permission. She pulled on her gloves and left. This wasn't a two-man job. It was something she needed to do by herself. Her gut told her Ingrid would be more likely to talk to her than the Kommissarie.

The drive to the church took less than five minutes. The streets were quiet now, the dimming sky cast shadows over the snowbanks piled along the sidewalks. A fine powder had begun to fall again, softening the world into monochrome.

Avril pulled up outside St. Augustine's and killed the engine. The church was dark and silent, except for a narrow beam of light spilling from a side annex. Probably the vestry or one of the meeting halls. She climbed out, boots crunching through the snow, and approached the door.

It was slightly ajar.

Inside, the corridor was silent, except for the faint hum of fluorescent lights overhead. Somewhere nearby, Avril could hear the gentle rustle of water and the clink of glass against porcelain.

She followed the sound.

The door to the kitchen was open, and inside stood Ingrid

Berglund, sleeves rolled up, drying porcelain teacups with a linen cloth. She looked up sharply when Avril stepped into view.

"Oh, you startled me!"

"I'm sorry," Avril said, "but I wanted to catch you alone. Do you have a moment to talk?"

Ingrid hesitated. "I shouldn't. My husband wouldn't want me to."

"This isn't about your husband," she said, even though that was a lie. "I want to know about you. Henrik won't know you've spoken to me."

Ingrid set down the cloth and sighed but gestured toward a small table tucked against the wall. "Close the door behind you."

Avril did.

They sat opposite one another, the table between them covered in a thin plastic cloth patterned with faded flowers. A floral cookie tin sat in the center, unopened.

"I know this is difficult," Avril began. "You told us you hadn't spoken to your daughter in months. Was that true?"

Ingrid stared at the tabletop. Her lips parted, then closed again.

Avril waited.

Finally, Ingrid whispered, "No."

Avril kept her voice steady. "You saw her recently?"

"She came to see me... the day before she disappeared."

Avril felt her heart skip. "Where?"

"Here. At the church. It was just before Bible study. She knew Henrik wouldn't be here yet. She said she needed to speak to me privately."

"What did she say?"

Ingrid glanced toward the door, then looked down again, as if ashamed. "She said she was worried about me." Her voice caught. "She wanted to make sure I was safe."

That surprised Avril. "Safe? From what? From your husband?"

Ingrid hesitated again, then reached up and brushed a hand beneath her eye. Her wedding ring caught the light. "Yes," she whispered.

"Is he violent toward you?" Avril asked, her gaze narrowing.

"Sometimes, but only if I forget to do something. The church is very important to him. He cares about his parishioners, and likes to create a warm, welcoming environment."

More than for his family, by the sounds of things.

"That doesn't make it right," Avril murmured.

She clutched her hands together on the table, her knuckles pale. "I know."

"Was he ever violent toward Lara?"

Tears welled. "I think so. I think that's why she left. He drove her away. My only child, and he drove her away from us."

There was a shuddering silence, as Ingrid fought to compose herself.

"Why do you stay with him?" Avril whispered.

"Because he's my husband and I have nobody else." She choked back a sob. "Now Lara's gone too—"

"Mrs. Berglund, did Lara say anything to you about a case she was working on for the newspaper?"

Ingrid swiped at her eyes but shook her head. "No. Why do you ask?"

"I'm just trying to find out what she was working on before she disappeared."

Her eyes widened. "You think that had something to do with her—"

"I don't know," Avril said honestly "We're considering all angles." She hesitated, not sure how to bring this up. "You don't think... Henrik could have had something to do with it?"

Ingrid stared at her, horrified. "Heavens, no. My husband might be a lot of things, Kriminalinspektör, but he is not a monster."

Avril wasn't so sure about that. Monsters came in many guises. They weren't always the obvious ones.

"He would never hurt his daughter. He was angry with her, sure. Ashamed, maybe, but he was still her father. He might not show it, but he loved her. It devastated him when she renounced God and left the church. Devastated."

Avril could see Ingrid believed that.

"Why didn't you tell him you'd seen Lara?" she asked.

Ingrid's smile was hollow. "Henrik has never forgiven her for walking away. For the way she challenged him before she left. The things she said..." She shook her head. "If he knew she'd come back—if he knew she was speaking to me—he would have been furious."

Avril leaned forward, her voice low. "Ingrid, I have to ask you again. Where was Henrik the night Lara disappeared?"

"In his study. Like he said."

"You're sure?"

Ingrid nodded. "I wouldn't lie about something that important." But she had lied about other things, like seeing her daughter.

"It's just, at the house earlier, you glanced at Henrik as if to make sure you'd said the right thing. It made me think it might have been rehearsed."

She swallowed. "No, Kriminalinspektör. I was glancing at him because we hadn't rehearsed anything, and I wanted to make sure he was okay with me answering your questions. He would never ask me to lie for him. He's a God-fearing man."

Avril could see Ingrid truly believed that. She got to her feet. "Thank you, Ingrid. I appreciate you talking with me."

Ingrid nodded, then clutched her arm. "I need to know what happened to my daughter. You will find out, won't you?"

Avril gave a tight nod. "I'm going to do my best."

chapter
nine

Avril sat down and reached for the stack of folders Eva Strömberg had given her. She'd driven straight back to the station and briefed the Kommissarie who wasn't angry so much as disgruntled she hadn't told him where she was going. Again.

"I did say I wanted to talk with her." Avril had defended her actions. "You said not to do it here." He couldn't argue with that.

The first folder was slim, more notes than anything of substance. A handful of clippings from regional papers, some crude graphs of population statistics, and a scattering of interviews typed up on plain A4 paper. Avril flicked through them, her eyes catching on highlighted quotes.

"There's nothing to stay for here."
"If you want a career, you have to leave."
"It's a nice place to grow up, not to live permanently."

Most of the voices belonged to people barely out of their teens, restless and impatient with the confines of a small town. Avril scanned one transcript where a nineteen-year-old spoke about saving up for a one-way ticket to London. Another, where a nursing student described her frustration at being expected to return and take care of her parents' farm.

Avril sighed and leaned back in her chair. It was an important assignment, but not relevant. To a town like Norrdal, bleeding its youth would feel like a crisis, but from an investigative standpoint, there was no threat here. No scandal, no obvious motive for murder.

She closed the folder and pushed it aside. If Lara had vanished because of her reporting, it wouldn't have been because she'd asked teenagers why they wanted to leave.

Avril reached for the second folder, heavier than the first, its pages dog-eared from use. She flipped it open.

The headline of a local newspaper clipping stared back at her: "Council Awards Winter Contract to Nordberg Infrastruktur." Lara had underlined key phrases in red, circling "despite cheaper bid from rival firm" and scrawling WHY? in the margin.

Avril skimmed the article. Norrdal's council had recently awarded a lucrative contract for road maintenance and snow clearance to Nordberg Infrastruktur, a mid-sized construction outfit owned by a man named Olle Nordberg. Another firm—better qualified and with a significantly lower bid—had been passed over.

She turned to Lara's notes. Typed transcripts of council meetings. Background on the procurement committee. And then Lara's handwritten scrawl across the bottom of one page:

Kickbacks? Land purchases on outskirts? Nordberg + Councilor Håkansson = cozy?

Avril frowned. This was more than sociology. This smelled like corruption.

She flipped to a separate sheet with a profile of Nordberg himself. Mid-fifties, smiling in most photos. A patron of the local hockey team, donor to civic projects. Publicly, he came across as affable, almost jovial. But in the margins Lara had written: *Old ties to Umeå? Check sources.*

Another note highlighted Councilor Birgitta Håkansson, chair of the procurement committee. "Fiercely defensive of Nordberg," Lara had typed, with a reference to her shutting down questions at a council meeting.

Avril glanced up to find she was alone with Ekström. She'd been so focused, she had barely registered Lundgren going out. Something about chickens escaping. "Is Bergqvist in his office?"

Ekström shook her head. "No, he went out ten minutes ago. I'm not sure where." The young woman hesitated. "Is there anything I can help with?"

"Maybe." Avril swiveled in her chair to face the officer. "What do you know about Olle Nordberg?"

"You mean the chairman of Nordberg Infrastruktur?"

"That's him."

Ekström exhaled. "He's a pretty big deal around these parts. Half of the town relies on his company for employment in one way or another, and the other are hockey mad. Why do you ask?"

"Are there any rumors of corruption?"

Ekström's eyes widened. "Not that I've heard, although he is very well connected. Politically, I mean."

"In what way?"

"He's friends with the mayor. They're often pictured together at functions."

"What about Councilor Håkansson?" she asked.

Ekström shrugged. "I don't know about her, but I wouldn't be surprised if they knew each other."

Avril gave a contemplative nod.

"If you like, I could do some digging?" There was a hopeful note in her voice. Avril got the impression she was bored and underutilized.

Why not? Maybe she'd find something useful.

"Sure, that would be helpful. See if you can find any ties to organized crime."

Ekström's eyebrows rose higher, but she nodded and turned back to her computer. Moments later, her fingers flew over the keyboard.

Avril turned back to the documents. This was the kind of reporting that could upset people. Local corruption, dirty contracts, potential links to organized crime. It was enough to make enemies.

She closed the folder slowly, tapping her pen against it. Lara had been digging, but was this enough of a motive for murder?

Avril pushed the file aside, stacking it neatly next to the first. She'd bring it up with Bergqvist. See what he thought of Olle Nordberg and whether Håkansson had ever come under suspicion for anything.

But first, there was one last folder to look at.

Avril opened the third folder. This one was thicker still, a mixture of typed reports, photocopied permits, and a handful of printouts from environmental agencies. At the top sat a map of the Norrdal River and its tributaries, several sections highlighted in yellow marker.

She leafed through the first few pages. Skogviken Timber AB. One of the biggest employers in the region. On paper, they were reputable. Longstanding, politically connected, well-funded. But Lara had been pursuing a very different line.

Typed neatly in her notes was the allegation: Dumping of chemical byproducts into tributary east of Norrdal. Impact on fish stocks, contamination of wells. Local families affected.

Avril exhaled softly. That was serious. In a town this small, poisoning the water would ripple through the community fast.

She found another page. Lara's handwriting scrawled in the margin.

Were the reports falsified? Was the inspector compromised?

Beneath that, she'd written a name.

Erik Palmqvist.

Avril frowned. That was the local environmental officer who Lara clearly suspected of signing off on doctored reports in exchange for money.

Another sheet held a profile of Mats Vinter, CEO of Skogviken Timber. Avril studied it. Vinter was in his mid-sixties, well-connected, and sat on the regional development board.

Too powerful to ignore.

Then there was Hanna Sjöberg, Skogviken's PR manager. She would be media savvy, and able to kill bad stories before they saw daylight.

A final scribbled note pointed to Johan Evertsson, Nordberg's operations manager and ex-military. Lara had added: *Intimidation?*

This one was hot. Corruption, money, coercion, political cover-up. If Lara had started poking into this, she'd have been stepping on some dangerous toes.

Avril sat back, her mind racing. Between the council contract scandal and this pollution case, there was more than enough motive for someone to want Lara silenced. The youth exodus story had been nothing. But these? They were worth killing for.

It seemed they had several more avenues to investigate besides Pastor Henrik.

She set the folder down and rubbed her temples. Too many threads, too many powerful names. She'd need Bergqvist's take on all of them. Did he know these people? Did he have history with them? Could he trust them?

"Hey, Ekström?"

The polisassistent looked up. "Yes?"

"Can I add some more names to that list you're digging into?"

Her face lit up. "Of course."

Avril gave her Mats Vinter, Hanna Sjöberg, and Johan Evertsson.

The door clicked open. Bergqvist and Lundgren stepped inside, brushing snow from their coats. Avril's gaze flicked over them automatically. A white feather clung stubbornly to Bergqvist's shoulder, and Lundgren's trousers were caked with mud halfway to the knees.

Ekström masked a grin. "Rough arrest?" she murmured to her colleague as he walked past.

"They're faster than they look," he muttered, before sinking behind his desk, red-faced.

Avril didn't comment. Her mind was on more important matters. She closed the folder and looked at Bergqvist, who was tugging the feather free. "We need to talk."

chapter
ten

BERGQVIST SHUT HIS OFFICE DOOR BEHIND THEM, LEAVING the bustle of the squadroom muted beyond the frosted glass. He dropped into his chair while Avril spread the two folders across the desk between them.

"I've been looking into the cases Lara was working on, and I think these require further scrutiny." She tapped the covers with her finger.

Bergqvist glanced at the file headers, his expression tightening. "Nordberg Infrastruktur and Skogviken Timber." He exhaled slowly, rubbing a hand across his jaw. "What about Pastor Henrik?"

"He's on the backburner for now. Ingrid was adamant he was at home, so his alibi stands. I've got no way of disproving it."

Bergqvist nodded, and she saw his shoulders drop in relief. "What's that one?" he asked, nodding to the third folder.

"That's a youth exodus piece, but I don't think it's relevant," Avril said dismissively. "These two, however, are a different story."

She flipped open the Nordberg file and slid it toward him. "The council contract was awarded to Nordberg Infrastruktur despite a cheaper, better-qualified bid. Lara's notes prove she was looking into kickbacks and possible ties to organized crime. Olle Nordberg's public image looks squeaky clean, but Lara thought he may have had history in Umeå."

Bergqvist grimaced. "There are always rumors about Olle. He's been around long enough, and he's got friends in the right places. The hockey team, the council... half the town depends on him one way or another."

That's what Ekström had said.

"That's what makes him dangerous," Avril countered. "If Lara started asking the wrong questions, he'd have every reason to shut her down."

Bergqvist gave a weary nod.

Avril pulled the second folder across and flipped it open to the highlighted river map. "Then, there's Skogviken Timber. Lara was looking into the alleged chemical dumping into a tributary. Fish stocks, wells, and local families have been affected. Lara suspected falsified inspection reports."

Bergqvist's brow furrowed. "Mats Vinter." The name was almost a sigh. "He's been untouchable for decades. Old money, political board seats. He's a lot more dangerous than Nordberg. If he was dumping illegally, and Lara got too close to finding out the truth—" He broke off, giving his head a little shake.

"She'd be a problem he couldn't afford," Avril finished for him. She tapped Palmqvist's name in the margin. "She thought the environmental inspector was compromised. If he's on the take, he could have been the weak link."

Bergqvist glared at the files as though willing them to shrink away. "Nordberg, Håkansson, Vinter, Palmqvist... these are people who don't scare easily. If she confronted any one of them, it could have gone badly."

Avril folded her arms. "The question is who had the most to lose."

After a moment, Bergqvist shifted forward and folded his hands on the desk. "I agree. These are leads we have to follow. But we need to tread carefully, otherwise we'll be ruffling some very powerful feathers."

She opened her mouth to object, but he held up a hand.

"In Stockholm, you've got entire departments. Financial crimes, corruption units, environmental teams. Here, it's just us. Three officers and a budget that wouldn't cover the copier paper you use at Stockholm HQ."

Avril pressed her lips together and nodded. He had a point.

He gave a weary shake of his head. "People like Nordberg and Vinter sit on boards, fund community projects. They sponsor the regional hockey team, for Christ's sake. You understand me? They control jobs. If we make the wrong move and they lean on the council, our funding will dry up. We won't even be able to afford the basics like fuel for the patrol cars. We're on a shoestring as it is. Any reduction in our allocation would cripple us—and they know it."

Avril stared at him, her heart sinking. She'd seen politicians meddle with investigations before, particularly in D.C. The FBI had to deal with that bullshit on a nearly daily basis, but she wasn't used to the stakes being quite so high.

"One of them could be guilty or complicit in Lara's murder," she argued.

"I know, and if they are, we will do our best to find the evidence and apprehend them. But everything has to be above board. We need to make appointments, get warrants, find actual proof. We can't afford to put a foot wrong here."

Avril gave a slow nod, frustration gnawing at her. "I understand."

And she did. Really. But it was going to make this investigation a whole lot more difficult.

"Kommissarie, I'd like to talk with Nordberg tomorrow. Will you be coming with me?"

"Of course. We must follow up on these leads. Let's meet here in the morning, and we'll go together." With him driving, no doubt.

Avril nodded and turned to leave. It had been a long day, and she was looking forward to getting back to the guesthouse and taking a shower, before falling into bed.

"And Avril?"

She glanced back over her shoulder. "Yes?"

"Why don't you call me Hans?"

chapter
eleven

AFTER A LONG, STEAMING HOT SHOWER, AVRIL COLLAPSED on the narrow guesthouse bed, the radiator clanking faintly in the corner. Ekström had thrust several reports into her hands before she left, and she'd meant to spend no more than a few minutes looking them over. Instead, she found herself drawn in. They were good—surprisingly good. Detailed, thorough, even annotated with newspaper clippings. She made a mental note to tell the young polisassistent how impressed she was.

Making herself comfortable, Avril started with Olle Nordberg. Born in Umeå, he moved to Norrdal in the late '80s where he founded Nordberg Infrastruktur. From what she could make out, it was essentially a construction company that built roads and took care of snow clearance. Essential lifelines in a place like this.

Fast forward to the present day, and Nordberg was one of the biggest employers in town, heavily involved in community projects, and the main sponsor of Norrdal's talented and often-successful hockey team. That must be good PR.

Avril thumbed the edge of the folder. Generosity was rarely just generosity. Ekström had highlighted Nordberg's political ties. She held up a photograph of him grinning beside Mayor Öberg at a hockey game followed by one of him shaking hands with a regional party leader to whom he'd made substantial donations. Avril arched a brow when she saw Ekström's notes on the amounts.

Her eye caught the bottom line.

Rumored to have ties to Umeå crime syndicates in the '80s–'90s, although these claims are unsubstantiated.

She exhaled and flopped back against the pillows. Organized crime? And Lara had been investigating him. She gave a little shake of her head. A man like Nordberg would not welcome a young journalist poking her nose into his business.

Her eyes felt gritty, but she pressed on, flipping to the next dossier.

Councilor Birgitta Håkansson, Chair of the Procurement Committee and gatekeeper for every lucrative municipal contract in Norrdal.

Quite a responsibility.

At forty-nine years old, Håkansson was a lifelong resident of Norrdal, and a loyal ally of the mayor. Avril studied a photograph of her. She looked like the kind of official who smiled at ribbon-cuttings while wielding real power behind the scenes.

Avril scanned the last page. According to the numerous newspaper clippings Ekström had included, there were frequent sightings of Håkansson with Nordberg. A suspicious holiday in Tenerife, allegedly with his entourage, although she'd denied it. There was nothing in the file to prove otherwise.

Except, Lara had smelled smoke, and Avril trusted her journalistic instinct.

She stretched her neck and blinked away the encroaching fatigue. Avril thought about Lara spreading out similar research and making the same connections. A young woman investigating two powerful men's businesses.

Hell, yes. That could get you killed.

Avril felt her eyes closing. Sleep was winning. With a weary sigh, she stacked the files neatly on the bedside table, switched off the lamp, and let the darkness close in. Tomorrow, she would face Nordberg and Håkansson. Tonight, she would rest.

. . .

THE ALARM on her phone buzzed her awake at six sharp. Avril blinked into the dark, momentarily disoriented by the anonymous bedroom. Cream walls, thin curtains, radiator clanking somewhere near the floor. For a few seconds she forgot where she was. Then the memory returned.

Norrdal. Frostsjön.

The body in the ice.

She pushed herself upright, rubbing her eyes, and reached for the clothes she'd laid out the night before. A dark wool turtleneck and a fitted blazer, the kind of outfit that projected composure without drawing attention. Tailored trousers, boots polished just enough to look deliberate. No frills, nothing showy. Just the clean, disciplined lines of someone who meant business. Exactly what she needed for facing Olle Nordberg.

Her phone rang as she zipped up her boots. It was Bergqvist.

She answered. "Hans?"

"Hey, Avril." His voice was brisk, but beneath it she caught the strain. "I'm sorry, but there's been a change of plan. We've had an incident outside of town. A farmhouse break-in. I need Lundgren with me to process the scene. Can you manage Nordberg on your own?"

Of course she could handle Nordberg by herself, but she thought about how thorough the dossiers were on the would-be suspects. Ekström already had a good working knowledge of Nordberg and Håkansson.

"What about Ekström?"

A pause. "Ekström? She doesn't have field experience."

"Not yet, but maybe it's time she learned. I'll do the talking and she can observe and take notes. Better than me walking in there alone," she added, hoping that would sway him.

Bergqvist exhaled like he was giving in against his better judgment. "Fine. But don't push Nordberg. Remember what we talked about. Keep it friendly. We can't afford him turning this into a political crusade against us."

"Understood."

"You can give me an update later. Good luck." The line went dead.

When Avril arrived at the station, Ekström was waiting outside, scarf wrapped tight, cheeks flushed pink from the cold. She looked younger in the natural light, her fair hair escaping her beanie in loose strands. When she slid into the passenger seat of Avril's rented Volvo, her hands gripped her notepad like it was a safety blanket.

"Thanks for inviting me along," she said, as she buckled up.

"I needed backup." Avril adjusted the rear-view mirror. "And you know more about Olle Nordberg and Nordberg Industries than anyone else in the department."

"That's true." She gave a girlish laugh. "I'm just grateful for the opportunity to work beside a real FBI Special Agent."

At Avril's look, she added, "Oh, I know you aren't with the FBI anymore, but I was reading about you, and everything you've accomplished. You caught The Frost Killer and got justice for all those poor girls."

Avril shifted uncomfortably. She wasn't used to anyone looking up to her, let alone a younger police officer. While in the FBI, she'd been tolerated at best, sidelined at worst. She was regarded as too intense, too unorthodox. Nobody had ever looked at her like she was someone to admire. It unsettled her more than she cared to admit.

"Yeah, well, that's all in the past now."

"Well, I still think you're—"

"I need to focus on what we're going to say to Nordberg," she interjected.

Ekström nodded and stopped talking.

They drove out of town, the road climbing steadily north. After ten minutes, the forest gave way to a broad clearing and Nordberg Infrastruktur's headquarters rose into view.

It wasn't a pretty building. A squat complex of glass and steel, it had a wide forecourt lined with heavy trucks and snow-ploughs, their orange paint dulled by frost and rust. Each vehicle had the company name stencilled across its side in bold navy letters.

Avril slowed down and took it all in. High tech surveillance cameras ringed the perimeter. She spotted at least two security guards at the entrance, one stamping his boots against the cold, the other speaking into a radio.

"There's a lot of security for a road-maintenance firm," Avril murmured, pulling into the visitor's bay. She'd called ahead and made an appointment, so Nordberg knew she was coming. She liked the element of surprise, but Hans had been adamant. By the book.

Ekström looked around and nodded. "You're right."

They got out of the car and went into the gleaming lobby. Avril told the receptionist wearing a headset that they had an appointment, and they were wordlessly directed to a second-floor office.

"Hello, Kriminalinspektör Dahl. Welcome to Nordberg Infrastruktur." Olle Nordberg greeted them with the charm of a man used to winning people over. Mid-fifties, ruddy-cheeked, broad-shouldered, with the kind of handshake that went on a fraction too long. He wore a dark blazer and an open-collared shirt, with gold cufflinks glinting at his wrists.

"This is Polisassistent Ekström from Norrdal Police," Avril said, returning his handshake.

Nordberg's gaze flicked to Ekström. "Kommissarie Bergqvist couldn't make it?" His voice was warm but faintly mocking.

Ekström turned pink. "There was an incident in town."

"Ah." He gestured them to a leather sofa opposite his desk. "All right, then. What can I do for you ladies?"

Avril bristled, but sat down, as did Ekström. She drew in a steadying breath. This wasn't a suspect interview, it was an informal discussion. She had to go easy.

"We're actually here to talk about Lara Berglund."

"Lara Berglund?" His expression went blank for a moment, and then he blinked. "Wasn't she the woman who—?"

"Who was found out by Frostsjön? Yes. She was also a reporter looking into your company and the municipal contract you won last year."

"Was that her?" His brows shot up. "I'm sorry, I didn't make the connection."

Beside her, Avril could see Ekström frowning. The polisassistent had good instincts.

"Do you remember speaking to her?"

He rubbed his jaw, then nodded. "Yes, I remember. Blond hair like yours. Attractive. Very passionate in her quest to uncover the truth."

"And what is the truth, Mr. Nordberg?"

Cold Mercy

He chuckled. "I don't know what you heard, Kriminalinspektör, but our contract was a standard tender. We've been maintaining Norrdal's roads for over twenty years. Our bid reflected that experience. The council knows us and trusts us. That's why they chose us. I told all this to... Lara, was it?"

"That's right." Avril studied him. Did he really not realize it was the same woman?

"I believe there was a cheaper bid from a rival firm."

He shrugged. "Cheaper doesn't mean better. Snow-clearing isn't about saving money, it's about reliability. When the storm hits, you don't want to be waiting for amateurs to get their act together."

"Mr. Nordberg, when was the last time you spoke to Lara Berglund?"

He thought for a moment. "Well, it was over a month ago. She sat right where you're sitting now and interviewed me. My assistant will have the details, if you want a date and time?"

Avril felt a chill go through her, and beside her, Ekström crossed her arms in a defensive gesture. "That would be helpful." Avril paused, measuring her words before she spoke. "I'm sorry to have to ask this, Mr. Nordberg, but where were you on the night of December 16th?"

"Again, I'll have to look at my diary."

"It was last Tuesday, if that helps."

His gaze lightened, and he grinned. "It does. I was playing poker with a small group of friends. We get together every Tuesday night, if our schedules allow. Keeps us sane through these winters."

Private poker games between friends were common and legal in Sweden, as long as there was no commercial element. Avril remembered her parents inviting their neighbors around for spelkvällar—game nights —when she was a child.

"Is Councilor Birgitta Håkansson part of that group?"

Nordberg's smile deepened. "You've done your homework, Kriminalinspektör. No, Birgitta doesn't play. Mayor Öberg, however... now he's got a hell of a poker face."

The sly smile sent shivers down her spine. They couldn't question an alibi vouched for by the mayor himself.

But since he'd brought it up. "Do you feel your political connections influenced the council's decision in awarding you the contract?"

This time his smile cooled a fraction. "I make no apologies for supporting my town. Sponsoring the hockey team, donating to civic projects, helping Norrdal thrive. That's not corruption. That's being a good neighbor."

She let the silence stretch, just long enough for him to feel it. Then she nodded once. "Thank you for talking with us, Mr. Nordberg. We'll get out of your hair and leave you in peace."

As they walked out, he called after them. "You're barking up the wrong tree if you think I had anything to do with that woman's murder. I've got nothing to hide, Kriminalinspektör. I'm genuinely sorry she's dead. She seemed like a decent person. Norrdal needs more of those."

chapter
twelve

Once they were back in the rental, Avril started the engine.

Ekström was quiet for a moment, then blurted, "How did you learn to do that?"

"What?"

"The interview. He thought he was in control, but you put him in his place every time." Her eyes were bright.

Avril focused on the road. "That's just experience. You'll get there."

Ekström let out a small sigh. "If I ever get the chance. The Kommissarie doesn't see me as a real investigator. To him, I'm just someone who does research and writes up reports."

Avril kept her tone even. "Then prove him wrong. That dossier you pulled together was excellent. I still don't know how you managed it so fast."

Ekström's cheeks flushed. "I've got some database queries I use. My brother's a programmer. He taught me a few tricks when we were kids."

Avril raised an eyebrow. "Does Bergqvist know that?"

Ekström shook her head.

"You should tell him," Avril said flatly. "Skills like that can make a difference in a case."

They'd exited the compound and rounded a bend when a heavy truck thundered toward them. The driver swerved too wide on the icy road. Avril reacted instantly, wrenching the wheel. The Volvo spun, tires skidding across black ice, the world tilting in a blur of snow and metal.

Ekström gasped, her phone flying out of her hand.

The car fishtailed once, then steadied. They came to a stop sideways across the road. The truck roared past, sending a wave of dirty snow thudding across their windshield.

For a heartbeat, neither of them spoke. Avril's pulse hammered in her ears.

"You okay?" she asked finally, her voice low.

Ekström nodded shakily. "Yeah. What the hell just happened?"

"He went wide. Lost control."

Ekström fumbled in the footwell for her phone. "Idiot could have killed us. If it wasn't for your quick thinking—" She faded off, the rest unsaid.

Avril set her jaw, checked her mirrors, and guided the Volvo back onto the road. No harm done, but was that a careless error on the truck driver's part, or something more deliberate?

She didn't want to think ill of Nordberg, but what were the chances of them having a near-fatal accident upon leaving his company headquarters? In light of everything that had happened, the experience made Avril jumpy.

She didn't let on, though, not wanting to spook Ekström.

Back at the police station, Avril asked Ekström to look into Nordberg's alibi for the night of Lara's murder. "I want a statement from the mayor that he was with Nordberg all night."

Ekström nodded. "I won't let you down."

Bergqvist was back, and while Lundgren was on the phone, he called Avril into his office. "What's this about a near car accident?"

Avril filled him in and watched as his frown deepened. "It's got to be a coincidence."

"Probably," Avril agreed. "Nordberg remembered Lara but didn't know it was the same woman who'd been found in the ice."

"You believe him?" Hans asked.

Avril shrugged. "Not sure. There's a lot of surveillance cameras on the property. More than what seems normal for a company like that."

"You think they're hiding something?"

"I don't know," she sighed. "Ekström's looking into Nordberg's alibi, and she's already done a profile on him, and the other persons of interest."

He arched his brow. "She has?"

"Yes, she's quite efficient, but she needs to get out more. I think she'll make a great Kriminalinspektör one day."

He grunted, but didn't reply.

"I'd like to speak to Councilor Birgitta Håkansson next."

Hans gave a slow nod. "Is that necessary? She isn't a suspect, is she?"

"She's the one who awarded Nordberg the contract. If there was a kickback, she's got as much to lose as he does."

"All right, but this time I'm coming with you."

"Fine. Let's go."

They were about to head out again when Lundgren cleared his throat. "Excuse me, Kommissarie. The autopsy report just came in on Lara Berglund."

Both Avril and Hans turned toward him. Hans spoke first. "Ja?"

"The cause of death is confirmed as ligature strangulation. The medical examiner notes fracture of the hyoid bone and deep contusions consistent with manual force. Toxicology showed a high concentration of flunitrazepam in her blood."

Avril's head came up. "Rohypnol."

"She was drugged?" asked Hans.

"Yes, sir." He still wouldn't answer her directly.

He tensed his jaw. "That explains the lack of defensive wounds. There were no skin cells under her fingernails or bruising on her forearms."

"That's how he got her out of the pub," Avril blurted. "She must have been woozy. Anyone watching would think she'd had too much to drink."

Out of the corner of her eye, Avril saw Ekström glance down at her hands. Sadly, it happened all too often these days, and usually went unreported. Either women were too embarrassed or ashamed to tell the police what had happened, or they just wanted to move on as quickly as possible and put it behind them. A court case would only drag out the nightmare.

"Was she sexually assaulted?" Avril asked, her voice tight.

Lundgren glanced at the page again before answering. "There's no evidence of that."

"You're sure?" Hans asked.

"Positive, sir. There's no evidence of penetration, no trace of semen, no genital trauma. She hadn't been violated in that way."

Avril frowned.

"It was a way to get her out of the bar," Lundgren concluded.

"Had to be." Hans ran a hand through his hair.

"Did they give a time of death?" Avril asked.

Lundgren sighed as if her question was an imposition. Avril frowned. She might have to have a little chat with him. Whatever his problem was with her, it needed to be resolved. They couldn't carry on like this.

"The cold makes it difficult to narrow down, but the pathologist notes the high levels of Rohypnol still in her blood. That suggests she died not long after she was taken—probably within a few hours."

Ekström winced. "That poor girl."

"We need to find out where she'd met her contact," Avril said. "There are only so many bars in this town. We could visit them all after we talk to Håkansson."

"Good idea. There might be CCTV or a surveillance camera to help us identify the kidnapper."

Hans felt his pocket for his keys, then looked at Avril. "Ready?"

She nodded.

"Then let's go."

chapter
thirteen

Councilor Birgitta Håkansson lived in one of the larger timber houses on the south side of Norrdal, set back from the street behind a neatly shoveled drive and a hedge frosted white with snow. A polished brass plate beside the door displayed her name, a touch more formal than most homes in town.

Hans parked the squad car at the curb. He shut off the engine but didn't move right away, his eyes fixed on the house.

"She's stubborn," he said, tensing his jaw. "Likes to run council meetings as if she were running parliament. She won't give us anything easily."

Avril tugged her scarf tighter, already feeling the bite of the late afternoon cold. "We'll see about that."

The door opened almost as soon as they rang the bell. Birgitta Håkansson wore a burgundy cardigan and tailored slacks, her dark blond hair pinned into a precise chignon. Calm, authoritative, and faintly irritated at being disturbed, she looked every inch the local politician.

"Kommissarie, it's nice to see you again." She gave Hans a tight smile, then looked at Avril, her brow rising a fraction. "This must be the Kriminalinspektör from Stockholm."

Word certainly got around.

Avril extended her hand. "Avril Dahl. Thank you for seeing us on short notice."

Birgitta hesitated a beat before shaking it. "Come in. But I have another meeting soon, so please be brief."

The living room was warm and cozy, and smelled like Christmas. Family photographs lined the mantelpiece. Avril spotted the councilor with a man, who she took to be her husband, and two grown children. A stylishly decorated Christmas tree took up an entire corner, its lights glowing softly.

They sat on a cream sofa positioned along the wall opposite an electric fireplace. Birgitta perched on an armchair diagonally across from them.

Hans took the lead.

"We're investigating the death of the journalist, Lara Berglund," he began. "Did you know her?"

Birgitta nodded. "I heard they found her body. Frostsjön, was it? So tragic."

"How did you know her?" Avril asked.

Birgitta didn't hesitate. "She worked for the *Chronicle*. She interviewed me."

"In relation to what?" Hans enquired.

Birgitta shrugged, spreading her hands. "She wanted to know why we'd awarded Nordberg Infrastruktur the winter road contract. We did the due diligence and, frankly, they were the better company. She was looking for a story that wasn't there."

Hans kept his expression neutral. "When was this?"

"Let me see. It must be two or three weeks ago now. I can check my calendar."

"Please," Hans said.

She reached across for her phone, which lay on a low coffee table, and scrolled for a moment. "Ah, here it is. Thursday, December 2nd, at ten o'clock. She came to my office, in case you were wondering."

"Thank you," Hans said. "That is very helpful."

Was it? Avril frowned. It told them nothing, other than they'd met.

She faced the councilor. "Can you tell us where you were on the night of Tuesday, December 16th?"

Birgitta's gaze flitted across to her. "That was last week, wasn't it? Let me think..." She tapped a manicured finger against her lips. "I was at home. My husband worked late, but I had a meeting over video with the procurement subcommittee. We were reviewing next year's budgets. I'm sure there's a record of the call."

"Was anyone with you in person?" Hans asked, shooting Avril a look that said, *I've got this.*

"No, but the other people on the call will confirm I was there."

Avril watched her closely. Birgitta's answers were polished, almost rehearsed. She sounded confident and assured, putting them at ease with a practiced smile.

"We'll need their names," Hans said, his frown akin to an apology.

"Of course, Kommissarie. I would expect nothing less. I'll get my assistant to send them over in the morning. Is that all?"

"Ja—" Hans said, but Avril cut in.

"How well do you know Olle Nordberg?"

Birgitta gave a cool smile.

"I know Olle professionally, of course, but no more than the mayor, or anyone else in public service."

"So you didn't holiday with him in Tenerife earlier in the year?" Avril pressed, ignoring the warning look Hans sent her.

The cool eyes slanted, just a little, and she said, "You know, you remind me of that poor girl. She had the same... passion, as you do. It's a quality I admire, especially in women. We always have to try so much harder than the men, wouldn't you agree?"

Avril noted how easily she'd deflected. A politician's skill.

She stood. "Now, I really must get back to my family."

"Thank you, Councilor," Hans said. "We appreciate your cooperation."

She broke into a warm smile as she looked at Hans. "Of course. I'm always happy to assist Polisen."

Back outside, the snow had started falling again, fine flakes swirling in the glow of the streetlamp.

Hans didn't speak until he'd unlocked the squad car and they'd gotten inside. Once he'd started the engine, he turned to face her. "I told you we needed to tread carefully."

"And this is a murder investigation," Avril reminded him. "She could have been in it with Nordberg. I had to see how she reacted at the mention of his name."

"You practically accused her of having an affair."

"Which she didn't answer. Did you notice that?"

His hands gripped the wheel. "She has an alibi for the night Lara disappeared, just like Nordberg."

"Neither of which has been verified yet," Avril reminded him.

He pulled away from the curb, and the heating kicked in, warming the interior.

"We'll get Ekström on it when we get back, but my gut is telling me we're barking up the wrong tree with these two."

"Maybe." She gnawed her lip. They were both too smooth for their own good.

"Even if they are closer than they made out, that still doesn't mean they had any hand in Lara's disappearance," Hans said. "It's not our job to investigate the winter road contract."

She couldn't fault that logic.

"Okay, let's see what Ekström comes up with. We've got Mats Vinter and the team at Skogviken Timber to look into next." There was more than enough to keep them busy.

Hans nodded. "Ja, but it can wait until tomorrow. I'm not pissing off any more dignitaries tonight."

Avril almost smiled. For once, they were in agreement.

Back at the police station, Hans stopped to talk to Ekström, while Avril approached Lundgren. He was young and probably knew the watering holes in Norrdal better than anyone.

"Hey, can you give me a list with the addresses of all the bars in town? I want to see if I can find the one Lara went to the night she disappeared."

His gaze flickered to Hans, but he was focused on Ekström.

"Lundgren?" she prodded, regaining his attention.

"It's not a long list." He reached for a notepad on his desk and scribbled down five names, along with the roads they were on, not needing to look up any.

"Good," Avril said.

"There's one on the edge of town too." He added the final name, then slid it across the desk. "That's it."

"Six bars. What about hotels, resorts, that kind of thing?"

"Not in town. There are several resorts scattered around the general area, particularly out at the lakes. Do you want those too?"

She thought about what Tarek had said. Lara had left her bag and phone at home. She'd been on foot, in this weather. "No, I'm pretty sure she wasn't going anywhere that wasn't within walking distance."

He gave a curt nod and turned back to his screen. She hesitated.

A flash of irritation crossed his face as he glanced back up at her. "Was there something else?"

"Is there any CCTV in this town?" she asked.

He shook his head. "No, we're much too small. But some of the stores have surveillance cameras."

That's what she'd thought. "Can you contact all the bars on this list and find out if they have cameras? If they do, we need to look at the footage of the night Lara vanished."

Hans came over. "Everything okay?"

Avril told him what she'd asked Lundgren to do. He nodded at the polisassistent. "Good idea. Go ahead. Oh, I've just heard back from tech support in Östersund. They've downloaded the contents of Lara's laptop and will send the files in the morning."

"Same with the cell phone company," Lundgren added, looking at Hans. "They're sending her call records through first thing."

"Excellent." Hans gave a satisfied nod. Avril supposed two days wasn't long, in the greater scheme of things. They often had to wait weeks in Stockholm, where there was more of a backlog. Small-town cases had their advantages.

Hans nodded to the list of names. "Are we going to do this, then?"

She hadn't even taken off her scarf and jacket. Her beanie was still pulled down low on her head. "It'll be quicker if we split up." She didn't want to spend all night with Hans. He seemed like a decent police officer, if a bit laid-back, but she wanted to get home and read through the rest of the dossiers Ekström had put together and prepare for tomorrow's meeting with Mats Vinter and his team. Besides, she wasn't any good at small talk.

He rubbed his jaw where the five o'clock shadow was beginning to show. "Agreed." He glanced down at the list in her hand. "I'll take the top three, you take the bottom three. Call me if you get anything."

"Same to you."

"Will do."

chapter
fourteen

THE VOLVO'S HEATER BLASTED AGAINST THE WINDSHIELD, but Avril still felt the cold seeping through the glass. Even the short drive from the police station had reminded her why no one in their right mind walked in weather like this. At minus fifteen with the wind chill, exposed skin could freeze in minutes. She remembered her mother warning her about it when she was a kid.

She swung the car onto a narrow street lined with dark timber buildings, most of them shuttered against the long night. Only one glowed, its windows throwing out amber rectangles of light onto the snow-packed pavement. A hand-painted sign above the door read *Korpen*. The Raven.

Inside, the warmth was warm and encompassing. The low-ceilinged bar smelled of hops and wood smoke. A group of regulars sat around a table playing cards and drinking beer. They were jovial, and the sounds of their laughter lifted her mood.

The barman, a stocky man with thinning hair and a red wool vest, straightened when he saw her. He wiped his hands on a towel, his eyes flicking to the badge she held up before she spoke.

"I'm Kriminalinspektör Dahl," Avril said evenly. "I'm working with the Norrdal Police. Do you mind if I ask you a couple of questions?"

He eyed her warily. "What about?"

"This woman." She slid a photograph of Lara Berglund across the polished wood. "Do you recognize her?"

He glanced at the photo, then back at Avril. "Of course I know Lara. She came in sometimes with Tarek. Terrible what happened to her. We're all in shock."

Avril felt a flicker of hope. "What about the night she disappeared? Do you remember seeing her here on December sixteenth?"

He shook his head with certainty. "I was on duty last Tuesday, but she didn't come in. It was a quiet night. I'd remember."

Avril studied him, searching his face for hesitation. There was none. The flicker of hope fizzled. She believed he was telling the truth.

"Thanks for your time." She gave a short nod, pocketed the photo, and turned to leave.

"I hope you find whoever killed her," he called after her.

She grimaced. That was the plan.

Svartälgen was only a few streets away. Avril parked outside, savoring the heat for one more moment before facing the icy cold outside. Bracing herself against the sting of the wind, she dashed across the icy pavement.

Inside, the blast of heat and noise almost bowled her over. The air was thick with sweat, beer, and fryer grease. The place was heaving, but mostly with teenagers and twenty-somethings. They were crammed around high tables or leaning against the bar with drinks sloshing in plastic tumblers.

Two pool tables dominated the back corner, the crack of balls ricocheting above the thrum of Swedish pop and bass-heavy dance tracks blaring from tired speakers. Someone was trying to play darts against a board scuffed almost beyond recognition.

Avril pushed her way through, conscious of the glances she drew. She was older, sober, and clearly didn't belong. She found the bar top, noted there were two bartenders on duty, and headed to the closest one. His name badge said Igor.

Placing her ID and the photograph of Lara on the counter, she raised her voice over the din. "Do you know this woman?"

The barman, mid-thirties, wiry and red-cheeked, barely glanced at the photo before nodding. "Ja, that's Lara. Everyone knows Lara."

"Was she in here last Tuesday night? December sixteenth."

He frowned, shaking his head. "That the night she went missing?"

Avril gave a grim nod.

He frowned, thinking. "I don't remember serving her, but look at this place." He gestured to the crowd. "Everyone under thirty comes here, every night of the week. Tuesday's just as busy as Friday. There's nowhere else for them to go."

In this weather, in a town this size, it made sense.

She leaned in close to be heard. "You're certain? It's really important."

He shrugged and shook his head. "Sorry, I don't think so, but I was pulling pints for four hours straight. If she stayed in the back with friends, I wouldn't have noticed."

Avril glanced over at the other bartender. "What about him?"

Igor raised a hand. "Luke, come over here."

The second bartender handed a customer his drink and came over. He was flushed, with slicked-back hair. "Ja? What's up?"

Igor nodded at Avril, who gestured to the photograph still on the counter. "Do you know if Lara Berglund was in here the night of December sixteenth?"

He pushed out his lips, considering. "No, I don't think so. Tuesday, wasn't it?"

Avril nodded.

"No, sorry. I haven't seen her for a few weeks."

Avril bit back her frustration. Luke went back to his side of the bar, while she turned her attention back to Igor. "Do you have a camera system?"

That got a nod. "We do. I can get the manager to pull the footage when he gets in tomorrow. He's not here now."

"December sixteenth," she reminded him.

He nodded. "Gotcha. Anything to help find whoever took Lara."

That was something, at least. "Thank you."

She took one last glance around as she pocketed the photo. The music, the shouting, the clatter of pool balls. It was unlikely a journalist would choose this place for a quiet meeting with a sensitive source. They wouldn't be able to hear each other talk.

She pulled her scarf back over her nose as she stepped into the bitter air again. Two bars down, one more to go.

THE STAG BREWERY sat just beyond the town limits, a low timber building strung with warm amber lights that glowed faintly against the snow. The parking lot was almost empty, save for a few dust-covered SUVs and a delivery van tucked at the side. It was the kind of place that attracted upmarket clientele, and those who valued the quality of the beer over quantity.

Inside, the atmosphere was calmer than the previous bar. No thumping bass, no bodies pressed shoulder to shoulder. Just the quiet hum of conversation, a soccer match muted on the corner TV, and the clink of glassware being polished behind the counter. The smell of hops and yeast clung to the air, faint but distinctive.

Only a dozen or so patrons were scattered among the circular tables. Couples in their thirties, a group of men sampling a range of bottled beer, one group of middle-aged friends drinking pints in the corner.

The barman looked up as Avril approached. He was in his forties, broad-shouldered, with thinning fair hair tied back in a stubby ponytail.

She introduced herself and slid her ID and Lara's photograph across the bar. "Do you know this woman?"

He gave a sad nod. "Of course. That's Lara. Everyone here knew her." He hesitated. "Are you investigating her death?"

She gave a tight nod. "Do you remember seeing her the night she disappeared? December the sixteenth."

He flattened his lips as he thought about that. "No, she was in here the weekend before, but not that night."

"Oh?" Avril felt a surge of adrenaline. "The weekend? Which night?"

"Saturday night. I remember because she and Tarek were celebrating their anniversary. Three years." He gave a sad smile, then shook his head. "What a goddamn tragedy."

She didn't disagree.

"I'm Lars, by the way."

Avril nodded. "Did she seem happy?"

He gave a subdued chuckle. "Yes, they were both happy, despite everything."

"Everything?" She looked up at him over her glasses. "What does that mean?"

"You know, with her father. It's no secret he didn't like Tarek. Blamed him for Lara leaving the fold."

He sniffed. It was clear Lars liked to gossip.

"You know, when she disappeared, I thought she'd left, like Freya. It was odd that she'd run out on Tarek, though. Especially after they'd just celebrated their anniversary."

Avril frowned. "Who's Freya?"

"Lara's best friend since school. She moved to Stockholm last year. Lara was sad to see her go, especially since she didn't even say goodbye. Awful, considering they were so close. Can't blame Freya for leaving though. There isn't much to do in this town, and she wasn't close to her family. To be honest, I'm surprised she stayed as long as she did."

Avril tried to process this new information. "How do you know she went to Stockholm?"

"She left a note. Said she was shacking up with some guy."

"The note was to Lara?" Avril asked.

"No, her mother, which was kind of strange, since they didn't speak. She didn't say a word to Lara, but then we assumed the guy was married and Lara probably would have tried to talk her out of it."

Avril scratched her head over her beanie. It was making her scalp itch. "Why married?"

He shrugged. "Lara said Freya had been seeing someone in secret, but she didn't know who it was. What other reason is there to keep a relationship on the downlow like that?"

Avril stored away the information. "Do you know Freya's last name?"

"Lindholm. Freya Lindholm."

Avril jotted it down in the notes app on her phone, then studied the interior. "Do you have cameras here?"

"Of course. One for the bar, one for the main entrance, and the third out back at the loading bay."

That was good news.

"I'll need to see the footage from last week. Tuesday night, the sixteenth."

"But she wasn't here."

"We still need to check."

He nodded quickly. "I understand. I'll send it over in the morning."

Avril pocketed the photograph, giving him a friendly nod. "Thank you, Lars. You've been very helpful."

"Anything for Lara."

Avril shivered as she stepped back into the cold, but this time, it was because of the uneasy feeling gnawing at her like a dog with a bone it couldn't quite sink its teeth into.

Lars was right. There was something off about Freya's disappearance. Why hadn't she said goodbye to her friend? Why address the farewell note to her mother with whom she wasn't close? Who was the mysterious married man? And did any of this have a bearing on Lara's kidnapping and subsequent murder?

chapter
fifteen

AVRIL GOT TO THE POLICE STATION THE NEXT MORNING TO find a woman in her forties hurrying up the steps in front of her. She stopped when she saw Avril, her dark hair billowing out around her flushed, cherubic face. She a tote bag draped over each arm and shifted them to one.

"You must be the Stockholm Kriminalinspektör. Hans has been telling me all about you."

Avril halted. "Oh?" She had no idea who this woman was—or why the Kommissarie had been talking about her.

"Sorry, you must think I'm so rude." She thrust out a hand. "Freda Bergqvist, Hans's wife."

"Of course." Avril managed a smile, though it felt more like a grimace because she was so cold. "Good to meet you. Shall we go inside?"

The woman laughed. "Not used to our cold winters, I see."

They went into the warm interior of the station. Ekström was already at her desk and looked up as Avril entered.

"Morning, Kriminalinspektör Dahl, I've got some—" She broke off when she saw the woman. "Oh, hello, Freda."

"Hello, Maja." Freda reached out and squeezed Ekström's hand. "Is Hans in his office? He left his sandwiches at home this morning. I thought I'd drop them off on my way to the grocery store."

Avril met Ekström's eye, and the polisassistent tried not to smile.

"He is, yes. You can go through."

"Thank you. I see Erik's not in yet." She glanced at his empty desk and tsked under her breath. "I'll have to tell his mother to kick him out of bed earlier."

Avril watched, slightly bemused, as she walked into her husband's office without knocking.

Ekström nodded. "Yep, that's Freda. She thinks we're all part of her extended family."

Avril snorted. "She seems nice."

"She is, but as I was saying before she bustled in—I've confirmed Nordberg's alibi for December sixteenth."

Avril, who'd just taken off her beanie, swung around to face her. "You have?"

"Ja. He was playing poker with his friends, like he said. I got their names from his assistant. All four of them confirmed Nordberg was there, in person, the entire time."

"What time did the game finish?"

"Late. Around eleven-thirty. Nobody left early, either. They were all there right to the end."

Avril sighed and shook out her beanie. "Well, I guess we can rule him out then. What about the councilor?"

"Her assistant confirmed she was on a work call at that time. It was in the calendar. However, we only have her word for it. I've asked for the names of the other people on the call, and will follow up with them."

Avril took off her jacket. "Find out if there's a recording of the video call."

Ekström made a note. "Will do."

Avril moved toward her temporary desk. "Good work, Ekström," she said, giving the polisassistent a nod.

Ekström beamed.

Avril spent the next hour prepping for the appointment with Mats Vinter, CEO of Skogviken Timber. He'd agreed to meet them at eleven, which gave her time to work through Ekström's notes and Lara's file before heading out.

Vinter at sixty-two was older than Nordberg. A veteran of the timber industry, he'd started his career as a logger in his teens and worked his way up the ranks. That in itself was admirable. Many industry leaders came from landowning families with generational ties to forestry. Vinter, by contrast, seemed self-made.

Now he was CEO of Skogviken Timber AB, one of the largest employers in Jämtland, and consequently held a seat on the Jämtland Regional Development Board.

The only official blemish on his record was a "minor" environmental violation in 2017, when Skogviken was cited for dumping sawdust and wood byproducts into a tributary of the Norrdal River. The County Administrative Board had ordered tests. At the time, the results were presented as clean and the water deemed safe.

But Ekström had dug deeper. A researcher at Umeå University—one of the scientists who had reviewed the samples—later claimed the data had been falsified after submission. Oddly, when pressed by journalists, he retracted his statement, saying he had been mistaken.

Avril frowned. Could someone have leaned on him? Vinter himself, perhaps? Or a friendly voice on the development board who didn't want the county's flagship timber employer under fire?

She took off her glasses and rubbed her eyes with the backs of her hands. There was a pattern here. First the sawdust infringement, and now the chemical runoff. Both times, an environmental assessment had taken place. Both times, it had come back clean.

Referring back to Lara's notes, Avril found the name of the municipal environmental inspector who'd done the impact assessment last year: Erik Palmqvist. Palmqvist had signed off on Skogviken's paperwork earlier this year. His reports concluded that the water quality was normal, with no evidence of chemical runoff or contamination.

Avril pulled the photocopies from Lara's file and studied them. They matched what Lara had written in her notes. No sign of illegal dumping. She squinted at the form, trying to decipher the signature at the bottom. Palmqvist.

Leaning back in her chair, Avril considered the scenarios.

It was possible Palmqvist had simply done his job and found nothing.

It was also possible he'd been paid to look the other way.

She wanted to find out which.

"I MET YOUR WIFE THIS MORNING," Avril said to Hans as they drove the icy road north toward Skogviken Timber.

"Freda worries a lot," he replied, eyes on the slick tarmac. His hands stayed steady on the wheel, but she noticed the faint pink creeping into his cheeks. "We didn't have kids, so she... overcompensates."

Avril gave a short nod. That made sense.

"How about you?" Hans asked, his tone casual but edged with curiosity. "Married? Kids?"

She shook her head. "None of the above."

"Boyfriend?" He arched an eyebrow.

She hesitated, then gave a half-shrug. "Of sorts."

THERE WAS no way she was unpacking the tangled mess of Krister and her relationship here—not in a patrol car on a snowbound road. Hans didn't need to know that much.

They fell into silence again. Outside, snow came in light but persistent flurries, the flakes hissing across the windshield in thin, wind-driven streaks. Pines rose on either side of the road, their branches heavy with white, the forest closing in like a tunnel.

After twenty minutes, the woods opened onto a broad clearing. A compound stretched ahead. Chain-link fencing topped with barbed wire, security lights mounted high on poles, cameras sweeping the approach. A large sign announced: Skogviken Timber AB.

Hans slowed at the gate, flashed his badge at the guard in a fluorescent vest, and was waved through. The drive wound between stacks of neatly piled timber, the scent of resin faint even through the heater vents. Processing sheds loomed to one side, the hum of machinery muted by thick walls.

The main office building was modern. A low, concrete-and-glass structure with the Skogviken logo etched into frosted panels. Inside, the air was warm and smelled faintly of coffee and air freshener.

At reception, a young woman greeted them and asked them to wait.

After a few minutes, she returned with an apologetic smile. "Mr. Vinter won't be able to see you after all. He's tied up with an urgent board matter."

Hans didn't bother to conceal his frown. "We had an appointment."

"I understand," she replied smoothly, like she'd said this a million times before. "Hanna Sjöberg, our Head of Communications, will speak with you instead."

Avril exchanged a glance with Hans. Not what she wanted, but better than nothing.

Sjöberg arrived moments later, striding toward them in a tailored navy suit and three-inch heels. She was in her late thirties, with polished blond hair, immaculate makeup and radiated composure.

"Kommissarie Bergqvist. Kriminalinspektör Dahl." She shook their hands firmly, her smile professional but cool. "I'm sorry Mats can't make it, but he asked me to step in. I'll be happy to answer any questions you have."

Avril let out a frustrated breath and cast a glance at Hans. This, right here, was why she preferred surprise visits. He ignored her.

They followed Sjöberg into a sleek conference room with a long, glass and chrome table, twelve chairs, and a wall-mounted screen at one end. Sjöberg sat on one side, where her laptop was already open. Avril and Hans sat on the other.

Hans cleared his throat. "As you know, we are investigating the death of the journalist, Lara Berglund. Before she died, she was researching an article about illegal chemical byproducts being dumped by Skogviken Timber into the river. Do you know anything about this?"

Hanna's expression didn't flicker. "We receive inquiries from journalists all the time. I couldn't say whether her name crossed my desk specifically."

Avril leaned forward. "Did Lara Berglund come here? Did she request an interview with Vinter or yourself?"

"Not to my knowledge, no."

"What's your response to the claims of illegal dumping?" Hans asked.

Sjöberg have a small, practiced smile. "We are aware of the rumors, yes. They're baseless. These things circulate—particularly when reporters are eager to make their mark. We deal with several such allegations every year. It's part of doing business nowadays."

Avril's gaze stayed fixed on her. "Are you sure she didn't meet with Mr. Vinter directly?"

"No. Mats doesn't handle press inquiries. That's my role."

"Could she have met with anyone else here?" Avril pressed.

"Not to my knowledge," Hanna replied in a clipped tone. "But even if she had, I can't see how that would connect us to her murder."

"How do you know she was murdered?" Avril asked, studying Sjöberg.

Her gaze flickered—just for a second—before she regained her composure.

"Why else would the police be investigating?"

It was a micro-expression, but Avril had seen it. Sjöberg did know who Lara was. So why was she lying? Was it just to protect the company's image, or was there more to it?

Hans placed his hands on the table. "We do still need to talk to your boss. Could you ask Mr. Vinter to call us to reschedule?"

She shut her laptop with an uncompromising snap. "I certainly will. Now, if there's nothing else, I have to get back to work."

Meeting over, they got to their feet.

Frustrated, Avril glanced at Hans. How could he be so calm? Sjöberg had obviously just lied about knowing Lara—and the boss, the man they really wanted to speak to, had sidestepped them.

Sjöberg smiled, but it didn't touch her eyes. "Johan will see you out."

On cue, the door opened and a tall, broad-shouldered man stepped in. His close-cropped hair revealed faded tattoos curling up his neck. A heavy winter jacket hung open, revealing a black T-shirt stretched across a chest that had been honed in the gym.

His expression was dark, almost threatening, and his eyes lingered a fraction too long on Avril's face. If she had to guess, she'd say Johan was ex-military.

"Johan Evertsson, Head of Operations," Hanna said lightly, as if introducing a chauffeur. "He'll walk you back to your car."

Avril studied him as they followed him out. The tattoos, the stance, the quiet way he moved—all screamed armed forces.

As they reached the door, she spoke quietly. "Did you know Lara Berglund?"

He paused just long enough to register the question. Then a slow smile tugged at the corner of his mouth.

"No, sorry. Who's that?"

Good comeback. But Avril wasn't buying it.

He pulled the door open, letting the cold rush in. "Drive safe, Kriminalinspektör. Roads are treacherous this time of year."

Avril glanced at Hans, a scowl on his face, as they stepped past Johan into the snow.

chapter **sixteen**

"They're all lying," Avril blurted out as soon as they got into the squad car. "I could tell Hannah Sjöberg knew exactly who Lara was. I'll bet she did go there to talk to Mats Vinter. That brute Johan probably saw her off the property."

"We can't make assumptions like that," Hans said, although his forehead was still furrowed. "Proper police work, Avril. Evidence. That's what we need."

"We'll never get it," she fumed, clenching her gloved hands in her lap. "None of them will tell us anything. Vinter won't even see us."

"He will," Hans muttered, as determined as she'd ever seen him. "I'll make sure of that. Nobody is above the law."

Avril was glad he'd said that. Vinter giving them the run around had obviously annoyed him too. It was about time he showed some backbone.

Still, she understood his position. He had to live here, amongst them. They had sway over police budgets, and in his words, could cripple the department. She, on the other hand, would disappear back to Stockholm and not give this place another thought.

Homesickness hit Avril like a sledgehammer. It surprised her. That wasn't an emotion she'd experienced before. Maybe it was a sign she was finally where she was supposed to be. The thought calmed her, and she let out a long breath.

"I want Ekström to do background checks on both Hannah Sjöberg and Johan Evertsson. Particularly Evertsson. I think he's former military, and could be Vinter's unofficial enforcer."

"I've never met him before," Hans said, as if surprised. "I don't think he lives in Norrdal."

"Does Hannah?" she asked.

He shook his head. "No. Nor Vinter. I believe he has a big estate out near one of the lakes."

Avril threw him a sharp glance. "Not Frostsjön?"

"No, but not far away. We have many lakes in that area."

"He could be our guy," Avril murmured, thinking out loud. "Lara could have been chasing him for an interview. Maybe he finally agreed to meet her at a bar. He could have spiked her drink, driven her out to the lake, and strangled her." The thought left her breathless.

Hans kept his eyes on the road, snowflakes spiraling in the headlights. "It's possible. But would a man like Vinter do his own dirty work?"

"You're right," Avril admitted. "More likely he'd send Evertsson. That's what men like him keep people like Evertsson around for."

Silence fell, broken only by the squeak of the wipers. Then Avril muttered, "It's a pity we can't search their vehicles."

"We'd never get a judge to sign off on a warrant," Hans said. "A journalist asking questions is not probable cause."

She ground her teeth. He was right. "Even if she was there, the vehicles would have been cleaned by now. They wouldn't leave anything to chance."

BY THE TIME Hans and Avril trudged back into the station, the light outside had already given up, though it was barely mid-afternoon. They stepped inside, snow still clinging to their coats.

Ekström sat at her desk, eyes darting across her monitor, fingers flying across the keyboard. She straightened when she saw them. "How'd it go?"

Hans grunted, gave a small shake of his head, and disappeared into his office without slowing. Avril dropped into her borrowed desk opposite Ekström, tugging off her gloves. "Not good. Vinter wasn't there, or if he was, he didn't want to see us, so we met with his communications person instead. She denied even knowing Lara Berglund."

Ekström blinked. "Really?"

"Plus, we ran into their Head of Operations on our way out. Shady character. Can you do a background check on Johan Evertsson?" She said his name slowly. "Give me everything you can find on him. I suspect he's got a military history."

The younger woman's eyes widened. "Of course. I'll start right away. I've just finished combing Lara's laptop."

Avril leaned forward. "Did you find anything?"

"The files match what we already had from the *Chronicle*. I couldn't find anything new."

Damn. She'd been hoping for a name, a source. Someone who she may have met. "Nothing at all?"

Ekström shook her head. "If she had anything sensitive, it wasn't on that machine. I checked every file to see if there were any hidden folders or encrypted files. There weren't."

Avril frowned.

"I mean, she may have cloud storage," Ekström added. "In which case, we won't be able to access them. Not without her password."

And it didn't look like they were going to get that. Unless… "Call Tarek," Avril instructed. "See if he knows it."

Ekström gave a quick nod and reached for the landline.

Across the room, Lundgren tilted back on his chair, a phone cradled between his shoulder and ear. He muttered a curse under his breath, then hung up and let the chair fall forward. "I can't believe those guys. They promised the call logs would come through today, but nothing yet."

Avril glanced at him. "You manage to go through the camera footage from the bars?"

Lundgren wouldn't meet her eye. "I started with the Stag since I figured it was the more likely spot. Went through the footage twice, frame by frame. She wasn't there that night. Lars was telling the truth."

Avril hadn't really doubted Lars, but it was always good to check. "What about Svartälgen?"

He pointed to his screen. "I've got it downloaded and ready to go."

Before he could press play, Ekström spoke up again. "I've also confirmed Councilor Håkansson's alibi."

Avril turned toward her. "You have? Already?"

"Ja. She was on a video call that evening. The other participants have all confirmed. The meeting was scheduled for seven o'clock and would have been over by eight."

Avril shook her head. "That's too late. Lara went out before seven. We know that because it's the time Tarek got home."

Hans came out of his office. "The councilor is off our list, then?"

Avril nodded.

A sudden shout broke the rhythm of the room. "Kommissarie!"

They all turned. Lundgren, on his feet, pointed to his screen. His chair was shoved back, forgotten.

Hans crossed the room, while Avril shifted position, so she was standing beside him. On the grainy footage from Svartälgen, the bar's exterior awning flickered into view. The timestamp in the corner read: *2024-12-16 19:36:02.*

And there she was... Lara Berglund.

Clear as day, captured on camera as she pushed through the door and stepped into the bar.

chapter **seventeen**

For a moment, no one spoke. The only sound was the faint whir of the desktop tower as they all stared at the footage. Lara Berglund, frozen in mid-step, her scarf trailing behind her as she pushed through the door of Svartälgen.

Avril leaned closer to the monitor, her pulse quickening. "That's definitely her. The clothing matches that in the crime scene photos, and the timestamp puts her there less than half an hour after Tarek got home."

Hans drew in a breath. "That is the last sighting we have of her."

"Not necessarily," Lundgren cut in. "This is just the exterior. I've got the interior footage downloaded as well." He tapped the keyboard, and the view shifted. The camera over the bar was angled at the door, so they could see a row of bar stools and patrons drifting in and out of frame.

Lundgren forwarded it to the exact timestamp of the first one.

"There," Ekström breathed as Lara came into view. "That's her." They watched as she walked into the bar, looked around, then headed to the tables, stepping out of frame.

"Damn," Hans hissed. "We can't see who she was meeting."

"Let's watch everyone else come into the bar," Ekström whispered. "One of them has to be her killer."

They all stood around Lundgren's desk, staring at his screen. After nearly five minutes, Avril shook her head. "This is useless. It could be any one of these people." The bar was busy, the flow constant. For once, Lundgren didn't argue.

Hans gestured at the screen. "Is there any other footage?"

Lundgren shook his head. "This is all they sent through."

"Run it forward," Hans ordered, scowling. "Let's see who she leaves with."

They watched as the images sped up, racing across the screen in jerky movements. Nobody said a word until Lundgren had played it all the way to the end.

"She *doesn't* come out," Avril said, blinking to rest her eyes. "There is no footage of Lara leaving the bar."

"How can that be?" Ekström whispered, glancing between her and Hans.

"There will be a back door," Lundgren said. "Most bars have them for deliveries and to take out the trash."

"That's it." Avril straightened up. "Whoever took her snuck her out the back."

"He could have come in that way too," Ekström added. "Avoiding the front camera."

Hans put his hands on his hips. "We need full statements from everyone working that night. Bartenders, waitresses, chefs, anyone else on rotation. Somebody must have seen something."

"The place was packed and the bar staff were busy," Avril countered. "It's understandable if they didn't see her. What we really need is to canvas the public. Anyone who was there that night who saw Lara leave."

"I can put out a radio appeal," Ekström suggested, her eyes bright at the thought. "Or you could go on television, Kommissarie."

Avril turned her gaze to Hans. "That is not a bad idea. People here know you, they trust you. If you stand in front of a camera and ask for their help, they will listen."

Hans exhaled slowly and pushed a hand through his hair. "The problem is that could open us up to a flood of false leads. We don't want to end up wasting hours chasing stories that go nowhere. We do not have the manpower for that."

Avril inclined her head. "You're right, but I still think it's worth trying. This is not Stockholm. We won't get thousands of crank callers. The community here is smaller. Someone may have seen something, and if they trust you enough to come forward, we could get the break we need."

Hans was silent for a moment, considering. Finally, he gave a reluctant nod. "Very well. Ekström, call the local networks and set it up. I will make the appeal. Let's just hope it doesn't backfire on us."

Avril turned to Lundgren. "Any news on Lara's phone records?"

"Not yet." He couldn't hide his frustration. "I'll let you know as soon as they come in."

She frowned at his tone, then had an idea. "Can we request their cell-site records for that night? If Nordberg or Vinter's phones connected to a tower near the Svartälgen, it'll show up."

"That's smart thinking." Hans pointed to Lundgren's screen. "Add that shady Operations Manager, Evertsson, to the list."

Lundgren gave his boss a nod and turned to do as instructed.

"Oh, I almost forgot." Ekström turned to Avril. "I did some digging on Evertsson like you asked, and you were right. He is ex-Swedish Army. Served in Bosnia and Kosovo, and after that transitioned to private security. Two years ago, he joined Skogviken Timber as Operations Manager."

"Any red flags?" she asked.

Ekström gave a brief nod. "Only one. Shortly after he joined Vinter's company, Evertsson was accused of assaulting a protester at a logging demonstration."

Avril narrowed her gaze. "What happened?"

"Nothing. From what I can gather, the case was dropped for lack of evidence."

"Convenient," Hans muttered.

Avril agreed. "Very."

These people were protected. They thought they were above the law, but they were soon going to find out they were wrong.

Avril reached for her coat. "I'll head to the Svartälgen. Get started on those statements. Meet you back here in a couple of hours?"

Hans gave a quick nod. "Thanks, Avril."

As she walked out into the cold, she felt a surge of hope. Could it be that things were finally coming together?

TURNS OUT, she was wrong. Despite what was on the video feed, nobody at the bar remembered seeing Lara. None of the serving staff recalled her placing an order, and none of the bar staff said they'd served her. It was like she'd walked in and then vanished.

"How can that be?" she asked Hans when she got back. The afternoon had been trying and her head was pounding.

"There were a lot of people there," he allowed. "Plus, it's been over a week."

That was the real problem. Once time passed, witnesses' memories faded and became less reliable. Key leads were lost. She'd seen it too many times at the FBI. Line up ten onlookers, and you'd get ten different versions of the same event. By day three, those versions blurred even further, colored by suggestion, rumor, or simple forgetfulness. That's why the first forty-eight hours in a murder investigation were so crucial.

As Avril came in, shaking the snow from her coat, Lundgren looked up.

"I've heard back from the phone provider," he said, holding up a thin printed log. "The call data for Nordberg, Vinter, and Evertsson came through."

Avril set her bag down, tugging her scarf loose. "And Lara?"

He grunted. "Still nothing. They say there's a backlog in processing victim records."

Avril exhaled sharply. "Of course there is. What did you find?"

"Nordberg checks out. His phone was active at his friend's place, just like he said. But neither Vinter nor Evertsson's phones returned any signal at all that night. Both were either switched off or completely out of range."

Hans's eyebrows lifted. "Both of them?"

Lundgren gave a grim nod. "They both came back on around midnight."

"That is suspicious," Hans muttered.

"Doesn't mean they were together," Avril said, thoughtfully.

"Doesn't mean they weren't," Lundgren added.

She sighed. Really, she needed to talk to him and sort out whatever this beef was he had with her. "Were either of them on the camera footage from the bar?"

Lundgren shook his head. "Not that I could see, but I'll need to go through it again to be absolutely sure. I wasn't looking for them the first time."

"I asked Igor about the back entrance," Avril said, glancing up at Hans. "There isn't a camera covering it, so the killer could easily have used it. It opens onto an alley, but it's too late now to check for footprints. That's a well-used path."

"Damn it. Just when I thought we were making some headway."

Complex murder investigations often felt like one step forward, two steps back, but she didn't say as much to Hans. She'd never heard him curse before.

"At least we're further along than yesterday," she said. "We know where she met her killer, how he got her out without being seen, and once the appeal goes out, someone might come forward."

They could hope, at least.

chapter
eighteen

THE APPEAL WENT OUT ON THE SIX O'CLOCK NEWS, A CLIPPED segment with Hans at the podium addressing the camera. Avril and Lundgren crowded around Ekström's computer to watch it stream live.

My name is Hans Bergqvist. I am Kommissarie at Norrdal Polisstation.

On Tuesday evening, the sixteenth of December, at approximately 19:36, Lara Berglund was seen entering the Svartälgen bar here in Norrdal. That was the last confirmed sighting of her alive.

We know there were many people at the bar that night. Some of you may have seen Lara. Perhaps you spoke to her, perhaps you noticed who she was with, or saw her leaving. Even a small detail that you might not consider important could be vital to this investigation.

I ask anyone who was at Svartälgen that night, or in the surrounding area, to please contact us at the Norrdal Polisstation. You can call us directly or use the tip line. If you are worried about speaking openly, you can provide information anonymously.

Lara's family deserves to know the truth. We need your help to find out what happened to her. Please, if you saw anything, come forward.

. . .

Hans was in his office on the phone, being questioned by Mayor Öberg. They could hear fragments of his low, deliberate responses. The broadcast had rattled him, and now he wanted reassurances—what was being done, how soon there would be an arrest, how the council was meant to calm a town that suddenly believed a killer might be walking its streets.

News of an FBI agent working in Norrdal had already circulated, fueling gossip in a community unused to national attention, let alone foreign law enforcement in their midst. The murder of a young woman —one of their own—had cracked the calm surface of the town. People were uneasy.

With an election coming up, the mayor needed this one solved, and fast. Avril didn't envy Hans, but the mayor wasn't her concern.

"You ready?" Avril asked Ekström and Lundgren. They weren't sure how many calls they were going to get, but it had the potential to be a long night.

"Yep," Lundgren said in a clipped tone. Ekström nodded but looked nervous. Avril guessed this was a first for her.

"It'll be fine," she said, reassuringly. "If anyone sounds like they have real information, take down their name and number, or pass the call to me."

The polisassistent bit her lip. "Okay."

The first calls came quickly after Hans's appeal went out on the evening news. People rang in with half-remembered details, suspicions about neighbors, even sightings of women who vaguely resembled Lara. A man insisted he had seen her boarding a bus to Sundsvall. Another swore she had been walking along the river yesterday, even though she had already been found beneath the ice.

Avril kept her notes brief, each one marked off as unfounded. False leads, hearsay, confusion. It was the same pattern she had seen so many times before. Noise that had to be sifted through, even when most of it led nowhere.

By ten o'clock, the phones had slowed, and Avril wondered if they would get anything useful at all. An empty dish and several plates lay scattered around the office. Freda, Hans's mothering wife, had been in with a homemade *janssons frestelse*—the creamy potato, onion, and anchovy casserole that was a staple winter dish for every Swede—to keep them all going.

Hans was still in his office, writing reports and fielding calls from various departments including Serious Crimes. Avril had checked in with Krister earlier and knew Sundström would be calling him for updates.

Avril sighed and glanced at her watch. She was about to suggest they call it a night when Ekström snapped her fingers and shot Avril a frantic look.

"Speaker," she mouthed. Lundgren stopped what he was doing to listen.

Ekström's voice was breathy. "Could you repeat that?"

A young woman's voice came through, hesitant but steady. "I saw Lara at Svartälgen... on the sixteenth."

"Are you certain it was her?"

"Yes, I'm sure. We were at school together."

Avril grabbed a pen and scribbled on the pad beside her laptop.

"Did you speak to her?" Ekström glanced at Avril, who gave an encouraging nod.

"No, but I saw her sitting at one of the tables. She was with a man."

Avril felt her breath catch. Lundgren straightened, and Ekström clutched the phone like it was a lifeline. "Could you describe this man?"

The caller took a shaky breath. "Darkish blond hair, long black coat, average build. His back was to me, so I couldn't see his face."

Avril tensed, her pen poised over her notebook. She'd just described half the men in Sweden.

"How long did they sit together?" Ekström asked.

"Maybe twenty minutes? Something like that. I wasn't watching them the whole time."

"What then?"

"When I went back up to the bar later, they were gone."

Avril pointed to her watch.

"What time was that?" Ekström asked.

"About eight o'clock. Maybe a few minutes after. I remember, because one of our friends had just arrived."

"You didn't see them leave?" Ekström pressed.

"No. Sorry. When I looked again, their table was empty."

"Name?" whispered Avril.

A beat passed, then Ekström leaned closer to the speaker. "Thank you for calling in. Can I take your name and number so we can follow up if we need to?"

Another pause, then the woman said, "I... I don't want to get involved. I just thought you should know."

Then the light went dead.

"Sorry," Ekström said quickly, cheeks flushed. "I tried to get her name."

"Did we at least get her number?" Avril asked.

Ekström shook her head. "No. Caller ID was withheld."

Lundgren swore under his breath. "We can still get the metadata. I'll follow up with the provider. Again."

"They still haven't sent Lara's phone records?" Avril asked. Three days, maybe four, and still nothing.

Lundgren exhaled hard. "They're blaming strike action. Apparently they're down to a skeleton staff. They keep telling me tomorrow."

"There'll be no one in the office now," Avril sighed, as the door opened and Hans walked in. He glanced around.

"Any news?"

Avril filled him in, then said, "Lundgren's going to get her number, but she didn't have anything more than that."

"It's not much help," he grunted.

"It confirms she did meet someone at the bar, and we know him to be a person of interest." She shifted her gaze to Ekström. "First thing tomorrow, let's go through all the staff records of Nordberg Infrastruktur and Skogviken Timber and do a crosscheck. Anyone who fits the description, run their phone number and see if they were in the vicinity of the bar on the sixteenth."

Hans nodded. "That will help narrow down our suspect list."

Avril glanced over at him. "Johan Evertsson has dark blond hair."

Hans sucked in a breath. "But so does Mats Vinter."

"Nordberg's dark-haired," Ekström pointed out. "But we've ruled him out anyway."

Double confirmation never hurt.

"And Hannah is a woman, so it's not her," Lundgren said, stating the obvious. Nobody replied to that. They were all tired.

Eventually, Hans ran a hand through his hair. "Okay, let's call it there. We'll pick this up first thing in the morning."

As Avril packed up to leave, Ekström went around and collected the plates, a thoughtful look on her face. "Do you really think this is a lead?"

"It is," Avril said, shrugging on her coat. "This is how it's done, little by little, until the pieces start fitting together."

Ekström smiled.

"You did good today," Avril added, hefting her laptop bag onto her shoulder.

The younger woman's smile widened. "Thank you. I'm learning so much from you. I wish…" Her voice trailed off as her eyes flicked toward Hans's office door.

"I know," Avril said quietly. "It can't be easy here, where not much ever happens."

"One day I'll move to Stockholm and work for Serious Crimes. Just like you."

Avril hesitated. She thought about her life, about chasing killers, and living with the images of their brutal crimes in her head. She still visualized the victims' faces long after the cases had closed. It never went away.

This job left its toll on you. It hardened you, affected your sleep, your mental health, and killed any hope of normalcy. Not that she'd ever been "normal" anyway.

She opened her mouth to say as much, then looked at the excitement and passion on the young polisassistent's face and shut it again. Who was she to ruin her dreams?

Instead, she forced a small smile and said, "I'm sure you will."

chapter
nineteen

WHEN AVRIL ARRIVED THE NEXT MORNING, EKSTRÖM AND Lundgren were already at their desks, headsets on, working through the overnight messages. Calls that had gone to the voicemail system after hours were logged and returned one by one, each entry added to the tip sheet.

"Anything?" she asked, as she passed Ekström's desk.

The polisassistent nodded, but held up one hand, fingers splayed, as if to say, give me five minutes.

Avril nodded and went over to her desk. After taking off her coat and setting up her laptop, she logged on to the system and saw that Ekström had loaded the video call Councilor Håkansson had been on the night of Lara's disappearance. That was probably what she'd wanted to tell her. It hardly mattered now, since Birgitta was no longer a suspect, but it was good to have confirmation.

She hit play. The video conference filled the screen, four small boxes showing each participant. The timestamp matched the evening of December 16th. Avril clicked play, watching long enough to note Birgitta's posture, her occasional comments, the way she jotted notes on a pad beside her. Nothing suggested she had left the call.

She dragged the bar forward to the end, where the councilor was still present as the others signed off one by one. The timestamps were continuous. As far as Avril could tell, Birgitta had been there the entire time. Satisfied, she closed the file and turned to her next task.

Across the room, Lundgren was still on the phone, his voice low but impatient. Ekström got up, a folder in her hands.

"I have something," she said, coming over to Avril's desk.

Ekström slid the folder across, her expression intent. "I decided to do some digging into Mats Vinter and Johan Evertsson last night. I wanted to figure out why both of their phones were off the evening Lara disappeared."

Avril raised her eyebrows. "Did you find anything?"

She gave a quick nod. "The logs show that both phones went dead around seven-thirty on the sixteenth and didn't come back online until after midnight."

"They both came on at the same time too?"

Ekström nodded. "Whatever they were doing, they were doing it together."

Hans came out of his office as she spoke, shrugging into his jacket. He looked from Ekström to Avril. "What is this?"

Ekström repeated the findings, her tone steady but cautious. Hans listened, his jaw tightening. "I knew it. They were in it together. Vinter gave the order, but Evertsson carried it out."

"Actually, I don't think that is what happened," Ekström said.

Hans focused on her. "Explain?"

She cleared her throat. "One of the county's traffic cameras caught a Skogviken Timber lorry on a back road that night, heading north toward a restricted tract of woodland. It should not have been there. I checked the company's transport permits. That road isn't on any of their routes."

"You thought to look at the traffic cams?" Avril asked, glancing at Hans.

He jutted out his chin, clearly impressed. "You think Vinter and Evertsson were driving it?"

"Why don't we ask them?" Avril faced Hans. "Vinter still hasn't given us an appointment, and it's about time we spoke to him."

"We need to talk to them both," he growled. "Okay, enough with the games. Let's head over there now."

Avril got to her feet, flashing Ekström a grin.

"Well done," she whispered, when Hans was out of earshot. "Told you those computer skills would come in handy."

Avril sat beside Hans as he drove to Skogviken Timber. She watched the spruce forests flash past, the pale light barely holding against the encroaching darkness.

"Ekström did well, didn't she?" she said, pointedly.

He smirked. "You don't have to keep reminding me. I know she's a good officer."

"You might want to tell her sometime."

He sighed. "You know she's going to leave, right? Everybody does. A smart young woman like that? As soon as she's got a couple of years under her belt, she'll transfer to the SPA, or even Serious Crimes with you."

Avril knew he was right. Ekström had said as much herself. Perhaps that was why he held back. He didn't want to lose her.

"What about Lundgren?" she asked. "Will he leave too?"

A shrug. "Eventually, maybe. Right now, he can't. He's got a young wife and a baby at home. They rely on her parents for support."

She didn't know that. Lundgren never spoke about his private life. In fact, he barely spoke at all.

Eventually, they turned off onto the icy access road leading to Skogviken Timber.

"How d'you want to play this?" Avril asked. "We could talk to each of them separately, or together."

"I say we split them up," he said. "See if their stories match."

"Agreed. You want Vinter or Evertsson?"

"Since I'm Kommissarie, I should probably take Vinter. It'll be expected. Are you all right to handle Evertsson?"

"Of course."

They parked out front and marched inside, IDs ready. The young receptionist started to rise, but Hans strode past without pausing, holding up his badge. "We'll see Vinter. Now."

Avril followed, her boots silent on the carpeted floor.

Within minutes, the CEO himself appeared, all practiced charm in a pressed shirt and tailored jacket. Behind him loomed Johan Evertsson, sleeves rolled, tattoos running down his forearms like maps. Unlike his boss, irritation was written across his scowling face.

"Kommissarie, I'm so glad you took the initiative, I've been meaning to call you to reschedule our appointment. Apologies, this is an extremely busy time for us."

Hans's reply was brisk. "Good. Then we won't take up more of it than necessary. My colleague will speak with Johan. You and I can talk in your office."

Vinter glanced at Avril, then at Evertsson, and almost grinned. Avril felt herself bristle. If he thought this would be easy, he had another thing coming.

Vinter gestured for Hans to follow him down the corridor, his polished shoes squeaking as he walked. Evertsson remained behind, shoulders squared, jaw set. He looked at Avril like a cat about to pounce on a mouse.

Avril met his gaze with her cool one. "Shall we?" She nodded toward a side room.

"After you."

Inside was a large, round table designed for meetings of up to six people. Two windows let in a modicum of light, but it was weak and ineffectual. Avril flipped the switch as she walked in, and the fluorescent light hummed and flickered to life.

She took a seat, her back to the window, while he lowered himself into one opposite.

"Do you know why we're here?" she asked.

A shrug. He crossed his arms, tattoos flexing in a show of intimidation. It didn't work. Avril had met far scarier men than Johan Evertsson before, and it didn't faze her. It probably had something to do with the fact that she didn't feel the depth of emotion some people did.

At first she'd thought it was a failing, some weird genetic quirk that dialed down her empathy. Of course, her traumatic childhood might have something to do with it, or the decade she'd spent hunting her mother's killer. Either way, she'd become immune to fear, and was still waiting for it to come back.

"We're investigating the kidnapping and murder of Lara Berglund. I believe you knew her?"

That threw him. He scowled, his eyebrows hunching over his eyes. "What makes you say that?"

"She came here, asking to speak to your boss in the week before she died. You would have seen her out." She smiled, the implication clear.

It was a guess, but a calculated one. From everything she'd read, Lara struck her as the type of person who went after what she wanted. She wouldn't have been easily intimidated either, and Avril could picture her striding into the building, demanding to speak to Vinter—just like they'd done.

"It's possible. I escort a lot of people off the premises."

Avril gave a quick nod. "Mr. Evertsson, where were you on the night of December sixteenth?"

If he was surprised by the question, he didn't show it. "At home."

"Anyone who can confirm that?"

A shrug. "Not really. I live alone."

"What is your role here at Skogviken Timber?"

"I'm the Head of Operations."

"So you schedule all deliveries and transport of timber to and from the factory?"

"Of course."

"Could you explain why a Skogviken truck was spotted driving on the Fagerhult road, through the state forest north of Norrdal on the night of December 16?" Avril asked, her voice calm but edged. "That stretch is restricted. Heavy vehicles aren't permitted without a logging concession, and there are no active permits in that area."

The scowl was back. Evertsson didn't like being cornered. "It wasn't."

Avril leaned back and studied him. "A council traffic camera caught it. We've identified it by the logo on the side and the license plate. There is no mistake."

He tried to look unconcerned, but failed. "One of our drivers must have taken a wrong turn. It happens."

"You were driving, Mr. Evertsson. We have you on camera."

He stared at her, a pulse ticking in his temple. Avril didn't move. If he asked for proof, she was busted, but she was hoping he wasn't smart enough to question it, since it was most likely the truth.

He leaned back, forcing a scoff. "Then your camera's wrong. Like I said, I wasn't driving. Must have been one of my guys."

"Mats Vinter was with you."

A beat passed, and then he glared at her. "Okay. We took a wrong turn and ended up on the Fagerhult road. I didn't want anyone to know because, as you pointed out, we don't have permits to go up there."

Avril exhaled under her breath. Now they had confirmation the two men were together.

She tilted her head. "What were you two really doing there, Mr. Evertsson? I know your usual delivery routes don't take you out that way."

He stared stonily back at her. "I told you, we got lost. That's not a crime."

"No, but logging in the State Forest without a permit is. And a serious one at that."

He shifted in his chair but didn't answer.

"All right," she went on. "Here's what's going to happen. We'll need the GPS logs for every Skogviken vehicle on the sixteenth. That means delivery schedules, driver assignments, and fuel receipts."

His eyes narrowed. "You'll need a court order for that."

Avril allowed herself the faintest smile. "Don't worry, we'll get one. In the meantime, the County Administrative Board has already been notified. There's an inspection team in the forest right now."

He looked at her like he wanted to tear her limb from limb. Evertsson and Vinter were guilty all right, but it wasn't of murder.

She got to her feet. "Thank you for your time. We'll be in touch. I'll see myself out."

And she left the room before he could say anything else.

chapter
twenty

VINTER, ON THE OTHER HAND, HAD FREELY ADMITTED TO knowing Lara. He'd told Hans that she'd come in guns blazing two weeks earlier and had demanded his response to the allegations of illegal dumping of chemical waste.

"He passed her on to his PR Manager, Hanna Sjöberg, and claims that's the last he saw of her," Hans explained, back at the police station.

"What did he say about the night of the sixteenth?" Ekström asked.

Hans shrugged. "He claimed to be at home, with his wife. I'm sure if we ask her, she'll back up his statement."

"Except Evertsson admitted they were together," Avril cut in, with a grin. "You were right, Ekström, they were in the State Forest, engaged in illegal logging activities. The Environmental Agency has found evidence of tree stumps in the protected area, freshly cut, as well as stockpiles of logs hidden under tarps, ready to be hauled."

"So, they didn't have anything to do with Lara's disappearance?" Lundgren rubbed his jaw.

Hans shook his head. "Don't see how they could have. Frostsjön is miles away from where they were that night."

"It wasn't them," Avril confirmed. "But I wish I could see their faces when they compare interview notes."

Hans snorted.

Avril went back to her desk, still feeling the buzz of adrenaline. It was a small victory, but it felt like they'd done something good, despite it having nothing to do with solving Lara's murder.

"I finally got Lara's call records from the mobile provider," Lundgren announced, holding up a thin printout. His voice carried more relief than triumph. "I've been chasing them for days. Turns out she made and received several calls from the same unidentified number in the weeks before she disappeared. Always the same one."

Avril sat forward. "That could be our source."

Hans, halfway back to his office, stopped in his tracks. "What do you mean unidentified?"

"It's a *kontantkort*," Lundgren said. "Prepaid SIM. No subscriber details, no contract."

"A burner," Ekström murmured, eyes widening.

"More people are opting for prepaid SIMs these days," Avril pointed out reasonably. "They don't want to be locked into contracts."

Hans's expression hardened. "We need to know who it belongs to."

"Okay, I'll do some digging."

"Have you tried calling it?" Ekström asked.

Lundgren hesitated. "No. Should I?" He looked at Hans.

Hans pressed his lips together, considering. "If it was her source, we don't want to scare him off."

Avril spoke quietly. "Better to see where it is. If the phone is switched on, the network can ping the last mast it connected to."

Lundgren nodded. "I'll call the telecom liaison."

Hans muttered something about coffee and disappeared into the tiny kitchen. The hiss of the machine filled the silence while Lundgren made the call. Avril watched the muscles in his jaw work as he told them what he needed. A few moments later, he asked, "So where is it now?"

Hans came back with a steaming mug and leaned against Ekström's desk, waiting.

Lundgren looked up. "I got it. It's currently active and pinged to this address." He held up the note. It read: *Gråsten Gård*.

"We should go there," Avril said, jumping up. "This could be our guy."

"Whoa!" Hans held up his hand, coffee splashing onto the floor. "That can't be right. Are you certain it's the correct address?"

"Ja, I double checked it."

"What's wrong?" Avril frowned. The color had drained from Hans's face.

He turned to face her, his eyes haunted. "That is my brother's place."

HANS WAS UNDERSTANDABLY quiet on the way to Gråsten Gård. He'd explained that his brother lived on a farm on the outskirts of Norrdal. This was where the number had pinged.

"What is he doing there?" Avril asked after they'd been driving for about ten minutes. It had been snowing for the last two days, and the roads were compacted. The squad car, a V90 Cross Country made for this kind of weather, crunched as it drove over the packed snow.

"I don't know," Hans said, his voice low and cautious. "My brother is... let's just say he's always been a little wild."

Avril glanced across at him. "Wild in what way?"

"At school, he was always the one to act out. He struggled academically and rebelled against authority. Got a reputation as being difficult."

"School was a long time ago," Avril said.

"It got worse. Afterwards, he fell in with the wrong crowd, started drinking and getting into fights, experimenting with drugs... You know how it goes."

Unfortunately, she did.

"What does he do now?"

"A little bit of everything. In the summer he fishes and does construction work. In the winter it's snowplowing or road clearing."

"So, he could have been working for Nordberg Infrastruktur?"

Hans grunted. "He could have been working for just about anyone."

"How old is your brother?" Avril asked.

"Thirty-seven. He's younger than me. My parents had given up trying to have another child when my mother fell pregnant with Jonas. There's an eight-year gap between us."

"That must have been hard," Avril remarked. She'd been an only child, and she couldn't imagine what it must be like to have a sibling to share things with, to fight with, to talk to when bad stuff happened. She'd had a lot of bad stuff happen. It could have made all the difference.

"For Jonas, maybe. But not for me. I had my own friends, my own life."

"Sounds like he grew up in your shadow."

Hans let out a low breath, almost a laugh. "The first time he got arrested was after my mother died. Drunk and disorderly. I was a polisassistent then, and the Kommissarie at the time picked him up. I was embarrassed by my brother's behavior, but I also understood it. He was grieving, and whenever he was upset, he acted out."

"Did he serve any time?"

He gave a rueful smile. "No, thankfully. Guess who they called to smooth things over?"

"You," Avril said.

"Big brother to the rescue." The smile faded. "He hated me for it. Still does. But he wouldn't have made it this far without someone keeping him from falling all the way."

"You think he's capable of murdering someone?"

Hans hesitated. "I'd like to believe he isn't, but he's unpredictable. When Jonas feels cornered, he can lash out."

"You think Lara backed him into a corner?"

He shook his head. "I don't know. I hope not, but I just don't know."

chapter
twenty-one

A SHORT WHILE LATER, THEY PULLED UP IN FRONT OF A dilapidated farmhouse situated at the edge of the forest. Its paint had long since faded to a dull gray, the porch sagged to one side, and several cracked or boarded windows dotted the facade. Snow drifted in uneven piles against the walls.

"He lives here?" Avril stared at it through the windshield. There was no smoke from the chimney, no vehicle in sight, no tracks in the drive. Just a vast, icy silence.

"This is where the number pinged," Hans said, placing the car in park and staring out at the house through the windshield. "There isn't anything close by for at least a mile in every direction. It has to be him."

"Unless someone else is living here," Avril murmured.

Hans gave a small shrug. "The last time I spoke to my brother, he said he'd rented this place cheap and was saving for a house of his own. But Jonas has a habit of saying one thing and doing another."

They climbed out of the car, boots crunching through ankle-deep snow. Avril checked her weapon, holstered to her hip.

"Odin is still out there," Krister had told her before she'd left. Though she knew Odin was the last person to come looking for her, especially right now. He was still too hot. The leader of the eco-terrorist organization she'd infiltrated earlier in the year would stay hidden for at least another six months, until the heat died down. At this moment, he was probably sunning himself on a Caribbean island, while she was freezing up here in the snow.

"Looks deserted," she muttered, as they approached the worn front porch. The land around them was flat and exposed, a sweep of white broken only by the dark wall of forest at the horizon.

"I'll see if he's in." Hans climbed the steps to the front door, the boards groaning under his weight.

"I'll go around the back." Avril veered off. If Jonas didn't want to talk to his brother, he'd bolt, and she wanted to be ready. Turned out, she was a few seconds too late.

Halfway around the house, she caught sight of movement. A figure wriggled through the back window, boots hitting the snow with a dull thud.

"Hey!" she shouted, and broke into a run.

The man turned his head, startled. For a heartbeat their eyes met, and then he took off toward the treeline, snow spraying with every stride.

Avril saw he wasn't armed, so she kept her gun holstered. Instead, she took off after him.

It was slow going in the snow, and the frigid air made her lungs burn. She heard a shout, and then footsteps as Hans came racing after her.

"Jonas!" he yelled. "We just want to talk."

Avril's boot caught on a buried stone. She pitched forward, the ice ripping at her palms, her knee slamming into frozen ground. She spat a curse, then scrambled up, but Hans thundered past her, his face flushed with exertion. Or anger. She couldn't tell which.

"Jonas, stop!"

But his brother kept going. He cut a dark path across the white field, legs pumping, coat billowing out behind him. He was fast too. Faster than they were. Hans was losing him. Jonas got smaller and smaller as he gained distance. Soon he'd be under cover in the forest, and they wouldn't find him.

Avril stopped running. She'd never catch up to him now. Besides, she'd seen enough to know that he fit the hotline caller's description. Dark blond hair, medium build, and wearing a black coat.

Eventually, Hans ground to a halt. His boots crunched deep into the snow as he bent double, hands braced on his knees, breath coming in ragged bursts that steamed in the air.

Avril slowed, her own lungs burning, though she forced her breathing to steady. "Where do you think he's gone?"

Hans shook his head, sweat glistening on his brow despite the freezing air. "I don't know."

She turned toward the endless sweep of trees. The forest loomed dark and silent, the kind of wilderness that could swallow a man whole. "Maybe we can track his cell phone," she suggested.

Hans followed her gaze, then straightened slowly. His jaw was tight. "If he hasn't dumped it already."

THEY BEGAN the trudge back toward the car. The farmhouse was a distant blur a mile away. Every step was an effort, with the snow tugging at their legs and the wind buffeting them.

Avril's glasses fogged up, and she couldn't see through them. Frustrated, she took them off and thrust them in her coat pocket, eyes watering in the icy wind. Her fingers ached despite her gloves, but at least the cold had numbed her grazed knee. The pain would come back once she thawed out.

"I'll get Ekström to put out an *efterlysning*," Hans said, his voice weary. The wanted notice, or BOLO as they called it in America, would ensure every other police department in the region was on the lookout for Jonas Bergqvist. "He won't get far."

When they finally reached the farmhouse, Avril said, "We should station a man here in case Jonas comes back. There's no way he'll survive out there in these conditions." He'd have to seek shelter, or risk freezing to death.

Hans gave a tense nod. "I'll ask Lundgren to come over."

Avril wondered how that would go down.

Hans gestured to the farmhouse. "Shall we take a look inside?"

"Definitely. Let's grab some evidence bags from the car, just in case."

He pulled out his keys and opened the trunk with the press of a button. Avril ducked her head and retrieved a handful of bags of varying sizes. Hans tried the front door, but it was locked. She nodded toward the rear. "The window at the back is still open."

They circled the house, their boots crunching against the hard-packed crust. They stopped in front of the window. It was at least five feet off the ground.

Hans pressed his gloved palms onto the sill and hauled himself up with a grunt. His boots scraped the clapboard as he swung a leg over, pivoted, then dropped lightly into the room beyond.

"Need a hand?" he asked, looking back at her from the other side.

Thrusting the plastic bags into her oversized coat pocket, she nodded. "Thanks."

Hans reached down and grabbed her wrists, then lifted her until she could hook a leg over the sill. After that, it was easy. She swung herself in and dropped down beside him, brushing snow from her pants and grimacing when she bumped her knee.

"Thanks," she muttered, ignoring the pain and reaching into her coat pocket for her glasses.

The open window had let most of the heat out, and Avril shivered against the chill in the air. It smelled of damp and old firewood mixed with a lingering sweetness that she recognized as cannabis. Their boots echoed on bare boards as they looked around at what had once been a kitchen.

It wasn't much. A battered table with two mismatched chairs. A chipped enamel mug left on the side, ringed with dried coffee. The place had the air of abandonment, yet there were enough signs of life to prove Jonas had been living here.

They walked out of the kitchen and into the living room. Heat still lingered here. Ash scattered on the hearth and a half-burned log pushed to one side of the fireplace were the only signs of recent use. Possibly from the night before, as the coals were cold now.

"Look." She nodded to a thin mattress pushed into the corner. A crumpled sleeping bag lay on top, along with a heavy woolen blanket. Beside it was a scuffed novel and a couple of empty beer cans. Not enough to suggest addiction, just someone numbing the cold and the quiet.

Hans stared at the mattress.

"Jesus." He shook his head. "I can't believe he was living like this."

Avril crossed to the table under the window. It was littered with matches, cigarette butts stubbed straight into the wood, and a folded newspaper yellowed at the edges.

Two half-burned joints lay in an ashtray. A crumpled packet of weed sat beside it, but no sign of anything stronger. It wasn't the stash of a dealer, nor the habits of a hardened criminal, just enough to take the edge off. This was a man drifting, hiding on the margins, trying to stay off the grid.

In the midst of the debris lay a phone. It was small and cheap, the plastic casing scratched from use.

Avril lifted it up in her gloved hand. "Guess we won't be tracking his phone."

Hans came over to take a look. "Is it on?"

She pushed the "on" button and the screen lit up, but it was locked. "Needs a passcode."

"Maybe the tech team can crack it," Hans said. "Although, we already know from Lara's call records that he was in touch with her."

"But we don't know what they said to each other," Avril reminded him. "There might be text messages on here we can read."

"Send it away as soon as we get back," Hans said.

Avril nodded and slipped it into an evidence bag.

They moved through the rest of the farmhouse. It wasn't big, only one bedroom and a bathroom. The bedroom was empty and freezing cold. The bathroom was functional but needed a good clean.

They wandered back into the kitchen. Hans rubbed a hand over his jaw. Avril thought he'd aged in the last few hours. He looked worn down and weary, but then he'd had a shock.

He shook his head. "I can't see any sign of Lara. If he did take her, he didn't bring her here."

"We don't know for sure that he took her," Avril reminded him. "For all we know, they may have been friends."

Hans's voice hardened. "A friend who drugged, kidnapped, and strangled her?"

Avril met his eyes and could see how personal this was for him. The conflict between Kommissarie and his brother was etched into every line of his face. "Nothing here says murderer," she said, not as reassurance, but as fact.

Hans's shoulders sagged. "I know you're trying to be kind, but he's still our prime suspect. Why else would he take off like that?"

"Maybe he didn't want to face you," she said, though the words rang hollow even to her. She had hunted enough killers to know Hans was right about one thing—innocent men didn't run.

chapter
twenty-two

AVRIL WOKE UP AND WONDERED WHY HER KNEE WAS throbbing. Then she remembered. The farmhouse, the chase, falling in the snow.

Jonas.

She wondered how Lundgren was getting on. Peering at her phone with bleary eyes, she saw he'd checked in at midnight, and again at six AM. He must be going stir crazy by now. At least he had a warm squad car to sit in.

Before she'd gone to sleep, Avril had looked over Lara's files again, searching for any reference to Hans's brother, but there was nothing.

Was he a friend, or was he her source? She didn't know. Maybe Lara's colleagues at the *Chronicle* would be able to shed some light.

She debated calling Hans, but then decided against it. If anyone at the newspaper did know about Jonas, they might not want to talk in front of his police Kommissarie brother.

Ethically, Hans shouldn't be involved. If Jonas was guilty, and this did go to trial, the defense might argue that having Hans on the case was a conflict of interest.

Perhaps she'd run it by Krister later. She'd only spoken to him once since she'd gotten here. They'd texted a few times, but she was eager to hear his voice.

. . .

Cold Mercy

Avril arrived at the *Chronicle* just before eight. Despite it being early, not to mention frigid, several of the newspaper's employees were already at their desks. The sound of softly tapping keys punctuated the background.

Fred glanced up as she walked over to his desk.

"How'd you get in?" He bent his head to peer around her at the door.

"I followed that guy." She nodded to a long-haired man in a fur-lined jacket with a pencil tucked behind his ear.

"Oh, that's Carl. What can I do for you, Miss—?"

"Avril," she said. "Avril Dahl."

"Right. Are you any closer to finding Lara's murderer?"

Avril stood in front of his desk. "That's what I wanted to speak to you about. Did Lara ever mention a man called Jonas?"

"Jonas? Jonas Who?"

"Bergqvist. He may have been a friend."

Fred thought for a moment, then shook his head. "I don't think so. I've met most of her friends."

"What about a source, then?" she asked.

He frowned. "If he was, she didn't mention it to me. Why do you ask?"

"She called him a couple of times, that's all."

Fred spread his hands, helpless. "Then I can't help you. I never heard the name."

It was disappointing, but what she'd expected. Sometimes, you got lucky, but not this time. Avril thanked him and left the office.

On her way to the police station, she rang Tarek. He sounded groggy, like he'd just woken up. She asked him the same question.

"Jonas? No, Lara never mentioned his name to me. Who is he?"

"I'm not sure. That's what I'm trying to find out. Could be a friend, could be a source."

"Likely a source then. I don't know him." Avril thanked him and hung up. It was beginning to look that way.

By the time she reached the police station, the sky was white with snow. Flakes drifted steadily across Main Street, piling up on the sidewalk.

"Where have you been?" Hans asked, as she walked in the door.

"Late start," she said, without meeting his gaze.

He was holding a cup of freshly brewed coffee, which he took into his office and closed the door.

"He's upset about Jonas," Ekström said, nodding after her boss.

"He has every right to be," Avril remarked. She lowered her voice. "Will you do a thorough background check on Jonas? Give me everything you can find on him, including his work history. I believe he's had a number of odd jobs over the years. I'm looking for a Nordberg or Skogviken Timber association."

Ekström gave a little frown. "Shouldn't we check with the Kommissarie first?"

"No, I'm giving you the order. I'll talk to Bergqvist myself. I'm going to recommend he step away from the investigation."

Her eyes widened. "He's not going to like it."

"Nothing I can do about that. It's a conflict of interest. We can't take the risk that his involvement will jeopardize the outcome of the investigation."

"You mean he may hold back evidence because it's his brother?" She shook her head. "The Kommissarie isn't like that. He's by the book."

Avril shrugged. "The defense might not agree with you."

She blinked several times, then murmured, "I see."

"Get digging."

Lundgren walked in. He looked exhausted. "How'd it go last night?" she asked.

He shook his head, walked over to his desk and sank down. "Nothing. He didn't come back."

"Who's watching it now?" she asked.

"Hans sent someone from Östersund to relieve me. He took over at six o'clock this morning."

Hans hadn't told her that. He must have called last night, after he'd gotten home.

"You okay?" she asked Lundgren. He must have only had a couple of hours sleep.

"I'm fine."

She left him to it.

The squad room fell silent. Lundgren got himself a cup of coffee, not offering some to anyone else, then sat back down at his desk. He ruffled some papers, cleared his throat, and then said, "I have something for you."

Avril looked up. "For me?"

"Ja. Remember the caller who saw Lara at the Svartälgen? I've got her details now. The phone company released the number—it's registered to Angela Eklund, a local here in Norrdal."

She felt a surge of adrenalin. "Great. Can I see it?"

He grunted but handed her the note. She didn't recognize the address, but when she looked it up on Google maps, she found it was only a few blocks away.

Avril got up and went over to Ekström's desk. "Hey, I've got a job for you."

Ekström blinked, surprised. "You want me to look something up?"

"I want you to talk to someone for me."

Her face lit up. "Really?" Then she swallowed. "Alone."

"Yeah, you can handle it. Besides, it'll be good field practice." Avril handed her the address. "Speak to Angela Eklund. She's the one who called the tip line."

Ekström glanced down at the paper. "You want me to go now?"

"Yes, now. Take a photograph of Jonas Bergqvist with you and ask her if he was the man she saw Lara with."

"Oh, yes. Of course."

As Ekström hurried to get her jacket, Avril glanced over at Hans' closed door. She had a call to make, and then they were going to have another talk. One she wasn't looking forward to.

chapter
twenty-three

Krister picked up the call on the first ring. "Avril, hey. How's it going up there?"

It had been quite a few days since they'd last spoken, and he was eager to hear her news. He also missed her. Her strength, her candor, her refreshing honesty. The way she looked at him with that girlish smile honed decades ago. The one she'd give him when he showed her the den he'd built in the woods, or when he carried her home that day she'd fallen off her bike.

But that wasn't something he could tell her. She wouldn't understand.

Avril wasn't like other women. Her early experiences had made her less able to empathize, to understand. A built-in defense mechanism that he would break down over time. Every now and then he'd see a flash of delight, a surge of anger, or a flicker of fear—but they were few and far between. Still, he lived for those moments.

He also felt protective of her. He knew her better than anyone else did. She trusted him, and that was a lot for a woman who'd lost everything at the hands of one of the world's most prolific serial killers.

Mikael Lustig was serving life in prison, but from what Krister had heard, he was on his last legs. The disease that had ravished him over the last few years was winning out. And as far as Krister was concerned, it couldn't happen to a better guy.

"It's going—" She stopped, and he knew she was searching for the appropriate word. Avril and small talk went together like oil and water.

"That well, eh?"

She laughed, low and breathy, and it made him smile. "Yeah. How about you?"

Her standard response. The thing she said when she didn't know what else to say.

"You know. Same old. So what can I help you with?"

"How do you know I'm not just calling to say hello?"

"Because I know you." He grinned. "What is it? I'll see if I can help."

"I've got a problem up here," she began. "We've got a suspect who looks good for the murder, but he's the Kommissarie's brother."

"Did you say brother?"

"Yeah, younger brother. Estranged, or so it seems, but clearly there's a conflict of interest, no?"

Krister frowned. "You'd better tell me everything. I'm going to need some context."

As she talked, he leaned back in his chair and stared out the window. The snow fell, light and fluffy. It wouldn't settle, just add to the brown sludge piling up in the gutters and against the walls of the city sidewalks.

When Avril was done, he drew in a breath. "This guy, Jonas, is still in the wind?"

"Yeah, we have no idea where he is. We've got an efterlysning out, but so far there have been no sightings. I'm going to suggest they call in reinforcements."

"Your instincts are right," he decided. "Bergqvist has to stand down. Not only could he purposely compromise the case, but it could be a problem in court. Besides, it's standard procedure in cases like this. If you're really worried he won't, you can flag it. Then it'll be formally decided by the prosecutor."

"That's what I thought. Krister?" She hesitated. "How do I bring it up with him?"

He knew what she was asking. Not how to bring it up, but how to handle it. Her direct, get-straight-to-it approach wouldn't work in this scenario. She was a guest at their police department. She was supposed to be assisting with the investigation, and now she would be running it. Making all the decisions. Calling the shots. It required tact, and as good as Avril was at her job, tact was not something she possessed.

"Do you want me to get Sundström to call him?"

"It's not his department."

She was right. Sundström had no authority over Bergqvist. "What about higher up? Sundström can speak to his boss, and they can give him a call."

"That sounds like I'm going over his head."

"Which you are," Krister pointed out. "It's either that or the prosecutor."

She sighed. "No, that's okay. If Bergqvist is half the Kommissarie he's reputed to be, he'll understand. He'll know he has to step away from this one."

"Okay." Krister's focus sharpened, bringing his surroundings back to the forefront of his mind. He was staring at his colleague with a frown on his face.

"What?" the colleague mouthed.

Krister shook his head and turned away. "Okay, go speak to him, but play it cool. Remind him how close he is to this, and how it might compromise the investigation. Like you said, he should get it. If you have a problem, let me know. We can always take it up the line."

"Okay. Thanks, Krister. That helps."

He really hoped it did. "Take care, Avril. Be careful."

"I will. Bye."

In true Avril form, she'd cut the call before he had a chance to reply.

chapter
twenty-four

AVRIL KNOCKED ON HANS'S DOOR, IGNORING THE unsettling feeling clawing at her gut. She didn't want to do this, but she had no choice. She had to act in the best interests of the investigation.

"Ja."

She opened the door and stepped into the room, trying to act casual. Krister was right. He'd see reason. He had to.

"Can we talk?"

Hans stopped what he was doing, leaned back and nodded. "Sure. Take a seat."

Avril slipped into the chair opposite him.

"Lundgren told me you sent an officer from Östersund to replace him this morning."

"Oh, ja. I forgot to tell you because you came in late. I felt sorry for the kid. He'd been out there all night."

"It was a good idea."

He nodded. "What was it you wanted to talk about?"

"The case." She hated how nervous she sounded. It wasn't fear. She didn't mind confronting him, she just didn't want to offend him. She was well aware this kind of conversation was not her strong suit.

This was what Krister did so well. When they worked together, he always did the smoothing over, handled the difficult conversations. She never had the patience for that.

"The case?" He tilted his head back and studied her. "What about it?"

"Your involvement in it," she said, then bit her lip.

He frowned, and she saw a flash of wounded pride. "I don't understand."

He was going to make her spell it out.

"Hans, your brother is our prime suspect. You must see how that poses a problem."

He gave her a guarded look. "I'm not responsible for my brother. We aren't even close."

"I know that, but your relationship to the suspect could compromise the investigation."

"How?" He frowned at her, then his brow cleared. "You think I would assist him in evading capture? That I would be reluctant to apprehend him because he's family?"

Yes.

"No."

Maybe.

She didn't know. That was the whole point.

The tension built. The air in the room suffocated her. "I don't, but others might. A jury might."

He was silent for a moment as her words hit.

"You're saying my involvement could be used against us at trial."

"If it goes to trial, yes."

If we catch him.

Avril steeled herself with a deep breath. "Hans, if we flag this, a prosecutor will make you stand down. I think you should excuse yourself from this investigation voluntarily. You can't be involved. It's too risky."

"I'm already involved," he said in a low voice.

"But your brother wasn't a suspect then. It's different now. Don't you see? We can't take the chance."

Hans fisted his hands on the desk. "So, my brother's behavior will reflect on me as a law enforcement officer? People are going to think I'm tainted by association."

"Not all people," she was quick to add. "Everybody in Norrdal knows you're above reproach. It's the defense lawyers that will question it."

"But if we catch him, they must see I'm above board? He's my brother, for Christ's sake."

Why was he pushing this? He must know the rules.

"They will try to poke holes in our case," she said, and she could tell by his expression he knew she was right.

What she couldn't say was that if they *didn't* catch Jonas, there would always be a lingering suspicion that Hans had something to do with it. Had he warned him? Slowed the search? Looked the other way? She didn't want doubts.

"I take it you've spoken to your boss in Stockholm about this?"

"I got advice from a colleague, yes."

He sighed and threw up his hands. "So, what do you want me to do? Go home?"

Avril didn't know how to answer that. "It would probably be best, yes."

"And what do I do there? Knit? Twiddle my thumbs while the biggest case of my career plays out without me?"

"I'm sorry," she whispered. "I wish it wasn't this way."

He clawed at his hair, then hissed out a low breath. "No, no. I'm sorry. It's not your fault. I should have considered the implications myself. I'm not used to all this...procedure. Things are usually much simpler here in Norrdal."

"I understand," she said. A murder trial was outside his usual scope. That's why she was here.

He nodded and got to his feet. "Okay, then. I'll remove myself from the investigation and go home and be with my wife." He scoffed. "She'll be happy, at least."

Avril forced a smile and watched as he got up, placed a few items in his bag, and zipped it up.

"We called you in to help," he said with a self-deprecating snort, "and now you're one man down again. Do you think you can handle a manhunt this size without support?"

"Like you, I've decided to call in uniformed police from Östersund.

We need boots on the ground to handle door-to-doors and to search woodland and nearby farm areas."

He nodded. "Wise move. If this weather gets worse, call Ingrid at Missing People Sweden. They've got quads and snowmobiles, and they can rustle up some tough locals to assist with dogs. Under police supervision, of course."

Avril made a mental note. If the snow continued, that's exactly what they'd need. Searching on foot would take days, and they didn't have that kind of time.

"You okay?" she asked, as he slung the bag over his shoulder.

"Not really, but what choice do I have? I'm sure you'll do a fine job without me."

She followed him into the squad room, but he didn't stop. He walked straight through, nodding once at Lundgren, before disappearing out the door into the snow.

Only then did Avril relax.

THE MANHUNT GOT underway without any more delays. Inspektör Svensson from Östersund Polisstation came over and brought twelve uniformed men with him. He was curt and to the point, and Avril was confident he'd take control of the search.

"The suspect has a twenty-four-hour head start," she explained. She should have called in reinforcements yesterday, but they'd all been so shocked by the fact that their main suspect was Hans's brother.

Had Hans deliberately stalled on that? He must have known this was an option, yet he hadn't suggested it. He'd waited until she'd brought it up.

She shook her head. This was why it was best he was off the case.

Also, before she wasted a ton of state resources, she had to be sure Jonas wasn't just a friend of Lara's. That he was actually her source, and potentially her killer.

Svensson was using Hans's office as his base and had laid a large-scale topographical map out over the desk, sectors marked in red, the heavy pen strokes cutting the forest into neat squares that would soon be filled with men. Avril stood beside him, listening as he explained, his voice low but firm. It was the kind of voice that carried authority because it never needed to be raised.

"You said the suspect was last seen here?" He jabbed a thick finger to the stretch of woodland where they'd lost Jonas.

Avril nodded. "That's right. He disappeared into the forest."

"Okay. I've split the search area into grids. Each one has an officer assigned, and we'll do a systematic sweep. We have patrol cars covering the highway, and I've put checkpoints on the farm roads. Canine units are pushing north through this sector. If he's holed up in there, the dogs will flush him out."

"You brought dogs?"

"Ja, it's standard procedure for any regional manhunt."

She nodded, impressed. Svensson knew what he was doing.

"What if he's past that point, or on the move?" she asked.

"Then he runs straight into the perimeter. The rescue volunteers are covering the outer ring. Small trails, back roads and cabins. Everyone checks in every fifteen minutes." Svensson folded the map and slipped it under his arm. "They've been told to call it in if they see him, not try to apprehend him themselves. They know the drill. Many of them have done this before."

"Thank you for your assistance," Avril said, and she meant it. The reinforcements were better than she'd expected. Svensson had even enlisted volunteers, which she'd never have thought to do, coming from the big city.

In America, things didn't work the same way. The FBI discouraged the public's involvement. But out here, in the rural parts of Sweden, who better to help hunt down a suspect or missing person than a hardy bunch of locals?

"You're welcome. That's what we're here for." He nodded as he walked toward the door. "Your suspect can't have gone far. Not in this weather. It shouldn't be too long before we find him."

She hoped he was right.

chapter
twenty-five

"What did Angela Eklund say?" Avril asked Ekström when she came out of Hans' office. The polisassistent was back at her desk after her solo excursion, reading something on her screen.

She glanced up. "Oh, Kriminalinspektör. I didn't see you there. I was just about to call you."

"Did she identify Jonas?"

Ekström gave an excited nod. Her cheeks were still pink from being outside in the cold. "She did. At first she was upset that we'd located her, because she wanted to remain anonymous. Her boyfriend isn't a fan of the police."

"I see." That explained the nervousness on the call.

"I showed her the photograph of Jonas, the one we took from his old Facebook page. She confirmed it was him. Said she was a hundred percent sure."

Avril adjusted her glasses. That was a high percentage for an eyewitness account. "She said on the phone that she didn't get a good look at him, so how could she be so sure?" Avril had hoped the photograph would jog the witness's memory, but this was better than she could have imagined.

"She recognized his hair and the cut of his coat. Also, when he turned his head, she noticed his profile, particularly his jawline and nose. She's a portrait artist, so she remembers things like that."

A portrait artist. Finally, their luck was changing.

"There's something else," Ekström said, her eyes flashing.

"What's that?"

"I've been going through Jonas's bank statements, and you were right. There is a connection. He did some contract work for Nordberg Infrastruktur three years ago. Manual labor, by the looks of it."

Avril's breath hitched. "You're certain?"

"Absolutely. Look. These are the bank payments from Nordberg Infrastruktur AB to Jonas Bergqvist. They made weekly payments that continued for..." She trailed off, running a finger down the page. "Six months. Maybe longer."

Avril exhaled slowly. This was huge. "Jonas could have been blowing the whistle on Nordberg. He could have been Lara's source."

Ekström frowned, confused. "Then why did he kill her?"

"We don't know that he did." Avril's gaze drifted to the whiteboard and the photograph of Lara Berglund's body under the ice. "Only that he met with her the night she died."

"But Angela saw her leave with him."

Avril shook her head. "No, she didn't. She saw her talking with him. The next time she looked across, the table was empty."

"Oh, come on," Lundgren said, looking over. "Of course they left together. He drugged her and forced her to leave with him."

"I admit that does appear to be what happened." Avril pushed down her annoyance with his blatant disregard. "And for all we know that is exactly how it went down. All I'm saying is nobody actually saw Lara leave with Jonas."

Lundgren spread his hands. "Who else could have done it?"

Avril shook her head. "What we need is to speak to Jonas. Hopefully Svensson will bring him in and we can settle this. We also need to get a forensic team over to his farmhouse. Lundgren, can you handle that? We didn't see any evidence of Lara having been there, but that's not to say she wasn't."

"Jonas doesn't have a vehicle," Ekström pointed out. "How would he have taken her to the farmhouse?"

"Does he drive?" Avril asked. "Have you checked with the transport agency, and the rental companies? Maybe he hired a car."

"On it," Ekström said, turning back to her screen.

Lundgren let out a noisy breath.

Avril marched over to his desk and stared down at him. "Lundgren, can I have a word please? In Hans's office?"

He shot her a sullen look. "Now?"

"Yes, now."

She strode ahead and waited behind Hans' desk. Enough was enough. Lundgren's attitude was becoming intolerable.

"Close the door," she snapped, as he walked in behind her.

He did so, then turned to face her.

"What is your problem with me?" she asked, her impatience getting the better of her. To hell with tact. This needed to be confronted head-on.

"I don't have a problem with you," he said.

She fixed a frosty gaze on him. "Rubbish. You've been disrespectful right from the start. Have I done something to offend you?"

"No."

"Is it because I'm a woman?"

"No."

"That I'm from the SPA?"

He shook his head.

"Then what?" She threw up her hands, exasperated. "Because I've had it up to here with your disrespectful attitude."

He glanced down at the floor.

"I'm waiting for an explanation," she said. "Because we're going to clear this up, whatever this is, right now."

"Kommissarie gave me this job," he said slowly. "After he sent me to the police academy in Umeå."

Avril tried to understand. "He sent you to the police academy?"

"Yes. He paid for it and everything. I said I'd pay him back, but he didn't want it."

Avril was stunned. Neither had let on that they knew each other so well.

"Why did he do that?" she asked.

"Because he knew my parents... before they died."

Avril shook her head. "I don't understand. How did he know your parents?"

Lundgren heaved a big sigh, his shoulders stooping. "My father was a few years above him at school. When Jonas got bullied, Hans would step in to defend him. Sometimes they got into fights and my father would step in. He was older and used to box, so nobody messed with him."

It sounded like a rough school. "So Hans and your father were friends?"

Lundgren nodded. "When my parents died in a car wreck, Hans stepped in to help. I was sixteen at the time. I was reeling and didn't know what to do with myself. It was Hans that suggested the police force."

Understanding dawned. "So you owe Hans, is that it? He didn't want a Kriminalinspektör coming here from Stockholm and taking over his case, so neither did you?"

"It was his biggest case," Lundgren said. "A career-defining case, and not only did you take it over, but you kicked him out."

"That wasn't me," Avril said quickly. "That's standard procedure. Look it up. The SPA takes conflicts of interest seriously."

The sullen expression was back. "Still, you took over right from the start."

"That's why I'm here," she tried to explain. "This is why they sent me. Do you think I wanted to come all the way here in the freezing cold to work this murder? They sent me to get me out of the way."

He stared at her. "Why do they want to get you out of the way?"

She shook her head. "It's a long story. There's someone out to get me, and they thought that if I was here..." She broke off, not wanting to tell him too much.

"That they wouldn't find you?" he finished.

She gave a grim nod. "I'm sorry about your parents."

He sniffed. "I'm sorry I've been so difficult."

She exhaled and held out a hand. "Truce?"

He hesitated, then shook it. "Truce."

chapter
twenty-six

AVRIL DROVE THE HALF HOUR TO NORDBERG Infrastruktur in her Volvo, the tires crunching over a thick crust of packed snow that had fallen steadily since yesterday. The fields on either side of the road stretched out in white silence, broken only by the black silhouettes of bare birches and the occasional farmhouse.

This time she was alone, but it wasn't Olle Nordberg she wanted to speak to. It was his human resources department. After several calls had gone unanswered, she'd decided to go in person.

The winter sky might be darkening, but it was only midafternoon, which left plenty of time to talk to the HR Manager about Jonas Bergqvist. Avril turned on the radio and listened to the news. A politician had been shot in Ukraine, a bridge had collapsed in Värmdö, and a double shooting in Stockholm had left two men dead.

She spotted the approach road and turned off the highway. She had to reduce her speed, as the snow had made the road barely passable. Drifts spilled in from the fields, and the wind flung snow straight at the windshield in a blinding sheet.

Crap, this was bad. She turned off the radio so she could concentrate, but even with the wipers beating furiously, she could hardly see more than a few feet ahead. Twice, she almost came to a standstill, afraid of sliding off into the ditch.

Maybe this hadn't been such a good idea. It had been years since she'd driven in these conditions, and she didn't know the area and wasn't familiar with the roads. When the squat office block of Nordberg Infrastruktur came into view, half-hidden behind a bank of piled snow, she could've wept with relief.

Inside, the reception area was empty except for the woman sitting behind a desk. She looked up as Avril entered, surprise on her face. "You drove in this?"

She nodded. "Stupidly, yes. I've got to get back too."

"Hopefully the storm won't last too long. We've grounded all our vehicles until it passes."

She showed her badge and introduced herself. "Since I've come all this way, could I speak with someone in HR?"

The woman hesitated, then gestured to a small waiting area to the side. "If you take a seat, I'll call someone to get you."

Avril watched the woman pick up the phone and press a few buttons. Talking in low tones, she said something Avril didn't catch, then nodded. Avril was willing to bet that wasn't HR she was talking to. That it was her boss, Nordberg.

The receptionist pressed another number, spoke again, then said, "Ja, jag säger till henne." *I'll let her know.*

Her gaze drifted across to Avril. "The HR manager is on her way."

Avril thanked her and settled down to wait. A short while later, a petite woman approached, her dark hair falling straight to her shoulders, her skin pale from the long winter, her cheekbones sharply cut in a way that gave her face a striking, austere beauty. She wore a smart skirt suit and three-inch heels that did little to add to her height. Avril still towered over her when she got to her feet.

"Hello, Kriminalinspektör. I'm Elsa Holm. I am the HR Manager here at Nordberg."

"Is there somewhere we can talk?"

"Sure, follow me."

Holm led her to a small interview room situated just off the main reception area and gestured for her to sit down. The circular table and four chairs took up most of the room. Once they were seated, Holm said, "Now, how can I help Polisen?"

Avril took Jonas's photograph out of her pocket and slid it across the table. "I'm investigating one of your former employees, Jonas Bergqvist. Do you remember him?"

She frowned, her smooth forehead creasing. "No, I'm sorry. Many manual laborers come through here and I don't get to meet most of them. When did he work with us?"

"It would have been three years ago," Avril said. "For the winter months."

Holm nodded. "That's when we take on extra staff. Unlike most enterprises, the colder months are our busiest—for obvious reasons."

That made sense.

"Do you keep employment records for your contractors?"

"Not employment records as such, but we do keep their details on file. Name, address, payment information. Most of them are seasonal, so they return every year." She gave a soft snort. "It saves us having to enter them again."

"Would you have recorded any problems or complaints?"

"Of course."

That's what Avril had been hoping she'd say.

"Could you check Jonas Bergqvist's details?" She prodded the photograph. "Please, it's important."

"I should ask you for a warrant," Holm said, frowning at her. "But since you've come out here in this awful weather—"

Avril held her breath.

"I can't see what harm it'll do," the woman finished.

Avril sighed, relieved. "Thank you."

"I'll just be one moment."

Avril waited while Holm went to her office to get the information. When she returned, she carried a paper printout in her hand.

"This is what we have on file." She held it out to Avril.

On it was Jonas's full name, his address and contact details, including an email address. Below that was a brief résumé, followed by a comment by his line manager.

Jonas is a good worker, he's always on time, and picks up extra shifts.

"You didn't have any problems with him?" Avril glanced up.

"If we had, they'd be written on there. That's how we know whether to take them back the following year."

"Who was his line manager?" She couldn't make out the signature.

"That would be Anders Nyqvist, but I'm afraid he's no longer with the company. He left last year."

Damn. It would have been good to talk to him just to make sure.

"Any particular reason?" she asked.

"Yes." Holm broke into a smile. "His wife inherited a large sum from her father and so Anders took early retirement. We were all very happy for him, although we were obviously sad to see him go. He'd been with the company for fourteen years."

"That's a long time."

Her eyes sparkled. "That's the kind of loyalty we inspire here at Nordberg."

Avril picked up the photograph and got to her feet. This was a woman who really loved her job.

She stuck out a hand. "Thank you for your time, and for letting me see the file."

"No problem," Holm said, smiling. "Anything to help. I'll walk you out."

As she left the building, she couldn't shake the feeling that there was more to the Jonas-Nordberg connection than met the eye. Five months was a long time. Maybe Jonas had overheard something, like a secret meeting between Olle Nordberg and Councilor Håkansson. Or perhaps he'd found evidence of kickbacks to local politicians for awarding municipal contracts.

She thought of Lara Berglund, forever asking questions, and wondered if Jonas had been feeding her information on Nordberg. Then again, if he had, why was it only coming out now? And why kill her? It didn't make any sense.

By the time Avril got back to her Volvo, the snowstorm had tapered off, thank God. At least she could see through the windshield now.

She pulled out of the parking lot, then drove the short distance to the open gates. There wasn't a guard in sight.

The narrow exit road was little more than an icy track, and she hunched over the wheel, peering through the windshield as she drove out of the compound. The temperature gauge showed minus twelve, and the heating was only just kicking in.

As she navigated the narrow road leading to the highway toward Norrdal, she thought about Jonas, on foot in the wilderness. How long would he last without finding cover? An hour, maybe two? He could be dead already, frozen in his attempt to escape. He hadn't gone back to the farmhouse, so where was he?

Maybe Svensson and his team from Östersund would be able to track him down. So far, she'd had no reports of any sightings.

Avril didn't see the oncoming vehicle until it was almost upon her. A dark blur careening around the bend, headlights flaring. She tried to swerve, to get out of its path, but she wasn't quick enough. It clipped the side of her Volvo and sent her spinning across the road.

Avril screamed as she tried to regain control, but it was too icy. The tires locked up, and she flew off the road and into a ditch. The impact slammed her head against the doorframe and everything went black.

chapter
twenty-seven

WHEN AVRIL OPENED HER EYES, ALL SHE COULD SEE WAS white. For a moment, she thought she was blind, but then a dark figure loomed in front of the cracked windshield. Someone, or something, stood in the snow.

She blinked, trying to focus, but it was just a blur. Pain shot through her skull, and her stomach roiled. Touching her head, she encountered a large bump.

Shit. She must have banged it against the car door.

The figure took a step toward her, and in the light of one headlamp, she realized he was wearing a balaclava, and what looked to be a long, black coat.

A chill swept over her. She tried the door handle but found it jammed. And she still had her seat belt on. With shaking hands, she undid it while keeping her eyes locked on the figure. The snow was much lighter now, but it still obscured her vision, or maybe that was the bump on her head.

Gun. Where was her gun? Damn, it had fallen into the footwell on the passenger side. Now what? She needed to bend down and get it but couldn't risk the stranger making a sudden move when she wasn't watching.

Her heart thumped in her chest, in time to the pounding in her head. Now she was in a pickle. Plus, it was freezing out here. No way could she make it back to the compound.

While she was in a stare-off with the masked figure, a glare of fresh lights cut through the darkness, accompanied by a distant rumble. What on earth—?

She turned, trying to see behind her, but her neck was stiff. The rearview mirror was hanging by a cord, so she bent her head to peer into it. A snowplow rumbled into view.

Thank God. She felt a surge of relief, and glanced up to check where the stranger was, but she couldn't see him. Blinking, she stared into the darkness, the snow falling softly in front of the cracked windshield, but there was only empty space. The figure had vanished.

AVRIL MANAGED to retrieve her weapon as the snowplow grumbled to a halt a few meters behind her. She was just looking around for her phone, when a man jumped down. She heard his boots crunching through the drifts and braced herself. A moment later, he wrenched open her door.

"Du är okej?" *Are you okay?* He bent to pull her free, then saw the gun in her hand.

"I—I think so. Don't worry, I'm a police officer." She holstered the weapon and let him help her out of the car. Her legs buckled as soon as she stood, the world tilting before it steadied again. The throb in her skull was intense, and her stomach rolled with nausea. She wasn't sure if it was shock or the head injury.

"Did you see him?" She scanned the white blur around them.

The man glanced around. "Who?"

"The figure in the snow."

"No, ma'am. There's nobody else here."

"Someone forced me off the road," she said, her throat hoarse.

His gaze moved to the Volvo, half-buried in the ditch, where a long gouge of fresh paint and torn metal scarred the driver's side. His jaw tightened. "You want me to call Polisen?"

She patted her pockets. No phone. It must be somewhere in the vehicle. "Thank you. Norrdal Polisstation. Tell them Avril has had an accident and needs someone to come and get her."

He dug out his device from inside his padded jacket. "Can you stand on your own?"

"I think so." The freezing air fortified her, though it made her eyes water and her nose run. Snowflakes collected on her jacket, and in her hair. She shivered, gently at first, and then more violently.

"Now we know you're okay, you should get back inside." He nodded to the tilted Volvo. Steam hissed from under the hood, the smell of antifreeze sharp in the air.

She slid back into the driver's seat, pulling her coat tight, but her teeth still chattered. The dashboard lights glowed faintly against the dark, while the shattered headlight threw a weak, crooked beam onto the snow. Something hard prodded into her butt. Turning, her fingers curved around her phone. It had fallen into the back crease of the seat.

She might be okay, but the same couldn't be said for her Volvo. It would need towing, that much was clear.

The man bent down. "I spoke to Polisassistent Ekström. She said someone is on their way."

"Thank you."

"Are you sure you're okay? I could take you somewhere on my snowmobile. The closest place is the Nordberg compound. It's only a few miles back down the road."

"I just came from there." She leaned back against the headrest. For all she knew, they had summoned the car that had driven her off the road. No one else outside of the police station had known she was coming out here.

The Volvo's engine was still running. The heating was on and other than the pounding head, she was fine. The stranger in the balaclava had disappeared—if he'd even existed at all. She would be okay for the half an hour it took for Ekström or Lundgren to get here.

She grimaced at the thought of riding back with Lundgren. Still, she was lucky anyone was coming to get her at all.

"I'll be okay," she decided, turning to the man. "Thank you for your assistance."

"Okay." He shot her an uncertain look, then headed back to his snowplow. It rumbled to life, and a moment later, he'd overtaken her stationary car and disappeared into the darkness.

"Do you think it was someone from Nordberg?" Lundgren asked her as they drove back to the police station. He'd taken one look at her rental and called for a tow truck. They were due to arrive within the hour. She'd left the keys on the wheel and the hazard lights on. At least it was off the road, so it wouldn't pose a risk to motorists.

"It could have been," she said, closing her eyes. "Then again, it may have been a genuine accident."

"Except they rammed your car."

"The road was icy." She wondered whether to tell him about the figure she saw. He might think she was imagining things. Maybe she had been.

"I blacked out for a moment," she said, as he turned onto the highway back to Norrdal. "When I came around, there was this figure standing in front of the car."

He glanced sharply across at her. "A man?"

"I don't know. They were wearing a long, black coat and a balaclava."

His breath hitched. "Jonas?"

She shook her head. "I don't know. It could have been, but why was he out there by the Nordberg compound? It's miles away from the farmhouse. And if it was him, how on earth did he know I'd be there?"

Lundgren didn't reply. He just stared out of the front windshield, his hands tight around the wheel.

That was the problem. There were no answers. None of it made any sense.

"You got a phone call today at the station," he said. "Kriminalinspektör Jansson from Stockholm HQ."

"Oh? What did he want?"

"An update. Said he couldn't get hold of you on your mobile."

She reached into her pocket and grabbed her phone. There were several missed calls.

"How's Hans?" she asked, after firing off a quick text message to Krister explaining what had happened. She added that she was fine, and she'd call him later when she got home.

"Okay. He called to find out whether Jonas had been apprehended yet."

So he was still checking in. That was understandable, although not really allowed. "Any update on that?"

Lundgren shook his head. "Not yet. Svensson has been checking in with Ekström regularly, but so far nothing."

She dropped her head back against the seat. "Where the hell could he be?"

"He must know people," Lundgren said. "Someone is sheltering him. It's impossible to survive out there for long."

Didn't she know it? At least the squad car's interior was cozy and warm. She was starting to thaw out.

She must have drifted off, because when she opened her eyes again, they were outside a hospital. Lundgren parked in an emergency bay.

"What are we doing here?"

"Getting you checked out," he said.

"I'm fine."

"Then this won't take long."

He wasn't taking no for an answer. She was touched by his concern, especially when he got out, walked around, and opened her door. "You need a hand?"

She glanced up at him. This was a different Lundgren from the one she was used to. She climbed out, felt her legs give a little, then nodded. "Maybe just an arm."

He let her hold onto him for balance as they made their way inside.

"Thanks," she said, as he led her to a chair in the waiting room.

"No problem."

HALF AN HOUR LATER, one of the emergency doctors diagnosed her with a mild concussion. He'd given her an ice pack for the bump on her head, then told her to go home and rest.

She was about to object, when Lundgren said, "I'll see that she does. Thank you, doctor."

"You're very bossy all of a sudden," she remarked as he opened the car door for her.

He grinned. "Now the Kommissarie isn't around, I guess I'm next in charge."

That was true, just not of the murder investigation.

"Okay if I take you back to your guesthouse?" he asked, as he started the engine.

She sighed and adjusted the ice pack on her head. "Sure, as long as you promise to keep me posted on any new developments."

"I'm sure Ekström will." He pulled out and into the stream of traffic. "Oh, by the way, Jonas does have a driver's license, just not a car. At least, there is no record of one registered to him at present."

"What about rentals?" she asked.

"Nope. There is only one rental agency in town, and they didn't know him. Ekström checked every agency in a five-mile radius. None of them leased a vehicle to Jonas Bergqvist."

She watched as he switched lanes and headed back toward Norrdal. "What about forensics at the farmhouse? Did the crime scene techs find anything?"

"It was obvious Jonas had been living there," he said, "but there was no evidence of Lara. No DNA, no skin cells, nothing."

"So he didn't have a car, there was no trace of the victim at his home, yet he was seen in the bar with her moments before she disappeared. If he wasn't responsible, why'd he run?"

Lundgren just shook his head. "Maybe we can ask him when they catch him."

If they caught him. It had been almost seven hours since Svensson had taken over the manhunt. Thirty, if you counted from the time Jonas had evaded them at the farmhouse. He could be out of the country by now.

Avril struggled to keep her eyes open. Waves of tiredness swept over her, a combination of shock, pain, and the short time she'd spent out in the cold. Maybe she did need sleep.

Cold Mercy

Lundgren dropped her outside the guesthouse.

"Thanks for coming to get me," she said.

He nodded, but his lips were curling into a grin. "See you tomorrow, Kriminalinspektör."

chapter
twenty-eight

AVRIL TOOK A PAINKILLER AND CLIMBED INTO BED. EVERY part of her ached, including the knee she'd landed on the day before. The ice pack had done its job and the bump on her head wasn't so egg-like, even though it was still tender.

She tried to sleep, but every time she closed her eyes, all she could see was the dark figure standing in the snow.

Had he meant her harm? Or had he been checking to see if she was okay?

He'd been on foot. That meant he either lived nearby or had come from somewhere close. Unless he had been the driver who forced her off the road. But the snowplow operator swore there had been no other vehicle, and out there, with nothing but open ground for miles, there was nowhere a car could have been hidden.

Outside, the snow had stopped, but earlier she'd gotten a text alert from the local weather bureau saying another storm was rolling in and would hit late tomorrow morning. As it was, the town was blanketed in white. It was quite beautiful, and she may have enjoyed it if she didn't feel so battered and bruised.

She thought about the Östersund police and the volunteers out there searching for Jonas and wondered when Svensson would call off the search. They couldn't continue indefinitely, and with every passing hour, it looked less likely they would find him. Svensson would probably give it one more day and then call it quits.

Jonas was in the wind.

Eventually, she drifted off but was plagued by dreams. Stumbling blindly through a whiteout, her legs sinking into the deep snow. A sense of fear, like someone was chasing her, a figure, dressed in black. Her breaths came in gasps, her heart pounding so hard she thought it would burst out of her chest. Someone calling her name. He was gaining on her. She cried out, unable to move. She sunk into the snow like quicksand. Terror gripped her. The figure gained on her. She turned and saw his eyes through the slits in his balaclava. He held a knife. Raised it above his head.

"Avril, open up. It's me."

She woke up to pounding on the door. "Avril, it's Krister. Are you okay?"

Krister? What was he doing here?

For a moment she was totally discombobulated, then she remembered where she was.

More banging.

"Coming," she called, and threw back the covers. She was drenched in perspiration. Her heart raced, but she could get it under control. It was just a bad dream.

Opening the door, she stared into the worried face of Krister.

"Why are you here?" she asked.

"Christ, you look awful."

"Thanks."

"No, seriously. Are you okay? I heard you scream."

"I don't scream."

"I heard you."

She hesitated. "I had a bad dream. Why did you come?"

"I got your text message. I was worried."

She tilted her head to study him. "You drove all this way just to check up on me?"

"Sure. When you see the text message you sent me, you'll understand."

She rubbed her forehead, teetered, and walked back to the bed. "I hit my head."

"I gathered." He walked in and dumped a bag on the floor. "This is quaint."

"It'll do." She leaned back onto the bed.

He looked around. "Can I get you a glass of water?"

She nodded. "What's the time?"

"Eleven. It's the soonest I could get here." He grinned. "I put the siren on."

She took the glass of water and watched as he walked around to the other side of the bed. It was a large double, with plenty of space for both of them.

"Now," he said, as he leaned back against the pillows. "If you feel up to it, I want to hear everything that's been going on."

Avril told him everything, but she didn't finish her story. She got to the part where Jonas had vanished when her eyelids began drooping. As independent as she was, she had to admit, it was wonderful having Krister with her.

He put his arm around her shoulders, and she leaned her head against his chest. It was a nice chest, she decided, broad and firm. He smelled good too. Like the sea on a warm summer's day.

"It's okay, you can tell me the rest tomorrow," he said, as she drifted off.

For the first time since the accident, she didn't see the man in the balaclava when she shut her eyes. Instead, Krister was there, his presence strong and reassuring.

The last thing she remembered was him stroking her hair and whispering that everything would be okay. He'd never done that before. She kind of liked it.

chapter
twenty-nine

Krister woke up with Avril curled in towards him, her pale blond hair draped over his arm. She looked like an angel, and he was hit with a longing so fierce it took his breath away. She stirred, and he shifted away from her, until he was sitting on the edge of the bed.

"What time is it?" she murmured, rubbing her eyes.

"Eight. You slept like a baby."

She groaned and sat up. "I thought I'd dreamed you were here."

"Nope." He stood, spreading his arms. "In the flesh."

Her clear blue eyes fixed on his face. She could read him as easily as he read her. "You didn't have to come, Krister. I can take care of myself."

He pulled out his phone and handed it to her. "Read this."

She scanned the screen. It was the garbled message she'd sent him yesterday after the accident. A tangle of half-formed words and letters that meant nothing.

"I can't believe I sent that. It made perfect sense at the time."

"That's how I knew you were in trouble. I called the station and spoke to... Ekström, isn't it?"

Avril nodded.

"She told me you'd had an accident and someone was on their way."

"Yes, Lundgren picked me up. The other polisassistent."

"Anyway, I came as soon as I could. Does this place serve breakfast? I'm starving."

"You're always starving."

He grinned. "Come on, let's go downstairs. You can finish the story you started before you fell asleep."

"Oh, God. I did, didn't I?"

He chuckled. "Mid-sentence. To be fair, you had a concussion."

"Mild," she said, touching the bump on her head. It was nearly gone. "My head feels clearer today."

"That's good."

They went down to the dining room, where breakfast was served from six until nine. They chose a small table by the window. Outside, the world was white, the church steeple rising from a blanket of snow. Powder lay untouched on the ground, unmarked by vehicles or footprints.

"The plows will come through soon," the manager said, bringing over their plates. Scrambled eggs, bacon, and fried potatoes. "You'll be able to reach the highway in an hour or two."

"You're going back today?" Avril asked. He saw a flicker of disappointment in her eyes, and his chest tightened.

"Ja, I have to. There's a double shooting in the city center. Looks gang-related."

"I heard about that on the radio."

"Still, I don't have to leave for another hour. So tell me what happened yesterday. They haven't found Jonas yet?"

"Not that I know of. Ekström would have called."

"And the crash?"

He listened as she described Nordberg, the car coming out of nowhere, the smash, the ditch. When she spoke of the figure in the snow, his frown deepened.

"Do you think it was Jonas?"

"Maybe. It doesn't make sense, though. Why would he be there? More likely someone from a nearby farm checking if I needed help."

"Then why vanish the moment help arrived?"

"I don't know." She shook her head. "I went over it a hundred times last night. I can't work it out."

"I don't like this, Avril. The sooner they catch him and you can come home, the better."

She sighed, and he felt her frustration. "There's no guarantee they will, and even if they do, we won't know if he's the murderer until we speak to him. There was no trace of Lara at his house, and no one saw him leave the bar with her."

"What about Nordberg?" he asked, scratching his head. "What if they knew Jonas would give Lara something incriminating, so they killed her and tried to silence him? What if he ran because he was scared they'd come after him?"

Avril studied him, thoughtful. "It's plausible," she admitted. "But he could have told Hans. Hans was right there at the farmhouse. Why not stop and talk?"

Krister shook his head. "I can't explain why he ran. Makes no sense to me either."

"Storm coming," the manager said, refilling their coffee. "Just heard on the radio. Best be on your way before it hits."

Krister glanced out. Snow was falling again. "Dammit. Does it ever stop up here?"

"You'd better go." She looked worried. He was touched by it. "If it's like yesterday, you don't want to be caught out. Trust me."

He shrugged. "I'll be halfway to Stockholm before it gets bad. Don't worry."

"I have to get to the station anyway," she said, standing. She'd finished her eggs but barely touched the rest. "This case isn't going to solve itself."

That was his cue to leave. "All right, but promise me you'll be careful. No more trawling the countryside in blizzards."

"I promise," she said, and judging by her tone, he believed her.

"And if you need anything, call me. My team is at your disposal."

"Thanks, Krister." She leaned over and pecked him on the cheek. He resisted the urge to hold her. She wouldn't be comfortable with that. "You're the best."

And that was as much as he could hope for.

chapter
thirty

Avril met with Svensson later that morning. Once again they were seated in Hans' office, the map spread out on the table.

"We're running out of places to look," Svensson told her, his expression grim.

"He must have help," she concluded. "Someone is sheltering him."

"If they are, they're keeping it under wraps. We've been door to door in all the suburbs surrounding where he went missing, and nothing flagged."

Avril sighed, her gaze shifting around the office. It fell on a photograph of Hans as a teenager, his arm around another boy. Could that be Jonas? She'd never noticed it before.

"Do we have a man stationed outside Hans Bergqvist's house?" she asked suddenly.

"No, why would we do that?"

"He's his brother."

"The Kommissarie is the suspect's brother?" Svensson blinked at her, surprised.

"Yes, I thought you knew."

"I didn't make the connection, but now that you mention it... Same last names. Of course."

"That's why he's not around." Avril nodded to the vacant leather chair over which Svensson stood. "Conflict of interest."

Svensson frowned, his brows drawing together. "You think the Kommissarie could be sheltering him?"

"I don't know, but you've looked everywhere else. I'm not saying he is, I just wondered if we were watching his house."

"We're not." He smoothed a hand over his buzz cut. "But we should be. A family member would be an obvious choice. I'll get on it straight away."

"Keep us posted."

THE WEATHER FORECAST WAS CORRECT. The wind picked up, and soon the snow started falling heavily again. Avril, with Ekström's help, was doing a deep dive into Olle Nordberg's past when her phone rang. It was Svensson.

His voice sounded terse down the line. "I've just been to Hans Bergqvist's house, but he's not there. His wife said he left a short while ago, but nobody seems to know where he is."

That was concerning. "Did his wife say if he'd had any visitors?"

"She said she got home yesterday, and he was locked in his den. Didn't come out until late last night. He was in there again this morning, then walked out and she hasn't seen him since."

"Did you check the den?"

"Ja. It looks like someone had slept there overnight. There was a sleeping bag on the floor. The wife said it isn't something her husband does. She couldn't understand why it was there."

"Jonas," she whispered.

"Ja. You were right. Bergqvist was harboring his brother. That's a serious offense."

Shit. What was Hans doing? He was ruining his career over this.

"We'll try to trace him," she said. "Stå kvar." *Stand by.*

"Understood."

AVRIL INSTRUCTED a bewildered Lundgren to get onto the mobile network's liaison and run a trace on the Kommissarie's phone. "He wouldn't do that," he blustered, his face stricken like his mother had just told him Santa Claus didn't exist.

"I'm afraid it looks like he did." Avril glanced at Ekström, who chewed her thumb.

"I can't believe it," she said. "It's so unlike him not to call it in."

Avril nodded. They were loyal to Hans, she got it, but he'd committed an offense, and it wasn't looking good.

"His car is missing too," Avril said. "Let's put out an efterlysning on that."

Ekström gulped. "I'll get right on it."

Avril went back to her desk. She was about to sit down when the front door burst open, and in strode Hans. Ekström gasped and set down the phone. Lundgren stared at him.

"Kommissarie?"

Avril stood up. His hair was ruffled and dusted with snow, he wore an old sweater, and his coat collar was crooked. It was like he'd thrown on whatever he could find before rushing out of the house.

He looked at her and ran a hand through his hair. "I need to speak to you."

Avril followed him to his office and sat opposite him, except this time she was in his chair. It felt strange.

"We know you sheltered your brother," she said. "The police are at your house now, searching it."

He nodded, not even trying to hide it. "He came to me last night, begged me to take him in. I refused, but he was so cold, so broken, I didn't have the heart to refuse him. I wanted to call you, ask you to come over, but Jonas was in a state. I managed to calm him down and agree to come in, to talk to you. He claims he's innocent."

Avril fixed her gaze on him. She'd never seen him this way before. Agitated, upset, not in control of his emotions. It was a far cry from the Kommissarie she'd first met.

"Everybody claims to be innocent," she pointed out. "Do you believe him?"

His shoulders dropped. "I don't know."

"So where is Jonas now?"

"When I got up this morning, he'd gone. I'm sorry. I know I've screwed up, but I was trying to do the right thing."

"By sheltering him when you knew there was a massive manhunt going on?"

"By trying to talk him into coming in. He was going to, I swear. He must have gotten cold feet."

"So now he's on the run again."

Hans nodded.

Avril studied him. "Hans, you know him better than anyone. Where would he go?"

"That's why I'm here," he said, his expression haunted. "I think I know where he's gone."

Avril leaned forward and put her elbows on the desk. "Where?"

He glanced around. "Got a map? I'll have to show you."

chapter
thirty-one

Avril had gotten Ekström to call Svensson back, and now the four of them were gathered around Hans' desk staring down at the topographical map. Hans pointed to what looked like an expanse of green near Myråsen, a marshy area surrounded by forest.

"We used to have a family cabin there." His voice was flat, devoid of any emotion. "It's abandoned now, but I think he could have gone there."

Avril looked at him over her glasses. "You only thought to mention this now?"

He shrugged. "We don't own it anymore. Nobody does. It sits on elevated ground surrounded by marshland. Totally inaccessible this time of year. The lowland bogs freeze over and are unsafe to cross."

Svensson was frowning. "What makes you think he went there?"

"He took my snowmobile."

"You have a snowmobile?" Avril stared at him. What else hadn't Hans thought to mention?

"I keep it in the garage in case of emergencies. When I woke up this morning, it was gone. He'd need one to access the cabin. It's the only way to get there."

Avril looked at Svensson, who studied the map. "We can go part of the way by car, but we'll also need snowmobiles to go any further than here." He prodded a position on the map.

Hans gave a tight nod.

Svensson rubbed his jaw. "The volunteer organization might be able to assist."

"You're going after him?" Avril studied his face. Stoic, thoughtful, determined. "It's a long way to go if he's not there."

"We have to act on this intel." Svensson glanced at Hans. "You did the right thing by coming here."

Avril agreed. It would stand for something, when Hans faced the prosecutor. This, and his long history of service, might just keep him out of prison. Particularly if it led to Jonas' arrest.

"Ekström can help you organize it," Avril offered.

Ekström smiled. "Of course."

Svensson nodded. "Thanks, but I can manage. I've got a point man on the volunteer team. He'll rally the troops and they'll have the snowmobiles waiting for us when we get there."

Avril was impressed. Things worked differently out here, but they still worked.

"I would like to come," she admitted. "But I'd only slow you down." The concussion was still there, lurking behind her temples. Krister would kill her if she went on a snowmobile chase, especially in this weather.

"We'll keep you informed," Svensson said with a nod.

"I heard there was a storm coming in," she cautioned Svensson.

He grunted. "I know, but if he's there, we can't risk him getting away again."

"It's not worth putting your men in danger."

"Understood. We'll monitor the storm carefully."

Avril was satisfied he wouldn't take any unnecessary risks. The man was experienced, that was plain to see. She'd let him handle it. "Okay, then."

"We'll record the entry," Svensson said, folding the map. "I'll wear a GoPro. That way you can watch every step of the operation."

"Really?" Avril felt a surge of adrenalin. She wouldn't miss out completely.

Ekström's eyes glowed with excitement. Hans said nothing.

"Ja. We use it for evidence as well as accountability. If anything goes wrong, we'll have a record."

Avril walked Svensson to the door, while Ekström went back to her desk. Hans waited in his office, sitting at his desk, staring at it like a dog whose bone was just out of reach.

"What do you want me to do?" he asked, when she returned.

She hesitated. This was a dilemma. He'd committed an offense, and she should arrest him, but he was also the Kommissarie, and his information might lead to the capture of their suspect.

The squad room had fallen silent behind her, and she knew Ekström and Lundgren were listening for her response.

She thought for a moment. What would Krister do? She could call him, but he'd still be driving back and she didn't want to distract him.

No, *she* had to make a decision.

"You can go for now," she said, and watched as he let out a relieved sigh. "But don't go anywhere. There will be an officer outside your house at all times."

"I understand." He got to his feet. "Thank you, Avril. I mean it. You've been very lenient, considering."

"I couldn't stand looking at Lundgren's sulky face if I arrested you," she said.

He chuckled. "Erik's a good kid. He's just loyal."

"I know. He told me about your... history."

"Ah." Hans tilted his head back in a half-nod.

"Why didn't you say you put him through police training?" she asked.

He shrugged. "It's not relevant. Besides, that was a long time ago. He's all grown up now, with a family of his own."

Avril respected Hans for that. He was a good guy, a decent man. It wasn't his fault he had a brother like Jonas.

THE SCREEN FLICKERED in front of her, the lens jerking as the snowmobiles cut across the frozen wilderness stretched out in front of the cabin. The GoPro's perspective was raw and unsteady. Since Svensson was at the rear, they could see the deep tracks the machines carved through the drifts. Static laced the audio, but over it they could hear the heavy engines, straining but relentless, chewing their way across the landscape.

The cabin got closer. Avril leaned forward, elbows braced against her desk. Ekström and Lundgren hovered behind her, their faces pale in the artificial glow. The snow pelted down like tiny spears of ice. Even in the heated squad room, she felt a chill seep in through the screen.

The five snowmobiles came to a stop a short distance from the cabin, cutting their engines. Wind whipped at the mic, flattening the conversation into broken bursts. They could just make out Svensson's voice, low and steady, as he gave instructions to the three Östersund officers who'd accompanied him.

The cabin was a squat wooden structure, half buried, its roof sagging under the snow. The video blurred as the GoPro caught the swirling air, the lens smearing where flakes had frozen against it.

Avril felt her pulse tick up a notch.

There was a faint hiss against the microphone, and the crunch of boots as the men dismounted. Svensson's head swung the camera toward the front porch. Avril slanted her eyes, straightening to see. None of them uttered a sound.

The door was warped but closed. One shutter hung half-loose, rattling in the wind. A broken padlock dangled from the latch, its hasp bent back.

She saw one of the other officers make a gesture. A flat palm and then a cutting motion. The sound on the mic was clipped, but the meaning was clear enough.

Approach, weapons ready.

The camera jolted as Svensson advanced. Avril's breath caught when the doorframe filled the screen. Her fingers ached where she gripped the desk.

Another officer stepped up and gave the door a firm kick. The GoPro caught his leg movement, followed by the splintering crack of wood giving way. The door burst inward, the frame shuddering. For a moment, there was nothing but darkness.

The officers went in fast, the beam of their flashlights darting across the cramped space. The feed swung wildly. She caught a glimpse of a fireplace, a table, then floorboards. Avril blinked, disoriented.

Then they saw him.

Jonas.

Behind her, Ekström gasped, while Lundgren stiffened.

Curled in the far corner beneath a mound of blankets, shivering so hard the fabric trembled, was Jonas. His hair hung limp and stringy, his face blotched with cold. For a second, his eyes caught the light. Wild, red-rimmed, the look of an animal flushed from its den.

"They've got him," she hissed.

"Polisen!" Svensson barked.

Jonas flinched, hands twitching above the blankets as though he might bolt. The camera jolted again as Svensson crouched down.

They all leaned closer, eager to see his expression. Both Ekström and Lundgren's cheeks were close to hers.

"Hands where I can see them," Svensson ordered. The other officers fanned out, securing the rest of the cabin.

Jonas held up his hands, fingers red and cracked from the cold.

"He doesn't seem violent," Avril murmured, tilting her head.

"He just looks starving and exhausted," Ekström said.

"He's cornered," Lundgren added.

Svensson's glove entered the frame, tugging the blankets down to be sure Jonas wasn't concealing anything. Then a pat-down, brisk and impersonal, but there was no weapon.

The view steadied for a moment, fixed on Jonas' face. Avril caught every detail. The hollow cheeks, the stubble thick with frost, the jerky flick of his eyes toward the open door. She recognized the look. He wanted to run but lacked the strength.

Back in the squad room, nobody spoke.

"Jonas Bergqvist," Svensson said, his breath fogging in front of him. "You are under arrest."

The camera jolted again as he pulled Jonas to his feet. The suspect staggered, knees buckling, and one of the other officers caught him by the arm. The feed dipped as Svensson adjusted the camera strap, giving Avril a tilted view of the room. The dead hearth, the stripped table, the blankets strewn on the floor. He hadn't been there long.

Jonas muttered something, but it was too low to make out and half-swallowed by the mic. Avril turned up the volume, straining.

"I...didn't... her."

The rest was lost to static as Svensson and his team guided him out, his boots dragging against the warped floorboards.

Ekström let out a sigh of relief. "That was exciting."

Lundgren snorted, then returned to his desk.

Avril straightened up and drew in a breath. They'd bring Jonas back here for processing, and then they could finally hear his side of the story.

chapter
thirty-two

THE INTERVIEW ROOM WAS WINDOWLESS, THE ONLY LIGHT coming from an overhead strip that buzzed intermittently. Inside was a table and two chairs, nothing more. It was the kind of room designed to strip away distraction until all that remained was the suspect and the truth he chose to tell.

Avril stood outside for a moment, watching Jonas through the narrow glass panel in the door. He sat slouched in the chair, his arms folded, long hair pushed back from his forehead. He looked better now than he had on the GoPro feed. Warmer, skin no longer mottled with cold, though his face was still pale, eyes hollow.

He'd spent the night in the hospital—the same one she'd been to for her checkup. They'd treated him for mild hypothermia and given him intravenous electrolytes and food. This morning, after a hot shower and some clean clothes, he was deemed fit to be interrogated.

Lundgren stood by the door, his uniform neat, his expression tight. They'd never had a murder suspect in custody before, especially not one who'd done what Jonas was suspected of doing.

Ekström sat at her desk, watching the live feed. The small video camera and microphone placed in the top corner of the interview room and angled at the interviewee would record the interview that would be stored on the police server.

Avril pulled down the sleeves of her black jumper, then flexed her fingers. Interrogations were a balancing act. Too soft and the suspect walked all over you, too hard and they shut down or lashed out. She would have to tread carefully.

She leaned closer to the glass, studying him. He tapped one foot in a restless rhythm under the table, the only sign of energy in his otherwise hunched frame. He hadn't asked for a lawyer. He hadn't asked for anyone at all. Not even Hans.

Avril drew in a breath, steadying herself. She knew what Krister would say. Stay calm, keep the questions sharp, don't give him any wiggle room.

She turned to Lundgren. "Keep the door locked. No interruptions unless I call for you."

"Ja," he said, giving her a brusque nod. He was nervous too, she could tell. Everybody was eager to hear what Lara's alleged killer had to say.

Avril smoothed a strand of hair back behind her ear, pushed open the door, and stepped inside. The sound of it closing behind her echoed louder than she expected.

Jonas looked up, his eyes glassy but alert, as if he were trying to figure out who she was.

"Kriminalinspektör Avril Dahl," she said. "I'm the senior investigating officer on the Lara Berglund case." She set her file on the table, pulled out the chair opposite him, and sat down.

On the camera above her head, the red light blinked. The recording had begun.

"Do you mind if I call you Jonas?"

He shrugged but didn't respond. Avril went on. "Jonas, do you understand why you're here?"

"You've arrested me."

She nodded. "We've arrested you on suspicion of murdering Lara Berglund. Did you know Lara?"

He stared at her for a long time, then said, "I didn't kill Lara."

"That's not what I asked," Avril said patiently. "I asked if you knew her."

He rubbed the side of his face. "Yeah, I knew her."

"How did you know her?"

He frowned, his deep-set eyes masked in the shadow from his overhanging brow. "She was an acquaintance."

"What kind of acquaintance? Was she a friend? A lover? A work colleague?"

"She was... just someone I knew."

Avril opened the file and took out a photograph of Lara walking into Svartälgen bar. "Did you meet Lara at a bar on December the sixteenth?"

He stared at it and swallowed. "Yeah, we met for a drink. What's wrong with that?"

"Nothing is wrong with that, but you were the last person seen with her the night she disappeared."

His scowl deepened. "I told you already, I didn't kill her."

"But you were with her?"

"Yeah, I was there."

"Thank you for confirming that. Could you tell me where you sat with Lara that night?" She pulled out a piece of paper and set it down in front of him. "This is a diagram of the inside of the Svartälgen."

He leaned over and looked at it, then scoffed and sat up again. "Over there." He pointed to a two-seater table and chairs toward the back left-hand side of the bar.

Avril's gaze narrowed. It was where their witness had said she'd seen them sitting.

"Thank you. What time did you arrive at the bar?"

He rubbed his forehead. "I got there just after seven thirty."

"What did you do?"

"I waited for Lara to arrive."

"Why were you meeting her?"

He didn't reply.

"Would you like me to repeat the question?"

He sighed. "She wanted to ask me questions about Nordberg Infrastruktur. I used to work for them."

Avril nodded. It was good to have confirmation of that. "What kind of questions?"

"What it was like to work for them, whether they paid me well, what

Olle Nordberg was like, whether I'd ever seen him meet with anyone from the council... that sort of thing."

"Anyone from the council? Like Councilor Birgitta Håkansson?"

"Ja. How did you know?"

"Have you ever seen him with her?"

A shrug, but his eyes were shifty. "Once or twice."

"What were they doing when you saw them?" she asked, more quietly now.

He hesitated, then drew in air through his nose. "They were kissing, okay. I saw them kissing."

A beat passed. Avril processed this new information, then asked, "They were having an affair?"

He spread his hands. "I don't know. They looked pretty passionate to me, but how should I know if they were having an affair?"

Good point. She was asking him something he couldn't answer.

"Did you tell Lara this?" she asked, getting back on track.

"Ja, I told her exactly what I've just told you. She was very interested, like it was a big deal or something." It would have been a big deal if the councilor had awarded Nordberg the contract because she was sleeping with him.

"What did Lara do?"

"She paid me, then I took off."

Avril rested her hands on the table. "Paid you? You mean for the information?"

"She said she'd make it worth my while. I don't have any work, so I agreed."

Avril studied him. He looked able-bodied enough to hold down a job. "How much did she pay you?"

"Femhundra spänn." *Five hundred kronor.*

"That's not much."

"It's not nothing. Kept me in smokes for a week."

Avril pursed her lips. "Why aren't you working, Jonas?"

"I got fired, and if you hadn't noticed, it's the middle of fucking winter. Nobody is hiring."

"I see. I'm sorry to hear that."

He smirked. "No you're not. You don't care what happens to me."

"That's not true," she said. "We're just trying to find out what happened to Lara. You were the last person to see her alive."

"So I must have killed her, right?"

"Did you?" She fixed her gaze on him across the table.

"No, I didn't. I left after that. Went out the back to bum a smoke off the kitchen staff, then I went home. She was still sitting at the table when I left."

"How'd you get home? You don't own a car."

"I cycled. I go everywhere on my bicycle unless the snow blocks the roads."

She studied him. Was he telling the truth? "Where is this bike now?"

"It's at my brother's place. I left it there the other day."

"When you stole his snowmobile?"

He gulped but nodded. "I knew you were after me. I thought if I hid up at the cabin, you wouldn't find me."

They wouldn't have if Hans hadn't told them about it. Jonas would have been in the wind, and the case of Lara Berglund would have remained unsolved.

"Why did you run if you were innocent?" she asked him.

"Because I had drugs at my house, and I knew my brother would charge me for possession. He's always so by-the-book." Jonas scoffed and shook his head. "Goddamn boy scout."

Avril wasn't so sure about that.

"He didn't arrest you when you went to his house," she pointed out.

"He was going to. I swear. He tried to convince me to turn myself in. I said, for what? I haven't done anything. I met the girl in the bar, that's it. I smoked some weed. Now I'm being hunted like Sweden's Most Wanted."

Avril studied him. The guy was either a brilliant liar or he was telling the truth. She'd met manipulative killers before—hell, she knew them intimately—and she wasn't seeing any of the signs here.

"Have you ever purchased Rohypnol?"

He blinked. "The date rape drug?"

She nodded.

"Why would I do that?"

"Could you just answer the question?"

"No. Jesus. I've never bought or used roofies."

"Okay, thanks for clarifying." Avril pressed her lips together. "What time did you leave the bar?"

"I don't know. It must have been around eight thirty."

"And you went out the back?"

"Yeah."

"Did you speak to any of the staff? You said you went to bum a smoke. Did you get one?"

He shook his head. "Nah, nobody was on a smoke break. I hung around for a while, but in the end it was too cold, so I left."

"And nobody saw you leave the bar?"

He hesitated. "I don't think so."

"You're sure?" Avril pressed. "This is important, Jonas. It could clear you as a suspect in Lara's murder."

He frowned, his forehead creasing. A desolate sob escaped his throat, as he croaked, "I don't think so."

chapter
thirty-three

"We can't just let him go," Lundgren said, once Avril was back in the squad room. It was midmorning and what little light there was filtered in through the misted-up windows. "He could have killed Lara."

"Except we don't have any proof." She took off her glasses and rubbed her eyes. They felt gritty and tired. Last night, sleep had evaded her. Knowing Jonas was in the hospital and she'd be interviewing him today had left her with a sense of anticipation she couldn't quiet. She'd tossed and turned, questions churning through her mind.

Now, their prime suspect looked like he would walk. "I can keep him in holding for seventy-two hours. After that…" She shrugged.

Ekström spoke up. "Crime scene techs are at the cabin now, processing the place. If they find anything, they'll let us know."

"He can't have taken Lara up there," Avril reasoned. "He wasn't mobile. He'd need a vehicle to transport her, especially if she was unconscious."

"Then he borrowed or stole one," Lundgren muttered.

Avril turned to him. "Find it, then. Find me the vehicle, and we've got something to charge him with."

Lundgren got back to work.

Avril thought about what he'd said in the interview. She played the sequence of events over in her mind. He'd met Lara, they'd talked for a little under an hour, she'd paid him, after which he'd left via the back door. Nobody saw him go.

He could be lying, of course. Most killers did. But there was something in his manner, in his desperation, that made her pause. He didn't like his brother, that much was clear. He thought Hans would arrest him for possession of weed. It was illegal in Sweden, sure, but the small recreational amount in the house was hardly worth the effort.

Was Hans that much of a stickler? It certainly hadn't looked that way to Avril. Hans had barely looked twice at the contraband in the farmhouse. The phone they'd found was much more important.

The phone.

She walked back to the holding cell and pressed the buzzer that allowed her to speak to the inmate inside.

"Jonas, we need your passcode for your cellphone. Will you give it to us?"

She heard scuffling. "I don't see what business that is of yours. But sure. I've got nothing to hide." He gave her a series of six numbers.

She hurried back to Ekström. "Give this to the tech lab. It's the passcode for Jonas' prepaid phone. Tell them to send us all the messages and other data on there. Apps, social media, everything they can find."

"On it."

Maybe there would be something on there they could use. It might even exonerate him—or prove he was guilty. Either way, it was worth a shot.

SOMETIME LATER, Ekström called her over. The data had started coming in. The tech team sent it in drips and drabs, as per Avril's instructions. No point in waiting for the whole lot when they could get started straight away.

The first bundle came in as a compressed file. Ekström unzipped it and scanned the header.

"Messages app," she murmured, angling the monitor so Avril could see. "Last week, several exchanges with a saved contact—no name, just the number."

Avril leaned closer, her glasses slipping down the bridge of her nose.

The texts were plain, stripped of context, but the meaning was stark enough.

Tuesday, 16 December — 18:02

"Meet me at Svartälgen. 19:30. I'll make it worth your while."

Jonas: "Worth my while, how?"

"Depends on the quality of information."

Jonas: "Fine. I'll be there."

Ekström scrolled further. "There aren't any other messages, but there were two calls from Lara's phone in the week before.

"That would be Lara making contact," Avril guessed. "She's somehow learned he worked for Nordberg and has managed to get his contact details. From whom, I wonder?"

Ekström shrugged. "We could ask him."

"I will," Avril mused. "Anyway, this corresponds with the call logs from Lara's phone. She called him to initiate the meeting. She was the one who suggested Svartälgen and promised it would be worth his while."

"Lara had been chasing corruption and dirty contracts. Turns out, Jonas had some valuable information."

"The kiss?" Ekström asked.

"The kiss proved they were intimate. It means she may have awarded Nordberg the contract out of favoritism, not because they were the better company for the job."

"It is suspicious," Ekström admitted.

Another email came in. Ekström clicked through. "No social media installed. No WhatsApp, no Signal. Just the calls and the messages."

"Was he in touch with anyone else other than Lara?"

Ekström nodded. "Yeah, there's a few other numbers here I don't recognize. I'll have to look them up. He's got nothing saved in his address book."

"That's odd, isn't it?" Avril asked. "I mean, who doesn't have a few saved numbers on their phone?"

That was another question for Jonas.

Getting up, she went back to the holding cell. They went through the same process. She knocked, pressed the buzzer, and spoke to him through the intercom system.

"How did Lara find out you'd worked at Nordberg?" Avril asked.

"Through a friend. We were there at the same time, and he gave her my name. She called me about three weeks ago and asked if we could meet. At first, I said no. I didn't want to get involved in that shit, you know? But she called again, so I agreed, just to get her off my back."

"Why don't you have any saved contacts on your phone?" Avril asked.

"Because my last phone got stolen," he said. "I don't even know where. I was drunk at the time."

"So this is a new phone?"

"Ja. I bought it a month ago. I don't remember anyone's number to put in."

It was just pathetic enough to be true.

"Thanks, Jonas," she said, and left him to sleep.

She'd just gotten back to the squad room after stopping to make a cup of coffee when Ekström gave a little squeak.

Avril stopped at her desk. "What is it?"

Ekström's eyes were huge as she pointed to her screen. "Look. The tech team have found DNA at the cabin. Strands of hair and some dried blood. They don't know who it belongs to, but they're taking it back to the lab for testing."

Avril went cold.

Shit.

"Female?" she asked, her pulse kicking into overdrive.

Ekström nodded. "The hair is long. They're saying it most likely belongs to a woman."

chapter
thirty-four

IT WAS GONE SIX BY THE TIME THE LAB RESULTS CAME IN. The hair did belong to a woman, but it wasn't Lara's.

"It was dark hair," Ekström explained, after putting down the telephone. "With a reddish tint. They think the red was hair dye."

"So who does it belong to?" Avril asked.

"A woman called Freya Lindholm. I'm going to run her name through the database now to see if I can find out who—"

"Freya?" Avril paused, frowning. "I know that name."

"You do?" Ekström said.

"So do I," Lundgren spluttered, his eyebrows rising in surprise.

They both turned to him. "How?" Avril asked.

"She grew up here, like me. I mean, I didn't know her personally, but I knew who she was."

Ekström narrowed her gaze. "So did I, but I don't remember her."

"She was older than you," Lundgren said. "A bubbly, extraverted redhead. Always wore provocative outfits. I think she worked near to Svartälgen, at the music store."

Ekström shook her head.

Avril clicked her fingers. "That's it. Freya was Lara's friend. The barman at The Stag Brewery, Lars, told me about her. According to him, she left Norrdal last year to move to Stockholm—with a married man."

"So why is her blood and hair in a cabin in Myråsen?" Lundgren asked, coming over.

"Maybe she never went to Stockholm," Ekström whispered.

A chill crept down Avril's spine. "Lars at the brewery said she left suddenly, without saying goodbye. Apparently Lara was devastated."

"That is suspicious," Lundgren agreed. "Are we sure she left town?"

"She left a note," Avril said. "To her mother, I think. The details are sketchy. I meant to check up on her but I never got around to it."

"Shall I call The Stag and clarify?" Ekström asked.

"I'll do it. Lundgren, I need Freya's parents' home address and telephone number. ASAP."

He scrambled to look it up. Avril's heart beat painfully in her chest. Dried blood. Hair. That didn't sound like accidental DNA. That was from a crime scene. A long-ago crime scene.

"Ekström, call the lab tech back and ask how old that bloodstain was. Could it be last year, around this time?"

Ekström had picked up the phone before Avril had even finished talking. While they were busy, she called Lars at The Stag and confirmed what he'd told her.

"Ja, that is correct. Freya left in November last year, just before the snow got really bad. Why do you ask?"

"It's not important." Avril thanked him, then turned to Ekström. "Anything?"

"It wasn't fresh. They couldn't put an exact date on it, but not in the last six months. That's as much as they would say."

Avril stood still, an uneasy feeling clawing at her. "What if Freya was taken last year, just like Lara?"

"But the note—" Ekström said.

"The killer could have written it. Maybe he knew Freya had plans to leave town, so he made it look like she had."

Both Ekström and Lundgren stared at her.

"Or he could have gotten her to write it under duress," Avril added. "We need to see that note."

"I've got her parents' address," Lundgren said, tearing off the page and handing it to her.

"How far is this?" she asked, glancing at it.

"A ten-minute drive."

She peered out the window of the station. The road was gone, swallowed whole beneath a thick white blanket. Snowdrifts had piled high against the gutters, spilling over onto the pavement, erasing the line between street and sidewalk. Wind drove the flakes sideways in furious gusts, plastering them against the station windows.

The snowplows hadn't made it this far, and even if they had, the snow would have covered their work in minutes. To drive in this was unthinkable. Avril suppressed a shiver. She didn't want a repeat of what had happened before.

"I'll try calling them," she said, and headed to Hans's office for some privacy. Hopefully, they'd still be open to answering some questions over the phone.

"Is this Mrs. Lindholm?" Avril asked when the voice of a mature woman picked up.

"It is. How can I help you?" She sounded reserved but curious.

"My name is Avril Dahl, and I'm calling from Norrdal Polisstation. It's about your daughter, Freya."

"Freya? Is something wrong?"

Avril hesitated. "Do you know where your daughter is, Mrs. Lindholm?"

"She's in Stockholm." There was a note of longing in her voice. "Why?"

"Have you heard from her lately?"

"No, but we're not close. What is this about?"

"I believe she left you a note informing you of her plan to leave and move to the city?" Avril asked, still not answering her questions. She had to be sure before she told the woman what they'd found.

"Yes, she did."

"Do you still have that note?" Avril asked.

"No, I think I gave it to Lara."

"Lara Berglund?"

"That's right. She asked if she could keep it. I think she was upset that Freya addressed the note to me and not her."

They hadn't found a note in Lara's files, nor in the contents of her backpack or bedroom. It hadn't been on the itemized log she'd looked at.

"Do you remember what it said?" Avril asked.

"Unfortunately, I do. Ja. It is forever engraved on my heart."

Avril drew in a quick breath. "Tell me."

"It said, *"Dear Mamma, I've had enough of Norrdal so I'm leaving. I've met someone, and I'm going to live with him in Stockholm. I'm sure you won't miss me that much. Freya."* She ended with a gulp. "I haven't heard from her since."

Avril wrote that down, word for word.

"Was it in her handwriting?" she asked, once she was done.

"Yes, of course. What is this about?"

"If you'll bear with me, Mrs. Berglund, I'll explain everything in a moment."

There was a soft huff. "Okay."

"Do you know who she was seeing?"

"No, she wouldn't tell us anything like that."

"Why not?" Avril asked.

"Like I said, we weren't close." A sigh. "It's complicated. Her father passed away when she was little. We all missed him—he was a wonderful man. But then I met Steph. He made me happy, but Freya didn't like him."

"Why didn't she like him?" Avril asked.

"I don't know. They just didn't get on. Eventually, Freya left home. By then, Steph and I had a child of our own. A little girl, Anette. A few years later, William followed." She gave an exasperated sniff. "We'd hoped Freya would take to the children, but she didn't. In fact, she spent even less time at home and eventually stopped coming to visit altogether."

"When did she leave, Mrs. Lindholm?"

"Oh, let me think. Yes, it was around November last year. Over a year ago now." A pause. "Do you have news about her?"

Avril took a deep breath. "I'm sorry to have to do this over the phone," she began, "but I can't get to you in person."

"What is it?" There was worry there now. Fear. "She is all right, isn't she?"

"I don't know," Avril said honestly. "We recently found her DNA at a cabin out at Myråsen. Blood, and some strands of hair. We were wondering what she may have been doing there."

There was an audible gasp down the line. "Oh, God. Is she...? Do you think she's...?"

"We don't know that, Mrs. Lindholm," Avril was quick to respond. "There wasn't enough to say for certain. She may just have been injured."

That would be the best-case scenario.

Another ragged gasp. "What should we do?"

"Nothing, for now," Avril said. "We're investigating, and we'll let you know if we find anything. If you hear from your daughter in the meantime, let us know."

"Of course."

WHEN SHE CAME out of Hans's office, she found both Ekström and Lundgren waiting for her. On the whiteboard was a photograph of a laughing redhead. She had wild copper hair, sharp cheekbones, and sparkling green eyes full of mischief.

"What did she say?" Ekström whispered.

Avril gave a grim nod. "Freya left in November last year. Her mother gave the handwritten note to Lara Berglund."

Ekström's expression clouded. "I didn't see a note listed in her personal items."

Avril was pleased she'd picked up on that. "Neither did I. Will you double-check?"

Ekström nodded and sat down, swiveling to face her computer.

"What should I do?" Lundgren asked. His blond hair was mussed, and a worried frown creased his forehead.

"We have to find out who Freya was seeing," Avril said, walking back to her desk. "Lars at The Stag said there was a rumor he was married, which was why she never told anyone. Not even Lara, who was her best friend." She shook her head. "I don't know where to start."

Lundgren sucked in a breath. "This is a small town. Someone must know something. Freya was a popular girl. She was sexy and bubbly, the type people noticed."

Sounded like Lundgren had noticed her too. Avril's gaze returned to the whiteboard. She supposed Freya was sexy, with her hourglass figure and all that wild hair.

"Did you put that up?"

He nodded.

Avril thought for a moment, finger tapping on her lip. "Lundgren, can you ask around? Call your old friends, anyone who might have known her. Anyone who might have seen her with someone."

He nodded.

"Talk to Igor at Svartälgen," she added, "and check in with the other bars in the area, including the ones farther out of town, where there's less chance of running into someone you know. Send them that picture. Ask if they recognize her."

Maybe, if they got very lucky, someone would know who she'd been seeing. Was he their killer?

Avril sat down at her desk, deep in thought. Lara's murder might not have had anything to do with Nordberg, or Jonas, or the article she'd been researching. This could be about Freya, her mystery man, and a secret relationship that he would kill to prevent from coming out.

chapter
thirty-five

AVRIL SLID A PHOTO ACROSS THE TABLE. FREYA'S SMILE frozen in time. "Ever seen her before?"

"No," Jonas muttered.

Avril sat opposite him in the interview room again, in an attempt to find out more about Lara's friend. The radiator ticked in the corner, but the air still felt cold. He sat hunched over the metal table, in his standard-issue tracksuit, compliments of Norrdal Police Station. His hands trembled as he rubbed them together, not from the cold but from stress, the after-effects of his frantic expedition to the cabin, and lack of sleep.

"Lara ever mention a Freya Lindholm?" Avril asked.

"No. Only Nordberg. That's all she asked me about."

Avril narrowed her gaze. "Can you explain how Freya's blood and hair ended up in the cabin in Myråsen?"

He shook his head, but she could tell the news hit him hard. "I can't. I only got there that morning. Hadn't been in years, not since our family stopped using it. It's been abandoned for a decade. Anyone could have gone there in that time."

And that was exactly the kind of line a good defense lawyer would use. In Sweden, an abandoned cabin was never truly empty. Hunters, wanderers, campers, anyone desperate enough could claim it, even if only for a night.

She sighed and leaned back in her chair. As convenient as it was for

Jonas to be their killer, she couldn't prove it beyond reasonable doubt. Everything they had was circumstantial.

"What made you think to go there?" she asked, after a beat. "To the cabin, I mean."

He shrugged. "I was at my brother's house, in the study. There's a photograph there of us as kids at the cabin one summer. I thought it would be a good hiding place."

"So, you went on a whim? An idea you had on the spot?"

"Ja."

She shook her head. It was frustrating how one moment everything seemed to make sense, and the next, nothing added up.

"Okay. Thanks, Jonas."

He glanced up hopefully. "Can I go now?"

Avril shook her head. "Not yet. We're still looking into a few things. I'll let you know."

"You can't hold me forever," he said. "You've got nothing on me. I didn't do this."

"I can hold you for three days," she said in response. "And there are still two days to go. You might as well make yourself comfortable."

THE COLD HIT her like a wall the moment she stepped outside. The storm still raged, a white curtain swallowing the town whole. Wind drove snow across her face in hard, stinging flakes that forced her to lower her head and squint against it. Her boots sank deep into the powder as she trudged forward. All she could hear was the crunch of snow and the howl of the wind funneling between the houses.

She kept to the middle of the road, as Lundgren had suggested. The drifts along the sidewalks were knee-high, swallowing the benches so only the top half protruded from the snow. Even in the center, the snow reached mid-calf. It was heavy going, and she leaned into the gusts to keep her balance. It felt like wading against a tide.

It was only two blocks to Hans's house, but it felt like forever. The buildings were indistinct shapes, barely visible through the storm. Windows glowed faintly here and there, pockets of warmth in the endless white.

When she finally reached her destination, she stopped at the gate to catch her breath. It was the sort of home that suited a police chief in a rural town. Solid, practical, but not ostentatious. A two-story timber frame, painted in a deep red that stood out above the snow creeping up its walls.

The roof was pitched to bear the heavy winters and now carried a thick white burden that overhung the eaves. A light shone in the front window, casting a golden glow onto the snowy yard. The driveway was already hidden under a fresh drift, and she almost missed the white picket fence that ran along the front.

Tightening her scarf, Avril climbed the steps to the porch. The frigid cold had seeped into her bones. She needed to get inside, and quickly. She knocked hard, then brushed the snow from her hat and coat while she waited.

Footsteps... a man's voice, and then the door opened.

Hans stood there, wearing a tracksuit, in his socks and holding a mug of something steaming. "Avril. For God's sake, come in. You'll freeze out there."

Her teeth chattered, so she gladly stepped inside, breathing a sigh of relief.

"Let me take your coat. Freda!" he called, making her jump. "Freda, can you get Avril a cup of coffee? She looks like she needs one."

Freda appeared, apron on. There was the smell of something sweet and doughy baking in the background. "Of course. Oh! My dear, what were you thinking?"

Avril shot her a grateful smile. "Thank you, Mrs. Bergqvist."

She waved a hand in the air. "Please, it's Freda."

Avril handed Hans her coat. It was lovely and warm inside the house, and she felt her body untensing.

"I needed to talk to you," she said, as he led her into the living room. Freda disappeared back to the kitchen. "It's about the case."

"I'm not sure you should be," he cautioned, with a backwards glance over his shoulder.

"I know, but it involves something that happened last year, and I was hoping you'd be able to help me."

"Okay." He gestured to the sofa.

They both sat down. Avril perched on the couch and removed her gloves, while Hans lowered himself into a well-used armchair in the corner, facing the television.

"What is it?"

"Last year, a young woman named Freda Lindholm disappeared. She left a note for her mother saying she'd met someone and was going to Stockholm with him. Do you remember that?"

He frowned and pressed a finger to his forehead as he tried to recall. "No, I can't say that I do. Was she from Norrdal?"

"Yes."

He shook his head. "How is this relevant to the investigation?"

Avril hesitated. "She was best friends with Lara Berglund."

Understanding flashed in his eyes. "And you think the disappearances are related."

"I'm still trying to figure that out. There is no record of her living in Stockholm. Ekström has scoured every database available. Nothing. She's not on any housing register, hasn't applied for a loan, and hasn't accessed her bank account or credit cards in over a year. It's looking like she never made it to Stockholm."

"Hmm..." He rubbed his jaw. "That is strange, I agree."

"Nobody reported her missing to you?"

"No, but if she'd left a note, I guess everyone assumed she had done as she'd said. No need to call the police."

Avril gave a low hum. "Mm..."

"How's my brother doing?" Hans asked, studying her.

"He's okay. We're going to hold him for the full seventy-two hours."

"Are you going to charge him with murder?" He nodded, like he'd accepted it.

She cringed. "I can't discuss that, I'm sorry."

Freda came in with the coffee. Avril wrapped her frozen hands around it. "Thank you."

"You warm yourself up, dear." She cast a look at her husband. "Hans, let her take the snowmobile back. She can't walk in this. She'll catch her death."

Avril glanced up. "You got it back?"

"Yes, thank goodness. One of the volunteers dropped it off earlier today. Still in one piece, unbelievably. You're welcome to borrow it, of course."

She'd never driven one before, but anything was better than battling the blizzard. "Thanks. I might just do that." How hard could it be?

"Does my brother know this Freya woman?" Hans asked.

"Freya Lindholm, and no. He claims he doesn't."

His forehead creased. "Do you believe him?"

"I don't know. Do you think he could be lying?"

Hans shrugged. "Maybe. Jonas lies. He makes things up. Who knows what's going on in his head. I stopped understanding him a long time ago."

"What do you mean he makes things up?"

"He bends the truth, leaves things out, tells you one story one day and another the next." He sighed. "Once, I got called out to a fight outside a bar in Krokom. Jonas swore he hadn't touched the guy, but the cameras showed him throwing the first punch. I can't take anything he says at face value anymore."

She frowned. "When was this?"

"A long time ago, when he was in his early twenties. He went through a bad patch. Fights, petty theft, small stuff, but it added up. He even did a short stretch inside. And more than once I had to lean on colleagues, ask for leniency. Community service instead of a charge, warnings instead of custody. I thought I was helping him at the time. Looking back..." He shook his head, his mouth tightening. "Maybe I just made it worse."

Avril thought about the man in the holding cell. He'd seemed broken, yes. Down and out, certainly. But he didn't strike her as the lying hellraiser his brother made him out to be. Then again, people change over the years. They get older, lose the urge to act out. Mellow.

Hans leaned forward and set his cup down on the low coffee table between them. "Avril, may I give you some advice?"

She looked at him. "Sure."

"I know I'm not a Kriminalinspektör, but I've been a policeman for a long time. Follow the evidence. Don't try to find things that aren't there. At the end of the day, the evidence is what we have to present. Swedish prosecutors do not like suppositions or opinions. They like proof. The defense on the other hand..." He broke off, not needing to continue.

Avril got it.

"That's the problem," she said, still clutching her cup. "I know Jonas was in the right place at the right time, I know about his history, and I hear what you're saying, but there is no actual evidence tying him to Lara's murder. No witnesses, no Rohypnol found at his house. He doesn't own a vehicle, and most of all, he had no motive." She shook her head. "Why kill Lara? She was no threat to him. *He* was blowing the whistle on Nordberg." She paused for a beat. "And he didn't even know Freya."

His eyes lit up. "What are you saying? That you're going to let him go?"

"You said evidence, but we don't have any." She upturned her hand that wasn't holding the cup. "I don't see that I have much choice."

A long moment passed where neither of them spoke, then Hans broke into a surprised laugh. "Well, I guess that is good news. I mean, bad for the investigation, as you still don't have a suspect, but good for Jonas."

"And for you," she added, giving him a sideways glance. "If Jonas is off the hook, then you didn't harbor a criminal."

Hans dipped his head, a wry smile still playing on his lips. "That is true."

Avril downed the last of her coffee and stood up. "Do you mind if I see your study?"

"Er, sure. Why?"

"I want to see where Jonas slept, the night he was here."

"Of course. Follow me."

He led her down a short corridor toward the back of the house. On the left, at the very end, was a door. It stood ajar.

Hans pushed it open, stood back and waved his arm. "Come in."

She stepped into the room and looked around. The study was larger than she expected, square and orderly, with a single window that looked out across the snow-buried garden. Half-drawn curtains muted the winter light. A broad oak desk dominated the room, its surface tidy except for a pile of folders he'd obviously been looking through. She wondered if they were old case files.

Behind the desk stood a tall bookcase, filled with law texts and binders marked Norrdal Polisen, as well as a few well-worn crime novels.

A pair of certificates—his police academy graduation and a commendation for long standing service—were tacked up in simple frames. A plain rug covered the floor, its corners curling with age.

In the far corner stood the evidence of Jonas's visit. A rolled-out sleeping bag, and an empty glass on the side table. The air held the faint scent of stale tobacco, out of place in the otherwise clean room.

She walked over until she stood in the corner where Jonas had slept. Turning, she surveyed the room. There was no photograph of the cabin, and the two boys posing in front of it. Had Jonas been making that up?

"What's the matter?" Hans said, his gaze slanting.

Avril shrugged. "Nothing. Jonas told me in his interview that he'd seen a photograph of you both in front of the cabin. That's what gave him the idea to go there. But I don't see it anywhere."

"You mean this one?" Hans moved over to the desk, opened the bottom drawer and pulled out a silver-framed photograph. He stood it on the desk. "I put it away after he was arrested. The cabin didn't have the same... meaning anymore, if you know what I mean?"

She got that. The memories were tainted now. His relationship with Jonas had soured over the years, and now the intel Hans had given the police had led to his arrest. Whether Jonas was guilty or not, she doubted there was any going back from that.

Avril picked up the photograph and studied it. The two boys must have been teenagers. Hans at the tail end, while Jonas was only about eleven or twelve. They had wide grins on their sun-kissed faces, their shirts off, and swimming trunks on. Behind them, the cabin was drenched in sunshine. A far cry from the snow-beaten shack it had appeared to be on Svensson's GoPro camera.

"Nice picture," she said, setting it back down.

"Thanks. We had some good times there when we were young."

"Where is your father now?" she asked, only mildly curious.

"He passed away several years back."

"I'm sorry."

A shrug. "It happens."

Avril glanced at her phone. It was getting on. She had to head back to the station. "I should be going." She walked past him and out of the study. The smell of baking made her hungry.

He nodded. "Take the snowmobile. It'll be easier than the walk, trust me. You can park it in the lot behind the station. There's space there for staff vehicles."

"I will, thank you."

She followed him out a side door and into a narrow alley alongside the house. At the end was a small garage big enough for one car. Hans pressed a buzzer on a device in his pocket, and the front door rolled up. There, in the center, stood the snowmobile. "Have you ridden one before?" he asked.

She shook her head. "Nope."

Hans gave the faintest smile. "Luckily, it's not that hard. Imagine a motorbike, except it doesn't have wheels." He ran her through the controls — throttle on the right handlebar, brake on the left, a lever for reverse. He tapped the ignition switch with a gloved finger and the engine rumbled to life, echoing off the walls of the garage.

The sound was loud in the enclosed space, a steady, throaty growl that made the floor tremble. Avril pulled on the helmet he held out to her, fastening the strap under her chin. The padding muffled everything but the engine's roar.

"Climb on," he said.

She swung her leg over the wide seat and settled in, her boots braced on the running boards. The smell of petrol and oil clung to the air, sharp and unfamiliar. She tightened her grip on the handlebars, the cold rubber rough under her gloves. Hans gave a nod toward the wide doors, rolled up to reveal the white expanse beyond. The driveway had been half-cleared, compacted to hard snow by the plows and the tires of his own car.

"Ease it forward," he instructed.

She twisted the throttle gingerly. The machine lurched, treads scraping against the concrete before catching properly on the packed snow outside. Avril jolted, almost losing her balance, then steadied herself.

"That's it," Hans called over the engine. "Keep it smooth. Let the track do the work."

She nudged the throttle again, the snowmobile crawling into the open, skis cutting a neat line through the thin crust of new snow. By the time she reached the street, the controls felt less alien. The machine was heavy, but it wanted to go forward, and that was enough.

Avril kept to the center of the road, unable to hear a thing beneath the helmet and the churn of the engine. Snow whipped past her visor, stinging the gap where the seal met her cheek. She tried the throttle once more, a little braver this time, and the sled surged into the wind.

It didn't take long to reach the station.

chapter
thirty-six

No sooner had Avril walked into the station than Ekström glanced up.

"Kriminalinspektör, Tarek Khalil called. He found a box of Lara's things in the shed and asked if you wanted to take a look?"

Avril took off her gloves and beanie and shook the snow out of them. The ride back wasn't nearly as debilitating as the walk there, but she still needed to thaw out before she could think of going anywhere else.

"How'd you get back?" Lundgren studied her windswept cheeks.

She shook out her hair. Flakes fell to the floor. "I borrowed Hans's snowmobile."

He raised an eyebrow, impressed. "Didn't know you could drive one of those."

"I can't." she replied. "Not really. Hans gave me a quick lesson."

He smirked. "How is Kommissarie?"

"He seems fine. Did you find out anything about Freya's secret boyfriend?"

"Yes and no. I spoke to all my friends, everyone who knew Freya. Nobody remembers a recent love interest."

Avril slid her coat off her shoulders and hung it behind her desk chair. "What about the bars?"

"All the bar staff in Norrdal knew her." He gave a dry smile. "Like I said, she was a regular."

"What about out of town?"

His eyes widened as he looked at her. "That's where it gets interesting. I called every bar and restaurant I could find in neighboring towns, but nobody recognized her. Then, I thought, what about the hotels? Maybe they ate there, or stayed over, you know?"

Avril slanted her gaze, sensing something was coming. "And?"

"I got lucky. The hotel manager at Fjällvind Hotell recognized her face. Said she'd been there a few times last year."

Avril's heart leapt. "Really? They were sure it was her?"

Lundgren grinned. "A hundred percent. The manager has a thing for redheads."

"This is great." Avril rubbed her hands together, to warm them, and because she was so pleased. "Did the manager see who she was with?"

That was the million-dollar question.

Lundgren's face clouded. "He did, but only briefly. The man met her in the lobby and they went straight upstairs. He got a side-on look. Said he was tallish, average build, with dark blond hair."

Avril stared at him. "Does he have a credit card on file?"

Lundgren shook his head. "The booking was in Freya's name, I checked."

Avril ran a hand through her hair, still tussled from her ride back. "What about cameras?"

"They have but they reuse them. The footage is long gone."

"Shit," she muttered.

"The description fits Jonas Bergqvist," Lundgren said, cautiously.

Avril turned to Ekström. "Check Jonas's bank statements for November last year. If he had a different mobile phone, check those too."

Then she glanced back at Lundgren. "Get him in the interview room. I want to talk to him on record."

He gave a quick nod and got up. "He'll be ready in five minutes."

. . .

Jonas looked even more strung out than he had earlier. "Are you drinking water?" she asked him, concerned by the gray pallor of his skin.

"Yeah, that's all I'm bloody drinking," he moaned. "Don't suppose I could have a smoke?"

"Don't have any," she retorted. "Sorry."

He grunted. "What do you want now?"

"Jonas, where were you in November last year?"

He frowned. "You mean on a particular day, or just generally?"

"I mean were you here, in Norrdal?"

He frowned for a moment, then his face lit up. "Actually, no. I was in Marbella. I went on a cheap break with a friend."

"Who's the friend?"

"Björn Larsson."

"Will he vouch for you?" she asked, feeling the tension behind her eyes.

"Yeah. He lives in Umeå now."

"Can I have his contact details?"

He shrugged. "I lost my phone and I don't have them on my new one. That's why I haven't been able to get in touch with anyone. It's shit."

She could see how that would be problematic. "How'd you lose your phone again?"

"One night at the bar. I'd had a lot to drink, and when I got home, it wasn't in my coat pocket. Someone must have nicked it."

"When was this?" she asked.

"About a month ago. What's the big deal? It's just a phone."

She shook her head. "Okay, let's move on. How can I get in touch with Björn Larsson?"

Jonas thought for a moment. "He's a fisherman. Works in a factory up there. Industrial machinery, I think. He's a pretty smart guy."

"Know which factory?" Avril's leg was jumping. She wanted to check out Jonas' alibi. If he was out of the country on the dates Freya and her mystery man stayed at the Fjällvind Hotell, then he was in the clear. For that one, at least.

Any clarity she could get at this stage would be welcome.

He scrunched up his face. "No, sorry. Never paid that much attention to what he did."

She sighed. "Okay, thanks."

"How much time left?" he asked, as she stood up to leave.

"Huh?"

"How much longer am I going to be here?"

"A while still."

Lundgren arrived to escort Jonas back to the holding cell, while Avril went to speak to Ekström.

"Look up the exact dates Freya stayed at the Fjällvind Hotell, then get hold of this guy in Umeå. Jonas said he works at some sort of machinery factory. Ask him if he was in Marbella with Jonas in November last year. Cross-check the dates. Got that?"

Ekström made a quick note, then nodded. "Is that what he's saying —that he wasn't in Sweden when Freya went missing?"

"He's just remembered, yeah."

Her eyes lit with purpose. "I'll get right on it."

"Thanks." Avril adjusted her scarf.

"What are you going to do?"

"I'll visit Tarek Khalil. There might be something important in those things he found."

"On the snowmobile?" Ekström asked, arching a brow.

It was still coming down outside, the flakes plastering against the windowpanes.

"It's better than walking," Avril said. "And driving is out of the question."

Ekström smiled faintly. "You're becoming quite a local."

Avril wasn't sure about that, but she had to admit—she liked buzzing around on the thing.

Tarek opened the door in jeans and a purple sweatshirt with Lakers stamped across the chest in bright yellow. From inside, she caught the pulse of a soulful R&B track.

"I went there once," he said.

She blinked. "Excuse me?"

"Los Angeles. Loved it. Went to a game too." He tugged at his sweatshirt.

"Ah." She nodded. "You have something of Lara's for me?"

He stepped back to let her in. "I found it in the shed." He gestured toward the back of the house, where she assumed there was a garden. "I was trying to fix the sink, so I went out to get a wrench, and there it was, just sitting on a shelf. I don't remember seeing it there before."

She followed him into the kitchen, where he picked up a cardboard shoebox from the table and handed it to her. "It's filled with clippings, a notebook, and various other things. I took a quick look. Looks like she was searching for her friend."

Her heart skipped a beat. "Freya?"

"Yeah, Freya. She always thought it was strange how she'd just up and left without so much as a word. But Freya was like that, you know? Impulsive. She'd shack up with some guy, and then a month later, she'd be single again. She slept on our couch more times than I can count."

Avril glanced down. A battered blue notebook lay on top, with newspaper clippings, receipts, and scraps tucked beneath it. She was eager to find out what answers it held, if any.

"Okay. Thanks, Tarek. You did the right thing by giving this to us."

His mouth tightened into a thin line. "I don't know if it'll help you find out who did this, but at least it's something."

"I'll look through it all and let you know," she promised, pushing the box into her backpack. She'd brought it along deliberately, knowing she might need to carry evidence back. The snowmobile had no storage compartments that she could find.

It was getting dark when she left. The streetlamps glowed weakly against the steady fall of snow. She paused, pulling her hood tightly around her face. Was it her imagination, or did it seem to be easing? She hoped so. At this rate, she thought grimly, she'd be stuck in Norrdal until the spring thaw.

chapter
thirty-seven

When Avril got back, she found Lundgren had gone two doors down to an Italian takeout place and brought two enormous pizzas back. "I opted for one plain and one pepperoni," he explained. "Hope that's okay."

"It's perfect." She placed her backpack on the floor and took off her coat, gloves, and beanie.

"What did Tarek give you?" Ekström asked.

Avril reached into her backpack and pulled out the cardboard box. She put it on her desk. "He found it in the shed. It contains a notebook Lara was using, as well as a bunch of newspaper clippings and other items."

They both came over to take a look. Avril took out the blue notebook and flipped it open. The handwriting was neat, looping, and underlined in places where Lara had wanted to emphasize a point. The first few pages were filled with references to Norrdal's so-called youth exodus. The story Avril had once dismissed as little more than sociology. Dates, names, ages, brief quotes. Margins filled with comments: Stockholm? Umeå? Abroad? Why?

"Looks like a story she was working on," Ekström murmured.

Avril nodded and kept turning the pages. Suddenly, the pattern shifted. Lara had been narrowing the focus. Whole sections were dedicated not to statistics or migration patterns, but to one person.

Freya.

Ekström gasped. "Look!"

Avril nodded, studying the scrawled notes. "*Freya Lindholm. Last seen November 17. At Kafé Norrsken.*"

"*Spoke to her on November 21st. She was excited about something but wouldn't tell me what. Not yet, she said.*"

"I wonder what she wanted to tell her," Lundgren said.

Avril thought she knew. "She was leaving with her secret lover. They were going to Stockholm together. Or so she thought."

Ekström met her gaze. "You don't think he meant to take her?"

Avril shook her head. "Do you?"

Ekström gulped. "I guess not."

"They must have arranged to meet, but instead of a romantic getaway, he forced her to write that note, then... what? Killed her?" Lundgren asked, piecing it together.

"It looks like it."

"Then where is her body?" Ekström whispered. "If she's been dead for a year, it should have been discovered by now."

"Not necessarily," Avril said, thinking back to the Frost Killer case that had brought her to Sweden. Some of his victims had remained buried for over a decade.

Below, several names were listed, most of them with question marks: Petterson – serious? Johan L.? Oskar – fling?

"Lara was looking into past boyfriends," Avril guessed.

Further down, Lara had drawn a line and written "WHO?" in capital letters, circling it so hard the pen had almost torn the paper. An arrow led to another word, underlined twice: "Married???"

Avril's stomach knotted. Lara had clearly stopped treating Freya's departure as a case of lovers running off together. She had convinced herself Freya had not left voluntarily at all.

"This isn't just about the article," Avril murmured, more to herself than to Ekström. "She was looking for her friend."

They pored through the rest of the notebook together. Freya's history with men filled the pages. Boyfriends, flings, one-night stands, even names Ekström said she recognized from town. Some were crossed out, others left dangling.

"There were quite a few," Ekström murmured, brushing a strand of hair out of her face.

Avril rubbed her eyes. The letters had begun to blur, the loops and lines running into one another. The room was heavy with the smell of pizza and overly warm from the radiators. She yawned, then glanced at Ekström, who had dark smudges under her eyes. "That's enough for tonight."

Ekström glanced at the notebook as if reluctant to leave it.

Avril closed it. "Go home. Get some sleep. We can pick this up again in the morning."

The younger woman nodded, too tired to argue. At least the snow was lighter now, and they could walk home without being in danger of hypothermia or being blown away.

Ekström gathered her coat and bag, nodded to Avril and Lundgren, who was still munching his way through the last of the pizza, and left.

Lundgren wiped his hands on a napkin and stood up. "I'll stay. Someone needs to keep watch on Jonas."

Avril inclined her head. "Thanks, Lundgren. I'll relieve you at three." That would give her six hours of shut-eye.

"I'll be okay till six," he offered.

She smiled wearily. "Thanks, but you barely slept the other night. Happy to go halves."

He grinned. "See you at three, then."

BACK AT THE GUESTHOUSE, Avril showered, got into her PJs and lay on the bed with the notebook and her phone. First, she wanted to speak to Krister. She told herself it was because she wanted to check in, but really, she was just keen to hear his voice.

"Why don't you answer my messages?" he said, as soon as she'd said hello. "I was worried something else had happened to you."

"I'm fine," she reasoned. "I've been busy."

"Well, so have I, but I still have time to check if you're okay. You weren't looking so hot when I left."

"I know. I'm sorry." He wasn't wrong. It was careless of her. When she was working, she simply didn't think about things like texts or updates. Any distraction from the case felt like a luxury she couldn't afford.

He let out a frustrated sigh. "How's it going over there?"

"I think we're finally making progress," she said, not wanting to tempt fate. This case seemed to change direction faster than you could say "arrest warrant."

"That's good. Want to fill me in?"

She did. It felt good updating Krister. Familiar. Like they used to do. It helped organize her thoughts, separate the important details from the clutter. Isolate what was important.

"You think Lara was murdered because she found out who Freya's secret lover was?" he asked, when she'd finished explaining about the notebook.

"I do. I don't believe this has anything to do with Nordberg Infrastruktur, or Jonas Bergqvist."

Krister let out a long breath. "Well, if you can find out who she was seeing, you've got your killer."

That was proving more difficult than expected. "We've got a general description, but it's not much."

"Do you think this man has done this kind of thing before?" Krister asked.

Avril frowned. "You mean before Freya?"

"Yeah. A predator like that might have a history of affairs with younger women."

She was silent for a long moment, staring at the ceiling. Then: "Krister... do you have access to a police terminal right now?"

"Ja, I'm logged in. I was working from home when you called."

"Could you run a search for me?" She told him the parameters.

"One second." She heard the thumping of the keys as he entered the query.

Avril held her breath, the seconds dragging. Then came the pause, followed by his sharp intake of air.

"Oh, God, Avril. You were right."

"Tell me."

"There have been multiple disappearances over the last few years. Even more if you go back further. Same profile: young women, twenties, from isolated towns in northern Sweden. Disappeared without a trace."

Avril felt her blood chill. "Are they all within driving distance of Norrdal?"

"Uh-huh, yep. I think you've stumbled upon something much bigger than a single disappearance here, Avril."

She paused, her pulse racing. Adrenaline flying through her veins. Suddenly, she wasn't tired anymore.

"Lara found out about it," she whispered into the phone. "She found out who the killer was, and so he had to silence her."

chapter
thirty-eight

THE ALARM DRAGGED HER OUT OF SLEEP JUST BEFORE THREE. Avril dressed quickly in the dark, splashing cold water on her face to drive away the fog.

The streets were empty when she left the guesthouse, the storm finally spent. She was on foot, having left the snowmobile parked behind the station the night before.

The snow lay piled high on the sidewalks. The plow had already been through—probably as soon as the storm had abated—leaving the center of the road clear, but hemmed in by walls of ice. At this hour, the air was still bitter-cold, sharp enough to burn her lungs.

She scurried along Main, hands thrust deep in her pockets, backpack on, beanie pulled low. At the end of the street, the police station glowed through the darkness like a ship's lantern, beckoning to her.

Hurrying up the few steps at the entrance, she used the spare key she'd been given to let herself in. Lundgren sat slouched at his desk, eyes half-lidded, a paper cup of coffee gone cold beside him. He jumped a little when she came in.

"Is it three already?" he muttered, rubbing his face.

"Yeah, how's the suspect?"

"Fine. Gave him something to eat and checked on him a few times. He's asleep."

"Good. Now, get yourself home." He didn't argue. Pulling on his jacket, he grabbed his keys, then gave a short nod before slipping out into the night.

Avril stood for a moment in the quiet, listening to the wind moaning around the corners of the building. Suppressing a shiver, she checked the lock after Lundgren had left and pressed the bolt home, then headed down the corridor to the holding cell. She checked the video panel. Jonas was curled up on the bunk, his eyes shut.

Back in the squad room, she set her laptop on the desk and opened the files Krister had sent for her with a note. "These in the last year. K."

Three women stared back at her from missing persons reports. On the top page were names, photographs, and sparse notes from local police. Other pages contained more details taken from the person reporting the disappearance.

She began to read through them.

Emma Karlsson, 22. Student at Umeå University. Last seen leaving a bar with friends. Estranged from parents. "Friends thought she may have dropped out."

Ida Stenlund, 19. From Östersund. Described as rebellious. Worked part-time at a café, missed two shifts before being reported missing by her roommate.

Sofia Lund, 21. From Sundsvall. "Difficult relationship with father. Mother deceased. History of leaving home for short periods."

AVRIL STARED at them for some time. There was a pattern here. All three women came from troubled or restless backgrounds and had temperaments that meant people didn't look too closely when they disappeared.

She studied their photos, likely taken from social media. They were all attractive, overtly so, in a way that drew attention. All wore provocative outfits, showing ample cleavage. Two of the three had striking red hair, the third was fair, and they all had soft, youthful faces and big eyes. A look of innocence, though the reports told another story.

It was clear the killer had a type.

Avril pulled her notepad toward her and began cross-referencing. Last sightings. Circumstances. Anyone they were seen with. She checked the maps, marking each disappearance across Norrland. As Krister had said, the towns were scattered, but within driving distance.

From the reports, none of them had been listed as high-priority cases. Too many plausible explanations. No bodies found. No evidence of foul play. Dropout, free spirit, runaway. That was the assumption.

Avril leaned back, rubbing her temples. Had Lara gotten this far? Had she also recognized the pattern? Or was it just dumb luck that she'd found the man Feya had been seeing, not realizing he was a serial offender?

A draft crept through the windows, whistling faintly, making the fluorescent lights buzz. Avril rose and poured herself a coffee from the pot Lundgren had left, black and bitter, and returned to the files.

She continued making notes, her pen scratching across the page. If these girls were linked, she wanted to find the common denominator.

Outside, the night pressed on, cold and silent. The only sound was the hum of the heating and the occasional creak of the old building settling under the weight of snow.

Jonas shifted once in his cell, the clang of the bunk frame echoing down the corridor. Avril lifted her head, listening, but all fell quiet again. She returned to her screen.

By the time Ekström came in at seven-thirty, Avril had used Lundgren's computer to log into the police terminal and added two more names from the year before to her list, plus three from the year before that. There might well have been more cases that had gone unreported, but these were enough for now.

"What's all this?" Ekström asked, stopping dead to stare at the whiteboard. Avril had moved the photographs of Lara and Freya lower down and stuck the photographs she'd printed out of eight other women above them.

"These are more potential victims," she said softly.

Ekström turned to stare at her. "These women are all missing?"

"They all went missing over the last three years. It could go back further than that, but I stopped there."

Too much data could overwhelm them, and risk diluting patterns. These, Avril was eighty percent certain, were linked. "They're all from difficult backgrounds. They are similar in looks, style, and attire. They all disappeared without a trace. And they're all from towns within driving distance of Norrdal."

Ekström stepped forward and gazed at their faces. "So young," she whispered.

"Yes. Attractive, provocative, dressed suggestively. Five of the eight have red hair."

"Oh, God," she whispered, the color draining from her face. "Does this mean we're looking for a serial killer?"

"None of their bodies have been found," Avril said evenly. "Can you check the regional mortuaries and pathology labs for Jane Does? Bodies they've been unable to identify? Ask for unmatched DNA profiles, too."

Ekström nodded, swallowing hard, then dragged herself to her desk. Avril noticed her fingers trembling as she booted up her computer and began typing.

"So, Freya wasn't the first," Ekström croaked, looking back.

"I'm afraid not." Avril shook her head, then her gaze hardened. "But Lara will be the last."

"How are we going to catch him?" Ekström whispered.

"After you've done that, contact the investigating officers on each missing persons case. Ask about lifestyle, friends, boyfriends. Were they going out a lot? Bars, nightclubs, student unions? Did anyone report them meeting someone new? Get the names of venues. Track their last known movements."

Ekström was writing it all down in her neat script.

"I'd go in person," Avril added, "but the roads aren't clear." The local streets in Norrdal had been plowed, but travel across the north was impossible. Reports and interviews would have to be done by phone for now.

Avril sank down into her chair, staring at the faces on the board. She imagined them staring back at her, begging her to help them. God, she was tired.

When the coffee finally kicked in, she jotted down her own notes. The killer, if that's what he was, must have a job that allowed him to move between all these towns unnoticed. Something mobile. Something ordinary. A salesman. Delivery driver. A contractor.

An idea struck her. She sorted the disappearances into date order. Two women this year, three the year before and four the year before that. Lara was likely unintentional. The murderer had silenced her because she'd found out who he was, and what he was doing.

The killings—if they were killings—were slowing down, or maybe he was just getting better at hiding the bodies?

Avril looked at the dates on her calendar app.

"They are linked," she hissed, under her breath.

Ekström turned her head. "What?"

"Seven of the young women disappeared on a Friday, Saturday or Sunday, including Freya. Lara was the only exception."

Ekström thought for a moment. "He must be targeting them at a bar or club. That's how he's finding them." It was a logical assumption. "And Lara wasn't a target. She just got in the way."

Avril nodded. "I agree with you there. Lara is the only one who doesn't fit the pattern. She was his mistake."

"His mistake?"

Avril gave a stiff nod. "She doesn't fit his MO. That means he had to deviate from his usual pattern. He hadn't planned on killing her, but when she confronted him, he had to adapt. She could ruin everything for him."

"So, she had to go," Ekström whispered.

Avril kept talking, thinking out loud. "He didn't have time to dispose of her body like the others, so he dumped her in the lake. It froze over, and then the fisherman, Olav, found her. The killer didn't mean for that to happen.

"Luckily for us it did," Ekström mused. "Else we'd never know what happened to her."

Something prickled the back of Avril's brain, but she was too tired to grasp it.

Lundgren came in, looking a little more refreshed than he had at three o'clock that morning, although there were still shadows under his eyes.

"What's happened?" he asked, as soon as he walked in. He saw the whiteboard and paused, looking from Ekström to Avril and back again. "Will someone fill me in, please?"

"You do it," Avril said to Ekström. "I need to make a phone call."

She went into Hans' office for some privacy and sat in his leather chair. It was comfortable, much more so than the hard ones outside in the squad room. Taking out her phone, she dialed Krister's number.

"Hey, it's good to hear your voice," he said, which immediately made her feel calmer. "How is it going up there?"

"Do you mind if I run something by you?" she asked, massaging her forehead.

"Shoot."

Avril told him about the four additional women she'd found, as well as their disappearances occurring on a Friday or a weekend. "We think it's because he's targeting them at bars, when they're relaxed and having a few drinks. He slips them Rohypnol and takes them home. Well, not home, but somewhere."

"He's got a vehicle," Krister said, straight away. "He'd have to be mobile."

She nodded, not that he could see. "If he were staying overnight, he'd need a motel, but if he sexually assaulted them there, there would be DNA left behind."

"Except nobody knew to look," Krister finished.

"I doubt he'd use his credit card," she continued. "That would leave a paper trail."

"He'd pay cash," Krister agreed.

She sighed. "So, how can I find this man, Krister? All these locations, all these dates. There must be some way of finding out who he is?"

Krister was silent for a moment.

"Just because he didn't use his card for the motel doesn't mean he didn't use it for something else."

"Yes, but unless we have a suspect in mind, searching for a random credit card isn't going to tell us anything."

"Send me the list of locations," he said after a moment's pause. "I'll see what I can find."

"Thanks, Krister."

"Are you okay?" She heard the concern in his voice.

"Yeah. I'm tired but hanging in there. We've got to catch a break soon."

"You will," he said, confidently. "You always do."

She wished she felt as self-assured as he made her out to be.

"Look after yourself, Avril," he said, and suddenly he sounded very far away.

"I will. You too."

She said goodbye, hung up and left Hans's office to talk to Jonas. They were nearing the end of the 72 hours, but before she let him go, she wanted to make sure he didn't recognize any of the other women.

chapter
thirty-nine

"No, who are they?" Jonas stared down at the photographs spread over the table. Avril thought he looked better than he had since he'd been arrested. His skin had lost that deathly gray pallor, and the circles around his eyes had lessened. They weren't nearly as sunken or hollow as they had been. The dope and the alcohol had worn off, and he'd had two good nights' sleep. It wasn't the Hilton, but it was warmer than the farmhouse he'd been living in and the cabin he'd fled to.

She hesitated. "They also disappeared, just like Lara."

His eyebrows shot up. "What? All of them?"

"Over three years, but yeah."

"Are they dead?"

She tilted her head as she studied him. "What makes you say that?"

A shrug. "Well, Lara's dead. So was that other woman you asked me about."

She gave a sad nod. "I don't know, but I think it's likely."

"You think the same guy killed all these women?"

She took a slow breath. "Maybe."

He gulped, perspiration appearing on his top lip. "You know it's not me, right? I don't know any of these women."

"I know, Jonas," she said quietly. He might be many things, but she didn't think he was a killer. Apart from being out of the country when

Freya was murdered, he didn't fit the profile. He was too hapless, too unorganized. A man who'd murdered this many women, who picked them out in a crowded bar, bought them drinks, drugged them, before... No. That type of man was a planner.

Jonas was rash, impulsive, scared. It wasn't him.

"Can you tell me where you were on these dates?" She slid a piece of paper toward him.

He glanced at it, then shook his head. "You're kidding, right? Do you know where you were on these dates?"

Touché.

She masked a smile. "Okay, let's try this. Do any of the weekends stand out? I need a reason to let you go, Jonas."

"Oh." His eyes widened in understanding. "Like an alibi, yeah?"

"That's right."

"Okay, let me take another look." He scanned them more thoroughly this time. "Ja, ja." He sat upright, clicking his fingers. "I was in Stockholm on this date."

"How do you know?" Avril asked.

He gave a boyish grin. "Because it was the day before my birthday." He poked the date on the paper. "This was a Friday, see, because my birthday was on the Saturday. I went to the city with some friends to go to a concert."

"That's good, Jonas. We'll need their names." She pulled a pen out of her pocket and handed it to him. "Write them down on there."

Jonas printed three names in block letters, one of which was Björn Larsson. He glanced across at her. "Did you manage to get ahold of him?"

"We did," she said, taking the pen back. "He confirmed he was in Mallorca with you last November."

"Yes!" He fist-pumped the air. "So, I'm good to go?"

"You're good to go." She smiled as she stood up. "We've just got to process your paperwork, and then someone will come get you."

He looked at her for a moment, and she could have sworn she saw his eyes welling up.

"Thank you," he muttered. "For believing me. After Lara was found, and the DNA in that cabin, I thought I was done for."

"It's my job to consider all the evidence," she said awkwardly.

He glanced at his feet. "That's something Hans was never able to do. Believe in me. I was always the difficult one, the one that got into trouble, while he was always the star, the one people looked up to." She heard the bitterness in his voice.

"Why didn't he believe you?" she asked.

He shrugged. "He always thought I was guilty. I admit, I did some dumb stuff, but I never intentionally hurt anybody. He never gave me the benefit of the doubt, always assumed the worst. That's why when I saw him come into that bar, I got the hell out of there."

It took a moment to register. "Wait? Which bar? Svartälgen?"

"Yeah. Where I met Lara."

Her chest tightened. "Hans was there?"

He gave a nod. "Last place I expected to see him. Anyway, that's why I left."

Strange, he'd never mentioned it. Avril didn't recall seeing him on the camera footage either.

"Are you sure he was there?" she asked Jonas again.

"Yeah. I'm sure. Hey, can I get a coffee before I go, and something to eat? I still haven't had breakfast."

"I'll get Lundgren to bring you something." Distracted, she pressed the buzzer to be let out. The door clicked open, and she exited the interview room, leaving Jonas sitting at the table surrounded by photographs.

Why hadn't Hans told them he'd been at Svartälgen that night? They'd stood here watching the footage together, and he hadn't said a word. Had he not wanted to implicate himself? Had he been looking for his brother? Had he seen Lara?

Or maybe Jonas had gotten the days muddled up? If Hans was there that night, why hadn't they spotted him on the camera? Her mind swirled with questions. Unanswerable questions.

Unspeakable questions.

But she couldn't blow this out of proportion. There could be a perfectly reasonable explanation for why he hadn't told them. Hans was a good policeman. Well-respected in the community, rational, decent. His only crime, as far as she could tell, was attempting to help his brother—and even then, he'd tried to get him to do the right thing and turn himself in.

It had been Hans's statement about the cabin that had led them to arrest Jonas. He'd been trying to help.

Or had he?

In the end, all he'd done was point them in the direction of a frightened, innocent man. But perhaps that had been his intention all along.

The hairs on her arms stood up. The conveniently placed photograph of the two boys in the study... the snowmobile parked out back... the blood and DNA in the cabin. A cabin that used to belong to Hans's family.

Shit.

Had he been manipulating his brother all along? Using him as a scapegoat for his own crimes? Setting him up as the perfect patsy?

Jonas had priors. He had a history of troubled relationships, sporadic jobs, instability. He smoked weed and drank too much.

Plus, he was the last person to see Lara alive.

She frowned. That was the part that didn't make sense. If Hans had orchestrated all of this, how had he arranged for Lara to meet Jonas in the bar that night?

Had Lara come to him with her suspicions about Freya? Or her article on Nordberg Infrastruktur? A chill crept up Avril's spine. Maybe he'd suggested she contact Jonas since he'd worked there?

Oh, God. If this was true, it was more horrific than she'd ever imagined. Hans had been playing them all along. He'd manipulated every thread of this investigation to point the finger at Jonas.

She gasped and put a hand over her mouth. He could even have stolen Jonas's phone so he'd have to get a temporary prepaid one and couldn't contact his friends. She already knew Hans had threatened Jonas about his drug use, making him think that's why they were after him. Making him run.

He'd offered his help, but then through a clever association trick, he'd subliminally persuaded Jonas to go to the cabin, where he'd planted evidence.

Evidence of Freya's murder.

Avril began to tremble. Was it true? Or was her mind running away with her? Blowing this all out of proportion?

In a daze, she walked through the squad room and into Hans' office, closing the door behind her. She needed privacy to think.

Standing in front of his desk, she stared at his vacant chair. At the empty desk. Her eyes roamed over the bookcase, the shelves, the framed photographs. Colored fishing flies, Hans holding up a large pike. She felt the color drain from her face. He was a fisherman. That meant he'd take weekend fishing trips. She thought about the locations of the other disappearances. Small towns, northern Sweden, near lakes and rivers.

The weekend disappearances weren't because he was targeting them at bars, it was because that was the only free time he had to go hunting.

Hand shaking, she pulled out her phone and called Krister. He didn't answer, and it went to voicemail. He must be on an operation, or out of the office. Taking a steadying breath, she left a message. With a name, he might have more luck on that credit card search.

After hanging up, she walked around the desk and picked up the commemoration photograph. She might still be making a humongous mistake, but the more she thought about it, the more it made sense. In fact, it was the only scenario that *did* make sense.

She stared at Hans in his uniform, smart, handsome, the star. The one people looked up to, Jonas had said. Except the older brother, the one who everybody loved, was actually evil at his core, and the troublesome brother, who wore his heart on his sleeve, was the innocent one.

A knock on the office door pulled her out of her reverie. "Yes?"

It opened, and Ekström poked her head around. "Are you okay?"

Avril just stared at her, unsure how to answer.

"Do you want us to let Jonas go?"

Avril nodded. "Yes, he's the innocent one."

"Excuse me?"

Avril shook her head. "Never mind."

Ekström frowned. "Are you sure you're all right?"

Avril hesitated. She couldn't tell them her suspicions now, not until she had proof. At the moment, it was her bewildered brain stringing together connections that might not even be real.

Even if in her gut she knew they were.

But that wasn't enough. Hans had said it best himself.

At the end of the day, the evidence is what we have to present.

And so evidence is what she would find.

Avril glanced up at the polisassistent. "Ekström, I need you to do something for me."

"Sure, anything."

Avril stepped toward her, holding the framed photograph. "Can you call the manager at the hotel who Lundgren spoke to? The one who'd said he'd seen Freya come in with her lover."

"It would be better if Lundgren—"

"I want you to do it."

Her eyes grew large, then she frowned. "Is something wrong?"

"I hope not." Her voice was a whisper. "Ask him if this was the man he saw with Freya." She handed her the picture.

Ekström stared at it for a long moment, saying nothing. Avril could see her brain ticking over, the questions formulating, the confusion setting in.

"Don't ask me why," she said. "Just do it, okay? And tell nobody."

Ekström opened her mouth to object.

"Not now," Avril hissed. "First do it, and then we'll talk."

Slowly, Ekström nodded, but her face had lost all its color.

Avril walked past her, out of Hans' office.

"I'll be back soon," she called to Lundgren, as she grabbed her coat and hat. The gloves were in the oversized pocket, so she pulled them out and put them on. "Process Jonas and let him go. Time's up."

Lundgren looked like he was going to ask a question, but Avril didn't wait. She strode across the squad room, out the door, and into the street. There was something she had to check before she went any further with this harebrained idea.

chapter
forty

TAREK KHALIL WAS ABOUT TO GO OUT. HE HAD A BACKPACK slung over his shoulder, a camera around his neck, and was jiggling car keys in his pocket.

"Sorry to keep you," Avril said, as he stepped outside. "Can I just ask you a question?"

"Sure."

"Did Lara mention speaking to Kommissarie Bergqvist about anything before she disappeared?"

He thought for a moment, then his eyebrows rose. "Ja, actually now that you mention it, she did. I remember her saying he was going to help her with one of the articles she was writing. This was some time ago, though."

Avril felt her pulse kick up. "How long ago?"

"Three weeks, at least."

Avril massaged her forehead. The timing was spot on. That's when Hans would have mentioned his brother had worked for Nordberg. Lara had tried several times to contact Jonas before he'd agreed. Just like Hans had known he would.

If they'd met earlier, Lara would have died earlier. The thought left her cold.

"Did she go to him with her concerns about Freya?" she asked.

Tarek frowned. "I don't know. If she did, she never told me."

Avril stood back, letting him pass. "Okay, that's it. Thanks, Tarek."

He didn't move. "Why are you asking about Kommissarie?"

She thought fast. "I've taken over the case, so I just want to know what she told him."

He frowned. "Is there any news?"

"Nothing yet, I'm afraid. I will let you know if we find anything."

He gave a sad nod, as if that was to be expected, and walked past her to his car.

AVRIL WALKED BACK to the station, but her route took her past the Bergqvist family home. She slowed down, staring in the windows, but couldn't see any movement. Their car was missing, and she figured either he or his wife had taken it.

It was mid-afternoon, and the bleak sun made an unsuccessful attempt to shine down on the fresh snow that had fallen over the town.

The streetlamps were on, as they were for most of the day this time of year. It was still bitterly cold, but without the wind, it felt warmer. She might actually be acclimating.

Tarek's news had confirmed her suspicions, but she still didn't have any concrete proof. There was nothing linking Hans to the murders, other than Jonas's testimony that Hans had been at Svartälgen the night Lara had gone missing. And after what had transpired, Jonas would not be deemed a reliable witness.

Her phone rang as she passed the house. She glanced down and didn't recognize the number. "Hello?"

"Avril, it's Hans."

Her breath caught in her throat. She stopped, turned slowly, and stared at the house. The windows were in darkness. Was he watching her?

"Hey, how are you?" She tried but failed to sound normal.

"Okay." There was a pause. "Can we meet?"

Shit.

He knew.

He knew she knew.

She could tell by his voice.

"I'm just on my way back to the station," she said, turning around and quickening her pace. "What's this about?"

Now he was doing it, but she heard the inflection in his tone. "Nothing important. Just wanted to ask you about my brother. I believe he's been released?"

How had he heard? Had Jonas gone there? Lundgren?

"Yes, we just released him."

"I'm pleased to hear it."

Like hell you are, she thought. Everything he'd done had been to pin the murders on his brother. Everything.

"I could come to the station?" he suggested, hopefully.

She hesitated, just like he'd known she would. If she suspected he was involved, the last place she'd want him to be was at the station, where he had access to files, the whiteboard, information on the active case. Where he was surrounded by people loyal to him.

He was manipulating her now, trying to get her to suggest somewhere else, somewhere private.

He'd know she'd want to talk to him. Test out her theory. He'd read her file, he knew how she operated. She shot from the hip. Usually. Confronted suspects head-on.

Oh, he was a master, all right—but she'd met this caliber of manipulator before. Hell, she was a direct descendant of quite possibly the smartest serial killer the world had ever known.

She could play this game too.

"No," she said, carefully. "Not the station. How about my guesthouse?"

It was central, there were other people there, including the manager. She'd be safe there.

"Fine. Say ten minutes?"

He was watching her. He'd know that ten minutes didn't give her time to get back to the station and inform the others where she was going, or why. She could send a text, of course, but without context, it would sound crazy.

It was crazy.

What he didn't know, of course, was that she'd already shown her hand to Ekström, and while she'd been shocked, she was loyal enough not to repeat it to Lundgren, who Avril suspected was in regular contact with Hans. That's how he was getting his information.

A chill settled over her. If she didn't find proof of his involvement, or get a confession out of him, he would soon be back at work. With Jonas cleared, there was no longer any reason for him to extricate himself from the investigation.

Once he was back in charge of the case, there was no telling what he'd do.

Avril hung up, then changed direction at the end of the street and headed back to her guesthouse. While she did so, she called Ekström, who picked up on the first ring.

"You got anything for me yet?"

"Sorry, no," she said, her voice strained. "He was out, but I left a message for him to call me back."

"Okay, thanks. I'm stopping off at my guesthouse to fetch something, but text me the moment you hear."

"Will do."

Avril hung up. She'd purposely not told Ekström who she was meeting there because a show of force would scare him off. If she wanted to get to the bottom of this, she needed to have a heart-to-heart with Hans. No pretense.

For some reason, she knew he'd open up to her. The game was up. He knew it, and she knew it.

At least Ekström knew where she was, so that if anything happened, she'd be able to find her.

It was with a frantically beating heart that Avril let herself into the house. A sturdy double-story with a sloping roof, it was set back from the street with a snowy drive, a front yard, and neat borders that would be pretty in the spring. Right now, they were coated with snow, the stems frozen solid.

She'd hardly been inside for a minute when she heard a car drive up. Looking through the communal lounge window, she spotted the gray SUV.

Hans.

Her breath hitched. He was here.

The lack of voices inside the house made her frown. Why was it so quiet?

She turned and shouted, "Mrs. Hansen. Are you here?"

No answer.

Where were all the guests?

She poked her head into the dining room, but it was empty. Reaching down, she unclipped the safety strap on her holster, resting her hand on her service weapon. Just a precaution. Drawing it without cause was premature, but she needed to be ready.

Through the frost-blurred window, she saw Hans approaching, his boots crunching up the path. He raised a hand in greeting, catching sight of her silhouette framed in the warm glow of the interior light.

She didn't wave back.

Grabbing her phone out of her back pocket, she pressed the audio record button, before dropping it back into her coat pocket.

Then she went to answer the door.

chapter
forty-one

ACT NORMAL, SHE TOLD HERSELF, AS SHE PULLED THE DOOR open. Mrs. Hansen would be back any moment. She'd probably just run out for supplies. There were at least a handful of other guests, she'd seen them at breakfast—except that was two days ago. They could have left by now.

"Hans, it's good to see you." She pasted a smile on her face and stood back to let him in.

He smiled back, but it didn't reach his eyes.

"This is a strange choice," he said, stepping into the hallway and looking around. "I would have met you at the station."

"I know, but I was coming back here to fetch something." She met his gaze. "Besides, I thought it would give us some privacy."

"Where's the landlady?"

"She's around somewhere." The lie slipped easily from her lips. She just hoped he believed it. "Come in."

He followed her in. She noticed he held nothing in his hands, no visible weapon. He wore a long coat and didn't appear to have a holster or anything underneath. That was a relief, at least.

"Would you like something to drink?" she offered. Anything to stall the conversation in the hopes that someone else would arrive home in the meantime.

"Sure. Coffee would be good."

"Make yourself comfortable, and I'll be right back."

Avril poured two cups from the pot Mrs. Hansen had left on and went back to where Hans was sitting in the lounge. Thankfully, he'd chosen an armchair, similar to the one he had at home. Avril handed him a cup and then eased herself down onto the sofa. The poker was inches away, behind her heels.

"Was there anything in particular you wanted to discuss?" she asked him, taking a sip.

"Why'd you let Jonas go?"

"Lundgren tell you that?"

"I called the station to find out whether he'd been charged or not. He is my brother, after all."

"I had to let him go. His alibi checked out."

"Alibi? He was with Lara the night she disappeared. We've already established that."

"Not that alibi," she said, softly.

Hans stared at her. "What other alibi is there?"

"For Freya Lindholm's murder."

His gaze hardened. "You're assuming the two are linked."

"I know they are," she retorted. "And Jonas was out of the country when she disappeared."

"What proof do you have that they're connected?" he asked.

"Lara was looking into Freya's disappearance. She knew her friend hadn't gone to Stockholm like the note said. She also knew Freya was having an affair with a man. A man she suspected was married."

Hans's gaze sharpened. "How do you know this?"

"I found Lara's notebook. It documents everything. Freya's last movements, her final conversation with her, her last telephone call." She faded off, letting him think there was more there than there was. None of that would amount to anything in court. It was all supposition.

"I think you're wrong," he murmured. "Jonas was the one with her at the bar."

"So were a lot of people," she said, carefully, holding the cup up to her lips.

He met her gaze, and in that moment, she knew for certain. He'd done it. He'd killed them all.

"Why didn't you tell me you were there?" she whispered, lowering the cup.

"I forgot," he said, then snorted. "I know how that must sound, but it's the truth. I was looking for Jonas, went to the bar and saw him go in the back. I followed him in, but he was with a woman. Lara, as it turns out. I said hello to a few people, used the facilities, and left. Nothing more to it. Not worth mentioning."

Avril studied him. The confident demeanor, the self-assurance that came with being the Kommissarie for years. "You saw the victim in the bar the night she disappeared. Why is that not important? You also saw the prime suspect with her."

"He was still with her when I left," Hans insisted. "My being there would have changed nothing."

"It would have implicated you in the crime," Avril said softly. "And you couldn't have that."

He gave a dry chuckle. "What are you talking about?"

"Did you go up to Lara once Jonas had left? Did you buy her a drink?"

"No, I—"

"She came to you with her suspicions about Freya, didn't she? Did she ask for your help?"

"Avril, I think you're getting ahead of yourself here."

"I know, Hans," she whispered, looking across at him. "I know it was you."

This time he didn't laugh.

His eyes narrowed and he said, "You know what was me?"

"Everything. I know Lara came to you because she was worried something had happened to Freya. She wanted you to look into it, didn't she? Instead, you devised a plan to kill her."

He regarded her silently, saying nothing.

"So, you used your errant brother. The one who was always getting into trouble. The one who nobody trusted. You told Lara he'd worked at Nordberg Infrastruktur, knowing she was working on that story. Did she bring it up when she was talking to you? Did she call you for a comment?"

He remained silent, but his eyes had turned colder than the temperature outside.

"You knew she'd contact Jonas, didn't you? You just had to bide your time. Were you tracking Jonas's phone? Is that how you knew when they were going to meet?"

He hadn't moved a muscle, but his gaze was fixed on her face.

"You slipped in after Jonas had left, using the back entrance to avoid the cameras. You said hello, bought her a drink. Of course, she wouldn't have suspected a thing, you being the Kommissarie."

A flicker of an eyelid, just enough to let her know she was on the right track.

She continued, talking slowly so her phone would pick up the audio. "You slipped Rohypnol into her drink, which you probably got from the police evidence store, or you bought it online. When she got woozy, you helped her out under the pretense of taking her home. She wouldn't have protested, and no one would have questioned a police officer helping a drunk woman home."

She glanced across at him. "How am I doing so far?"

He folded his arms across his chest. "Well, it's a good story. I'm intrigued to find out what happens next."

The smug look on his face irked her. He was enjoying this. Enjoying the way she was telling it, enjoying hearing about his exploits. She had to get him to break, to admit what he'd done.

"You put her in your car and drove her to Frostsjön, where you strangled her and dumped her body in the lake. It was nearly frozen, so you knew it would be quickly covered up and wouldn't emerge until the thaw. Maybe not even then."

She paused.

"Is that how you got rid of all your other victims too?"

For the first time, she saw a crack in the armor. He frowned, heat rising into his cheeks.

"What do you mean?"

She held him with her gaze. "You know, all the other young women you drugged, raped, and murdered over the years."

He scoffed, "You're delusional."

"Am I? So the women in Strömsund, Hoting, Vilhelmina,

Hammerdal... They weren't part of your fly-fishing expeditions?" She was pushing him now, needing him to break. So far, she'd done all the talking.

His gaze narrowed, and for the first time, she caught a glimpse of the killer within. The rage directed across the room at her was frightening. His eyes burned with it.

Yet somehow, he managed to maintain his cool.

"What other women?"

"As soon as I found out Lara was looking into Freya's disappearance, I realized there might be a pattern. A predator targeting young women. You like them young, don't you, Hans? Young and curvy."

He didn't answer her, but a vein bulged in his temple. Throbbing so hard it looked like it was about to burst.

"When we checked, we found a similar pattern all over Nordland."

"We?"

"Ekström and me."

His eyebrows rose. "Ekström knows about this?"

She almost had him. It wasn't a confession, but it was close. He was worried who else knew he was responsible.

"Oh, yes," she said. "Why? Are you going to kill her too?"

He scoffed. "She won't believe you. You can't prove any of this. All you've got is a theory."

Not yet.

"You know what I thought was the smartest thing," she said, slowly.

He shook his head. "I can't wait to hear."

"The photograph. The one of you and Jonas in front of the cabin. You put that there on purpose, so your brother would see it and think to go there. You didn't have to say a word."

His lips curled back in a smile. "That photograph is always there. You can't prove otherwise."

She sighed. He wasn't giving an inch.

"You can stop playing games, Hans. It's only a matter of time before we have proof."

He watched her carefully, his legs crossed, his arms folded across his chest. Her phone buzzed, making her jump.

"You should lay off the coffee," he said, when she reached into her pocket for it. "It's making you jumpy."

It wasn't the coffee. She was face to face with a goddamn serial killer, and she hated those. They were the worst kind of scum. The kind that thought they held all the power. The kind that wanted to wield that power over another human being. Usually a woman. Some long-forgotten grudge that they couldn't get over. A jilted girlfriend, an abusive parent, a mother who simply didn't care. She'd seen it all in her ten years as an FBI agent working with the Bureau's Behavioral Science Unit.

That's why she knew Hans was a killer, and how she knew Jonas wasn't.

"You can get that." He gestured to the phone in her hand.

She kept the screen facing away from him so he wouldn't see she was recording and glanced down at the text. It was from Ekström.

"It's a positive ID. What do you want to do?"

A shadow fell over her.

"I'll take that." He reached for the phone.

Before he could, she dropped it and kicked it under the couch with the heel of her shoe. He growled at her, frustrated. It was too far out of reach for him to get it. If he bent down, he'd give her the advantage.

Her hand closed around her weapon, but he was too quick. He grabbed her arm and pushed it back onto the sofa. Using her free arm, she tried to push him off, but he was too strong. He grabbed that wrist too and held it above her head.

"Why did you have to be so good at your fucking job, Avril?" he hissed, as he pushed her back on the sofa. "Why couldn't you just let Jonas take the fall?"

"He's innocent," she hissed, lashing out with her legs, but he was too close and she couldn't get her knees up. He knelt across her thighs, still gripping both her wrists as she tried to wriggle out from under him.

"Ja, but he's a waste of space. I, on the other hand, am Kommissarie."

"You're a rapist and a murderer," she spat at him. "A despicable human being. You'll pay for this."

"Oh, yes? How do you figure that? With you gone, who's going to accuse me? Ekström? I don't think so. She doesn't have the guts. Was that her, by the way?"

Avril was too busy bucking and writhing to answer. She managed to knee him in the balls, and he grunted. "Agh, you bitch."

Letting go of one wrist, he whacked her so hard across the face that she saw stars.

"I should have killed you the day you had the accident. I was just minutes too late. That goddamn good Samaritan got there first."

His face swam in front of her. She blinked to clear her vision. "That was you?"

His mouth opened in a lurid smile. "See, there are some things you don't know. Yes, I followed you up there, mostly to keep track of the case, but you were quicker than I expected. I saw an opportunity and took it. I was hoping it would scare you off the case."

Her head pounded. "It was you? You drove me off the road?"

"Pity you only suffered a concussion." He huffed, as he pulled her to a sitting position. Grabbing her own handcuffs, he fastened her wrists together.

"Help!" she yelled. "Somebody help me!"

He laughed. "You're a terrible liar, you know that? There is nobody here."

She let out a sob. He was right. There was nobody to help her.

At least she could still get a full confession. He didn't know her phone was recording, even though it was useless to her now.

"Did you take Freya to the cabin? Was that where you killed her?"

"Ah, Freya." A faraway look came into his eyes. "She was my favorite. I enjoyed being with her. So adventurous, so eager to learn."

Avril felt repulsed. He was a monster.

They were all monsters.

"Did you strangle her too? Or did you stab her? There was blood in the cabin."

"You don't stop, do you?" He smirked. "If I tell you, will you shut up?"

She glared at him.

"I tried to strangle her, but she was feisty. She fought back. I had to subdue her, so I used the barrel of my gun and hit her on the head. She fell on the floor, there was blood."

Avril exhaled. Finally, she had her proof.

"Now," he said, in a menacing voice. "You're going to be a good girl and drink this." He pulled a tiny vial of liquid out of his pocket.

She knew what that was. Rohypnol.

He was going to drug her, like he had the others. Then he would take her somewhere and kill her. He was resorting to his standard MO.

She opened her mouth and screamed.

chapter
forty-two

KRISTER WAS HAVING A ROUGH DAY. FIRST, HE'D BEEN called out at the crack of dawn for another suspected gang incident in central Stockholm, without even having a cup of coffee first. Next, he and his colleague, Freddie Nyström, had walked into a bloody gun battle.

During which he'd been shot.

A bullet had grazed his shoulder, leaving a deep furrow in his arm. It hurt like hell. He'd just spent the better part of the afternoon at A&E getting patched up.

Freddie had just dropped him back at home, and Sundström had given him strict instructions to take the rest of the week off.

Krister had snorted at that one. It was already Thursday.

Using his left hand, he let himself into the house. One of the uniformed officers had driven his car back, which was the least they could do. Not that he was meant to drive, mind you.

He shoved off his jacket, which had been draped over his shoulders now that his arm was in a sling. It still hurt, but the doc had given him a bunch of painkillers to take the edge off.

He poured himself a small finger of whiskey—not enough to interact with his medication—and sat down at the kitchen table to drink it. Sometimes this job sucked.

He sighed and set the tumbler on the table. Its wooden surface was filled with scratches and deep striations from years gone by. He fingered one in particular. It had been made by Avril when she'd been a kid. They'd each carved their names into the surface. His mother hadn't been too pleased, but she'd left them there, a memento of a time when life was simpler.

He hadn't checked his phone all afternoon, but he'd felt it buzzing on numerous occasions. Now, he pulled it awkwardly out of his right-side pocket and held it up to his face. The screen lit up.

Eleven messages. Jesus.

Most of them were work notifications. He thumbed through them until he saw one from Avril. She'd left him a voice message.

He hit it, and her voice filled the room.

"Krister, I have a hunch. Could you check the hotels and convenience stores in those towns I gave you for a credit card belonging to Hans Bergqvist."

One thing he knew about Avril's hunches was always to take them seriously.

Hans Bergqvist. That name was familiar.

Holy shit!

He jumped out of the chair, spilling his whiskey. That was Kommissarie's name, wasn't it? Chief of Norrdal Polisstation. He sucked in a breath. She couldn't possibly suspect him, could she?

What the hell was going on? Last he'd heard, they had his brother in custody.

He dialed Avril's number, but after a few rings, it went to voicemail. Shit, where was she?

He strode into the spare bedroom, which he'd converted to an office. It was actually his old bedroom from when he'd been a kid. When he'd inherited the house from his parents, it had seemed fitting to make it into his study.

Opening his laptop, he connected to the police terminal. Where was that list?

He found it scribbled on a piece of paper in his in-tray. He scanned the locations. There couldn't be very many hotels or guesthouses in those villages. Using Google, he made a quick list. Next, he called them. This was the most time-consuming part. He had to verbally question every hotel manager and ask them to give him the information.

It would be far easier to obtain a warrant to look into Bergqvist's bank records, but he didn't have probable cause for that. Bergqvist, even excused from the case, was still Kommissarie with an up-till-now clean record. No judge would issue a warrant for him.

After an hour, he'd had more "no's" than he could count, so he took a break and poured himself a little top-up. Not surprising. As they'd suspected, the killer had probably paid cash.

The perp also had to be mobile, so he'd be using a vehicle, which meant he'd need gas. Maybe he'd gotten lazy and used his card at a gas station, not considering that it might lead back to him.

When Krister called the fifth gas station, he got lucky. The owner, a pleasant-sounding man, was happy to help the Polisen. "What is the name on the card?"

Krister gave it to him, then waited. To his surprise, the man grunted and said, "Bergqvist, you say?"

"Yes."

"Ja. He was here. He used his card on April fifth last year."

"Really?" Krister set the glass down, phone pressed to his ear. "You're sure it was on that date?"

"I'm sure. You want me to send you the receipt?"

"Yes, please. That would be very useful. Can you take a photo of it with your phone and message it to me?"

The man said he would, and a few seconds later, the photograph came through. Krister studied it hard, double-checking the date and time.

There was no mistake. Hans Elias Bergqvist had filled up his tank with gas on April fifth last year.

Avril had been right. It was him.

He tried calling her again but got her voicemail. Frowning, he dialed the police station instead. A female officer answered. "Can I help you?"

"I'm looking for Avril Dahl," he said. "It's Krister Jansson from Stockholm Police."

"Oh, Kriminalinspektör. I'm sorry, but she's not here."

"Do you know where she is?"

The officer hesitated. "I'm not sure I'm supposed to say."

"Tell me," he demanded. "It's urgent. She's not answering her phone."

"Oh, God. Really?"

"Where has she gone?"

"She went back to the guesthouse to pick up something."

"Bergqvist? Was she going to meet Bergqvist?"

"I don't know," the officer whispered.

"What's your name?" he barked.

"Ekström, sir."

"Ekström, I have found evidence linking Hans Bergqvist to the murder of a young woman in Hammerdal last April. Do you know what I'm talking about?"

"Yes, I do. Kriminalinspektör Dahl told me her suspicion. I too have found proof he was involved."

"Go to her guesthouse now," he told her. "Take backup. Call me as soon as you know she's okay."

"Yes, sir." She hung up and Krister pushed himself out of his chair with his good arm and began to pace.

He felt so goddamn helpless. He was a five-hour drive away. Not possible to get to her in that time, even if he could use his arm properly. A flight would be quicker, but once you factored in airport time, flying time, hiring a car…

Fuck it.

He grabbed his coat and his keys and headed for the door.

chapter
forty-three

EKSTRÖM GOT TO THE GUESTHOUSE IN TIME TO SEE THE Kommissarie's gray SUV nose out of the layby and head up the road, its rear lights winking red through the darkness. She braked hard, tires chirping on packed snow.

She let her Volvo idle as she watched the SUV crest the rise and disappear behind a stand of birch. The wind blew loose powder along the tarmac in ghostly veils. Getting out of the car, she ran toward the house. The front door was open, so she darted inside, calling out.

"Kriminalinspektör? Are you all right?" There was no answer. She ran through the rooms, her heart beating frantically. "Kriminalinspektör?"

The lounge showed signs of a struggle. She saw two half-drunk coffee cups, and a fire poker on the floor in front of the sofa. As she was looking around, she heard a soft buzzing sound. Where on earth was that coming from? It sounded like a phone.

Bending down, she peered under the couch. A faint light was on at the back. It *was* a phone!

She pulled the sofa out and saw that it was the Kriminalinspektör's. Picking it up, she answered, her voice trembling. "Ja?"

"Who is this?" came a male voice.

"Polisassistent Ekström," she replied.

"Where is Avril?" the voice demanded.

Ekström let out a sob. "I don't know. I came here to look for her like you said, but she's gone. There are signs of a struggle."

"Is Bergqvist there?"

"I just saw him leave." She gave a little gasp. "I think he's got the Kriminalinspektör."

A low growl brought her to her senses.

"Get after them," he shouted. "Now! He'll be heading out of town."

Heart racing, Ekström spun around and dashed out of the house, the Kriminalinspektör's phone still glued to her ear. She jumped into the Volvo, grateful she'd brought her own car and not the squad car, as it would be less conspicuous.

Once inside, she put Jansson on speaker and dropped the phone into the center console. "I'm in pursuit," she said, breathlessly.

"Find them, Ekström," he said, and she heard the borderline panic in his voice. She didn't know what the relationship was between the Kriminalinspektör and this man, but she suspected it wasn't just colleagues. The fear in his voice told her that he cared.

She sped down the street, turned onto Main, and floored it as fast as she dared to the end. The Kommissarie had a five-minute head start, but the roads were icy and drifts still covered large sections of them. There was a limit to how fast he could safely go.

"Any sign?" Jansson's voice filled the interior of her car.

"Not yet," she replied, her hands gripping the wheel. "But if he's heading out of town, there is only one route to the highway."

There was no response, but she could hear he was still on the line. A low hum accompanied by a rhythmic thumping noise—the sound that tires make over a bridge—told her he was driving too.

Confirming that, he said, "I'm still at least four hours out. I need you to find them, Ekström."

She felt the weight of that statement. It pressed down on her, making every part of her body tense. She let out a shaky breath, forcing her shoulders to relax.

Taking a left, she navigated an icy section, feeling her tires fight for traction, before digging in again. The storms had dumped half a meter

over the last few days, and even though the bigger roads had been plowed, everything smaller was still treacherous.

Slowly, she pressed down on the accelerator, gaining speed. The engine hummed, the heater fan a steady rush against the mist creeping up the windshield. Another bend, and she saw taillights. Inching closer, she drew in a relieved breath. It was the Kommissarie's SUV.

"I've got them," she breathed.

"Excellent. Keep them in sight. Make sure he doesn't see you."

"Okay." She sank a little lower in her seat, following the twin red dots up the long, gradual climb.

Ekström tried to remember her training. It was only a year and a half ago that she'd graduated from the academy in Umeå, but she'd never used anything on her physical course. Norrdal wasn't that kind of place. Its sleepy, insular routine meant most of her skills had gone unpracticed.

Her pulse raced, blood pounding in her ears. She knew, without a doubt, that if she failed tonight, if she lost them, the Kriminalinspektör would die, and she'd never get over it.

She stifled a sob. She couldn't let that happen.

How could the Kommissarie be the killer? He'd been her boss for little over a year now, and she looked up to him. Sure, he didn't give her much credit, but she was just learning—that was par for the course. Trust was earned, she knew that.

People trusted Bergqvist. Even her parents spoke highly of him. They'd been so proud of her when she'd gotten this job. Being a police officer in a town this small was about as prestigious as it got. You'd think she was the mayor by the way her parents went on about it, telling all their friends.

What would they say when they found out her boss was really a prolific rapist and serial murderer?

On the crest, the SUV's brake lights flared. Ekström coasted, letting the engine braking do the work. The SUV accelerated again, dropping into a shallow valley. On either side, the land flattened into farmland. Farmhouses hunched in the darkness, while fences buried up to their top wire sped by in a blur.

Ekström wondered if the Kriminalinspektör was in the back. Was she okay? Had she been drugged? Was she even alive? She gulped over a lump in her throat.

Please let her be alive.

"Are you still behind them?" came Jansson's voice. She jumped, forgetting he was there.

"I am. You were right, he's about to turn onto the highway."

"He hasn't spotted you?"

"I don't think so. I'm keeping well back."

"Good. Hang in there. Have you got backup? Someone you can call?"

"There's Lundgren."

Oh, my God. Lundgren.

She ought to fill him in. He didn't even know that the Kommissarie was Lara's killer. Not just Lara. All of them.

He'd be devastated. She was devastated, and she wasn't nearly as close to Bergqvist as Lundgren was.

"Where is he?"

"I don't know. He should be at the station, but he may have gone out for food." Lundgren was always hungry.

"Call him. You can't tackle Bergqvist by yourself. Give him your location and—"

"I don't know what my location is. I don't know this area. Oh, God. How is he going to find me?"

"Calm down," Jansson said, although he sounded anything but calm. "You're going to open the map app on your phone, look for a blue dot. Press it and see the coordinates that come up. You're going to share those with him. You got that?"

Oh, yeah. She remembered now. Panic clouded her brain. She had to get a grip.

"I got it."

"Good. And watch for any road signs. There are bound to be some. You can call those out to him too. He'll find you."

"Okay." She hadn't even thought about what she would do when the car in front of her stopped. The panic rose like bile in her chest, sharp and stinging. She tried to push it back down, to take some ragged breaths, but it kept rising back up again.

"Call him, Ekström. Now. I'll stay on the line."

"Okay." His voice brought her back to her senses. Enough so she could scramble in her pocket for her own phone. Keeping one eye on the road, she navigated to her recently dialed numbers and pressed Lundgren's name. It rang a couple of times, then he answered.

"Ekström, where the hell are you? I got back and you were gone."

"Lundgren. Oh, God. It's the Kommissarie—"

"What is? Ekström, where are you? You sound weird."

"He's the killer. Lundgren, he's got the Kriminalinspektör in his car, and he's going to kill her." She was babbling, not making any sense.

"What are you talking about?" he said. "Have you completely lost the plot?"

Jansson's voice. "Polisassistent Lundgren, this is Kriminalinspektör Jansson from Stockholm Police. I assure you, your colleague is right. We have proof that Hans Bergqvist killed Lara Berglund, killed all those women."

"What women?" he asked.

She realized he didn't know any of it.

"I'll tell you when you get there. I'm in pursuit. I'm going to need backup."

"In pursuit of who? The Kommissarie?"

"Yes. He has the Kriminalinspektör in the car." At least, she thought he did. She hadn't actually seen him force her into it, but she knew in her gut she was there. She'd never understood that term before. Gut feeling. As a person who relied on facts and data to guide her, she didn't put much stake in what her gut was saying. Except for now.

"Lundgren, get in the car now. This is it. You have the killer in your sights and your colleague needs you. Don't let him get away."

Ekström appreciated the pep talk. She heard shuffling as Lundgren kicked into gear. The scrape of his chair, the jingle of keys, and then the slam of a door. A moment later, panting as he ran to the squad car. "Keep the sirens off," Jansson advised. "He mustn't know you're onto him. Don't give him any reason to panic and kill Avril."

"Kill her? Jesus."

"Hurry, Lundgren," Ekström pleaded. "I'll send you my coordinates."

Glancing down, she opened the map app and shared her location.

"Got it," Lundgren barked, but she could hear the uncertainty in his tone. He was confused, and he had every right to be. This was a shock. At least she'd had some prewarning from the Kriminalinspektör. He'd had her bumbling at him like an idiot.

Thank goodness Kriminalinspektör Jansson was there to assist.

When Ekström looked up, the road ahead was in darkness. "Oh, shit," she muttered.

"What?" Jansson's voice.

"They're gone."

chapter
forty-four

"They can't be gone," he barked, the strain evident in his voice. "Find them, Ekström."

She leaned forward and peered into the darkness, her breath fogging the windshield. The highway made a lazy meander, and then she breathed a sigh of relief.

"He's slowing down. I think he's turning off the highway now, onto a secondary road."

"Don't lose them again," Krister cautioned, but she heard the relief in his voice. "You're all she's got, Ekström."

He didn't have to tell her that.

"I know," she murmured, her eyes burning. "I know."

"Are you armed?"

Her eyes darted to her hip. The SIG lay heavy in its holster, a weight she usually forgot about until moments like this.

"Yes."

"Good. Take it out. Keep it on the seat next to you—safety off. If he stops or approaches you, you want to have it in easy reach."

She swallowed. Unclipping the holster, she pulled it free. The pistol felt cold in her hands. She set it on the passenger seat, angled toward her, close enough to grab in an instant. Her palms were already sweating.

There were barely any other vehicles on the road. The wind blew loose powder along the tarmac in ghostly veils. She watched as the Kommissarie's taillights veered to the right and he took an off-ramp onto an arterial road. Slowing down, she followed.

"I'm on the highway," came Lundgren's clipped voice. He too was on speaker in the console beside Kriminalinspektör Dahl's phone. It felt like they were both in the car with her.

"He's turned onto Skogsvägen," Ekström said, catching sight of a signpost just before the off-ramp. It flashed past so fast, and she was concentrating on the vehicle ahead, that she almost missed it.

"Copy that," Lundgren said.

Up ahead, Bergqvist turned onto the smaller road. She hung back, not wanting to give herself away. The off-ramp was well lit, but at the end, where the turning was, it faded to black. She waited until he'd turned before she put her foot down. At the end, she spotted the taillights about a quarter of a mile down the road. She followed.

"You still with him?" Jansson asked.

"Yes," she whispered, although she wasn't sure why. The silence outside seemed to call for it. A village slid by. A cluster of houses around a bus stop, a general store closed and in darkness. Beside it stood a small red and white church with a lamp burning in the window. She drove past the graveyard with the stones wearing little white snow caps and then a bus stop. The sign in front read: Välkommen till Lillträsk.

This was a smaller road. She had to be careful, or he'd spot her. There wasn't much traffic this time of the evening, in these conditions. She turned off her high beams, opting for the cover of darkness. The run of his taillights would be enough.

The town morphed into rolling fields blanketed with snow. Drifts piled high at the sides like frozen waves, making the road seem narrower. Beyond the fields, spruce and pine forests loomed in a dark wall. A moose sign flashed by.

"Where are you now?" Lundgren asked. "I'm approaching Skogsvägen."

Thank goodness, he was gaining on her. He must be moving at pace, but then he'd always been a confident driver.

"East at the off-ramp," she said. "I've just passed Lillträsk church."

"Copy that."

The wind shoved at the little Volvo, and she corrected, her fingers too tight on the wheel. She made herself loosen them.

Breathe.

The SUV kept going at the same pace, cautious but not nervous. That was almost worse. Bergqvist knew what he was doing, whereas she didn't have a clue. She was so far out of her depth, it was crazy.

Another gust, and her car buffeted, hitting a patch of black ice. Ekström slowed down. Her wheels spun for a few heart-wrenching seconds, but then she was through it. The SUV had drawn a few car lengths farther ahead.

Don't lose him.

He took the next junction without signaling. A sudden left, a quick swing of his rear like a dog changing its mind mid-run.

"He's turning off," she murmured, just loud enough for Jansson and Lundgren to hear.

"Keep him in your sight," Jansson replied.

"What's the turnoff?" Lundgren asked. "I'm a minute or so behind you."

She looked for a signpost.

"Um, I'm not sure," but she sighed in relief upon hearing his words. Thank God. She wasn't alone anymore.

"I can't see you," Lundgren said.

"I've got my high beams off," she muttered, glancing in the rearview mirror. Lundgren's squad car came up behind her. As he got close, he doused his lights too. The road plunged into darkness.

Ekström turned after Bergqvist, her tires bumping over a snowy seam. The road along here had not been plowed, and the ruts were shin-deep, the center ridge a glued mass of snow and gravel.

"You okay, Ekström?" Lundgren's voice.

"My car's not equipped for this terrain." The little Volvo lurched and pitched in the grooves like a boat.

"I'm overtaking. Hang back."

She did as instructed and slowed down so he could pass her. In the cruiser, his tires handled the thick crust and tracks better than hers could.

"I've got point," Lundgren said.

"Don't lose him, whatever you do," came Jansson's reply.

"Copy that."

A pair of barns loomed, both old, their doors closed. Beyond them, a fence line and the skeletal outline of an orchard, its branches spiked with frost. The SUV's taillights flickered through the trees, then disappeared down a shallow dip.

"He's turning again," came Lundgren's voice. "It's a farm lane. Proceed with caution."

"He must be at his destination," Jansson said. "Let me know when you see Avril."

"Will do." Ekström strained her eyes as she tried to see where Bergqvist's SUV had gone. The lane to the left ran along a ditch, then dipped between two low rises. No taillights. Nothing.

"He's turned onto a dirt track maybe eight hundred meters ahead of me," came Lundgren's voice. "Looks like it leads to a farmhouse. I can see a barn and some sort of shed."

"Send me your final location," Jansson said. "I'm still hours away, but just in case—"

"Sending now," she said, slowing to a stop behind Lundgren's cruiser. She didn't want to think about 'just in case,' or what they had to do now. Thank goodness Lundgren was here. He was young too, but he had a good five years' experience under his belt. She would follow his lead. "I'd better go. We're here."

"Copy that. Good luck, and let me know when you have her," Jansson said, before disconnecting the call.

They killed the engines one after the other. Ekström sat very still, her breathing the only sound in the sudden silence. The farmhouse crouched in the distance, dark against the sweeping backdrop of the fields. Its roof was heavy with snow, illuminated by the moonlight.

Other than that, the only light came from the SUV's taillights as it slowed, crunched into the yard, and stopped in front of the porch.

Ekström saw Lundgren get out of the cruiser, and grabbing her service pistol and both phones, joined him.

Heavens, it was cold.

She zipped her jacket right up to the top as her breath misted in front of her. It might be freezing, but visibility was clear without snow falling.

"Ekström, what the hell? How is Bergqvist involved in all this?" His gaze was questioning, and she didn't have time to give him all the answers now.

"It's a long story," she whispered. "Kriminalinspektör Dahl figured it out. She found more disappearances, women who'd gone missing all over Nordland."

Lundgren stared at her. "More?"

"Much more. On a hunch, she asked me to show the hotel manager Bergqvist's photo. At first I couldn't believe it, but when I did, he identified the Kommissarie as Freya Lindholm's mystery lover."

Lundgren shook his head. "I just... I just can't believe it."

"Believe it, Lundgren," Ekström told him. "He fooled all of us."

"But... he helped me and my family. He sent me to Police College. Why would he do that?"

She laid a hand on his arm. "I don't know, I'm sorry."

The sound of a car door closing carried across the still air. They ducked behind the hedge and watched the blurry figure they knew to be Bergqvist, broad-shouldered and all in black, step out into the yard.

He went around to the rear passenger side, pulled the door open, and leaned inside. When he reappeared, he had Avril in his arms, limp and unresisting.

Ekström stiffened. "It's her."

Lundgren gave a grim nod. Even at this distance, they could make out the pale line of her hair as Bergqvist hauled her out of the SUV. He cradled her against his chest like a child, her head lolling, then hitched her higher in his arms and started toward the farmhouse. His boots crunched on the snow.

"Jesus," Lundgren whispered. His voice was hollow in the eerie silence between their cars. "What's he done to her?"

"She's drugged," Ekström whispered back, her pulse pounding in her ears. "I'm guessing it's Rohypnol."

They watched Bergqvist mount the porch steps. He adjusted Avril's weight, put a booted foot against the door, and kicked it open. The darkness inside swallowed him whole. Then the door closed, the sound sharp and final as it carried across the frozen yard.

For a moment, neither of them spoke.

Ekström glanced over at Lundgren. "What do we do?"

He exhaled hard. "We can't wait. He could... he could hurt her. We'll have to go in." He glanced at her. "You ready?"

She sucked in a breath.

No!

How could she ever be ready for this?

She swallowed and gave a swift nod. "Ja."

Their boots crunched softly in the rutted snow as they made their way up the track to the farmhouse. The wind whipped around the corners of the barn, making a low whistle. Ekström shivered.

They kept low, moving together toward the edge of the yard, where the barn and a sagging shed provided some cover. From there, they studied the farmhouse. Two windows at the front, a faint glow now showing from one of them.

"How do we do this?" Ekström whispered.

"Let's check out the back." They crept around, the wind blowing cold air into their faces. Ekström's eyes watered. She blinked the tears away and froze in place, staring at the vast expanse beyond the farmhouse.

"It's a lake."

The ice stretched as far as she could see, broken only by the dark reeds along the shoreline. The surface appeared to be solid, but she knew lakes like this could be treacherous, covered by pockets of thin ice and hidden currents beneath.

"A frozen lake." Lundgren's voice was low, edged with unease. He turned back to the house. "There's a back door."

She dragged her gaze away from the mirror-like surface gleaming in the light of the moon and focused on the task at hand.

"Is that a good thing?"

"It means you have to cover it while I go in the front. If he makes a run for it, you know what you have to do."

She gulped. This was it. This was what she'd trained for. Glancing down at her gun, she checked it and gave a nod. "How will I know when you're in?"

He snorted. "Don't worry, you'll know."

Feeling like she was about to have a heart attack, she watched Lundgren sneak off again, back to the front of the house and out of sight.

She was on her own now.

chapter
forty-five

EKSTRÖM PRESSED HER BACK TO THE ROUGH BOARDS OF THE shed, her fingers clenched so tightly around her pistol that her knuckles ached. Her breath misted in short, uneven bursts.

Calm down. Keep it steady.

She had to stay in control.

She adjusted her stance, her boots sinking a little into the packed snow. From here she had a clear view of the back door, a crooked rectangle with peeling paint and a drift of snow piled against the step. The farmhouse was dark in front of her, save for the faint line of light bleeding from a window on the far side.

Then it began.

From the front came the dull creak of hinges. A pause. A muffled shout:

"Polisen! Visa händerna!"

Police! Show your hands.

Boots pounded on wooden floorboards, followed by a crash as something overturned inside.

Ekström flinched. What was going on? Was Lundgren okay?

She wanted to run in, to help him, but she knew she had to stay where she was. If Bergqvist bolted, she had to be in position. She couldn't afford to screw this up.

Cold Mercy

The sounds of a struggle followed—heavy movements, the thud of bodies colliding, a grunt of pain. Her heart hammered against her ribs.

How could she stay out here when her partner might need her?

But her legs wouldn't move.

She froze, her training slipping away in a surge of panic. She had never faced anything like this before—never a real suspect, armed and dangerous, while a colleague fought to apprehend him, only meters away.

The gunshot shattered the night.

Ekström got such a fright that the pistol nearly slipped from her grip. Her ears rang with the echo of it.

No! What if Lundgren had been hit?

She forced her legs to move, pushing away from the shed and running toward the farmhouse. She was almost at the back door when it was flung open with a splintering crack.

Hans Bergqvist exploded through it, slamming into her and sending her flying. She landed on her backside on the snow.

"Go after him!" called Lundgren's voice from within, followed by a groan.

"Are you hurt?" she asked.

"Go! He's getting away."

She turned back to the fleeing fugitive, indecision paralyzing her. Lundgren was obviously injured, the Kriminalinspektör was in there too, but Bergqvist was escaping. He was fast, his coat flaring behind him, his boots biting into the hard ground.

In that split second, she made a decision. Getting to her knees, she raised her weapon, and yelled, "Stop, or I will fire!"

Bergqvist didn't halt. He bolted onto the frozen surface of the lake, a black shape cutting across the pale crust of ice.

Ekström sighted down the barrel. Her finger tightened around the trigger.

The crack of her shot echoed through the night air.

She missed. The ice spat up a few meters to his left. Her heart lurched.

Come on... You can do this.

Remember your training.

She adjusted, focused, and tried to still her breathing. When she was ready, she fired again.

This time the round hit. Bergqvist staggered, his stride faltering. His hand shot down to his thigh, gripping it, but he didn't stop.

He pushed on, limping now, dragging himself across the frozen ice. His figure grew smaller against the looming tree line beyond. If he made it across the lake, he'd get away.

Ekström surged to her feet and gave chase, the cold wind slashing her face. Her boots skidded on the slick surface as she followed the ragged line of his footprints. He was only twenty meters ahead now, his movements jerky, desperate.

"Kommissarie, please!" she cried again, though the whipping wind snatched her voice away.

He didn't stop.

She was closing the gap, her breath burning in her chest, when she heard an awful, splintering crack. Everybody who lived in these parts knew that sound. She skidded to a stop and froze, her hands out.

Bergqvist yelled out as the ice gave way beneath him. He seemed to be suspended in space for a brief moment, before the crack opened up and he dropped out of sight. Water splashed where he had been standing.

"No!" Ekström dropped to her stomach, sliding forward, pistol clattering against the ice.

Bergqvist clawed at the edges of the hole, his fingers scrabbling for purchase on the slick surface. The ice groaned and broke away in chunks beneath his grip. His face twisted in panic as his eyes met hers.

She stretched out one hand toward him. "Take my hand! Hold on!"

The shock, the fear registered on his face, then his weight shifted as his soaked coat dragged him down. His hands slipped, nails raking across the ice.

"Kommissarie!" she shouted again, her voice breaking. She crawled closer, her chest pressed flat to the ice, one arm outstretched.

But he was gone.

With a final heave, the lake swallowed him. Horrified, she watched as his shadow disappeared beneath the ice, before dissolving into nothingness.

Ekström lay there, unable to move, her arm stretched out towards the jagged hole. Her whole body trembled. From cold, from adrenaline, from shock.

She had failed to stop him.

Or maybe the lake had done it for her.

chapter
forty-six

KRISTER PUSHED THROUGH THE SLIDING GLASS DOORS OF the hospital just after nine o'clock that night. He'd made the drive from Stockholm in five hours and ten minutes and had blue-lighted it all the way.

A nurse at the reception desk looked him over as he approached. "Do you need to see a doctor?"

"Huh?"

"Your arm?"

He glanced down and saw blood dripping down the inside of his sleeve, staining his gray sweatshirt red. Shit, the wound had started bleeding again. He quickly slotted it back into the sling.

"I was shot, but it's just a graze. No, I'm here to see Kriminalinspektör Avril Dahl. She was admitted a few hours ago."

Her eyes widened. "We have an emergency doctor on call."

"What? No, it's fine. Which room is Avril Dahl in, please?"

She frowned and checked her screen. "Ward C, second floor. Room twelve. Follow the signs." He nodded and headed for the stairs.

"Please," she called after him. "Come back afterward to see the doctor."

Krister raised his good arm in response. Even though Ekström had phoned to say Avril was alive, drugged but stable, he wouldn't feel satisfied until he saw her with his own eyes.

The stairwell was quiet, his boots echoing against the linoleum. Upstairs, though, it was busier. A few patients waited in curtained bays. A nurse wheeled a cart past him, nodding politely before moving on.

He found Room 12 and paused at the door, forcing himself to breathe. Then he pushed it open and stepped inside.

Avril lay propped up against white pillows, her hair pale against the sheets. She looked smaller somehow, more fragile, but her eyes were open. They seemed dilated and unfocused, but she was alive. Relief crashed through him so strongly he had to grip the doorframe to steady himself. "Avril."

She turned, hearing his voice, and a smile flickered across her lips. "Krister?"

"I'm here." He crossed to the bed in two strides and took her hand. It was cool, but her fingers curled around his with surprising strength. The tension inside him eased, replaced by a deep, unshakable gratitude. Thank God she was all right.

Behind him, someone cleared their throat. Krister turned to see a young female police officer get to her feet. Her cheeks were flushed, and her uniform was wrinkled. She looked exhausted. "You must be Kriminalinspektör Jansson."

"And you must be Polisassistent Ekström."

He smiled, walked over, and shook her hand. "Thank you for what you did to save Avril."

She gave a small, almost self-conscious nod. "It was my job, and my pleasure. Thank you for your advice. You kept me calm when I... when I wasn't sure I could do it."

"You did good," Krister said simply.

Her face colored, the hint of a smile breaking through as she thanked him. "*Tack*."

Avril shifted, her voice rough. He got the impression she'd only just woken up. "What happened after he put me in the car? I thought..." She swallowed. "I thought I was going to die."

Krister reached out and squeezed her hand, but it was Ekström who answered.

"We tracked you to the farmhouse," she said, voice low as she approached the bedside. "Lundgren went in the front, but the Kommissarie—Oh, I mean Bergqvist—resisted arrest. Lundgren got shot, but it wasn't fatal. Bergqvist escaped out the back. I pursued him and shot him in the leg, but he kept going. Out across the ice." Her expression tightened, the recount coming in erratic bursts. "It gave way beneath him. He went under. I tried to save him... but he was gone."

Avril closed her eyes for a moment. "He's dead?"

"Yes," Ekström whispered. "It's over."

Avril looked at her. "Thank you. You saved my life."

"It was Lundgren too. Not just me."

"But you followed me. If you hadn't—" She broke off.

Krister scowled. That didn't bear thinking about. "The important thing is she did, and you're going to be fine."

Ekström's cheeks turned pink again. She dipped her head.

The door opened, and Krister turned to see a man he didn't recognize walk in. "I'm sorry to interrupt," he began, hat in hand.

"Who are you?" Krister asked, giving him a hard look.

"This is Jonas Bergqvist," Ekström said, by way of introduction. "The Kommissarie's brother."

Krister tensed. "What's he doing here?"

"He's okay." Avril squeezed Krister's hand and looked past him at the visitor. "Jonas, how are you?"

Krister could hear by her voice she didn't consider this guy a threat. He studied the killer's brother. He was younger, thinner, more worn-looking, but his gaze was steady.

"I heard what happened." Jonas took a tentative step forward. Krister shifted his position, moving closer to Avril. "The whole town knows already. My brother—" He shook his head. "I can't believe it was him all along."

"He set you up," Avril said. "He manipulated you. He sent you to that cabin where Freya had been murdered knowing we'd find her DNA and think it was you."

Jonas gave a sad nod. "I realize that now. I figured it out once I heard."

"He even planted that photograph in the study the night you were there, to remind you about the cabin. I bet he mentioned his snowmobile too?"

Jonas hung his head. "He did. Said he'd just fueled it up, ready to go because of the storm."

"The man was diabolical," Krister muttered.

"I'm sorry for what we put you through," Ekström interjected, offering a sympathetic smile.

"That's okay. You were just doing your jobs. I can see how it must have looked." He grinned at her. "Now that I'm sober."

Krister raised his eyebrows. There was so much he didn't know.

"What will you do now?" Avril asked.

"I'm leaving Sweden," Jonas said, squaring his shoulders. "I've decided to go to Barcelona. Start over. That's why I'm here. I wanted to thank you for what you did, and to wish you a quick recovery."

Avril smiled. "Thank you, Jonas. I think that's a great idea."

Krister supposed he couldn't stay in the small town now. Not after what his brother had done. Everyone would look at him, wonder if he was cut from the same cloth. It would be torture.

He gave a soft snort. "The best part, is there's no risk of hypothermia there."

Avril laughed, as did Ekström. Krister didn't understand the reference, but he was pleased everyone was happy.

Jonas was about to leave when another officer walked in. Once again, Ekström made the introductions.

"This is Polisassistent Lundgren," she said, as the man with his side bandaged turned to Krister. "Lundgren, this is Kriminalinspektör Krister Jansson from Stockholm."

Krister shook the young officer's hand. "Thank you, for everything."

"Hey, that's my job," Avril said weakly.

Lundgren went over to her. "I'm just glad we got to you in time."

Krister drew in a silent breath. It irked him that he couldn't have gotten to her sooner. Luckily, she'd had these two looking out for her.

"I'm sorry my brother shot you," Jonas said, studying Lundgren's wound. "Does it hurt?"

He cringed. "Ja, but it wasn't your fault."

"I know, but still... I know you two were close."

Lundgren closed his eyes for a moment. Krister didn't know what the story was, but he could tell the man had something on his chest.

"What I don't understand is how he did all that for my family—for me—yet murdered all those women. It doesn't make any sense."

Jonas shook his head. "Hans always had a dark side. Even when we were kids. He bullied me, but in front of our parents he was the perfect big brother. Once, he hit his girlfriend. I saw her crying afterward, but he threatened her, so she never told. On the surface, he was respectable and upstanding. But underneath, he was always... a bad apple."

Lundgren stared at him. "But he put me through college."

"That was for him," Jonas said bitterly. "He liked being respected. Liked people thinking he was generous. It was never for you. It was for what people saw."

Krister could see how much that upset the young officer. Lundgren looked like he was about to burst into tears.

Avril spoke then, her voice calm but firm. "It doesn't matter why, Lundgren. At least something good came from a bad situation. You got your qualification and became a police officer. A good one. Besides, we'll never know for sure. Maybe he really did want to help. People can be complicated. Even killers."

The room fell quiet.

A nurse entered, brisk and efficient. "Kriminalinspektör Dahl? The blood tests came back and everything looks okay. The doctor says you can be discharged now."

"That's great news." Krister turned to her. "Come on. Let's get you out of here."

They said goodbye to Jonas, who actually gave Avril a gentle hug. That was a first for a former suspect. Krister smiled at the shocked look on her face. Avril didn't really go in for hugs.

Next came Ekström, another hug. "Thank you for everything, Kriminalinspektör."

"It's me who should be thanking you," Avril said awkwardly.

Lundgren shook her hand. "I'm sorry I gave you such a hard time in the beginning," he said gruffly.

She shrugged. "Forget about it. You had your reasons."

He grunted. "They seem stupid now."

"He fooled us all, Lundgren," she said, glancing at Krister. He nodded to back her up. "It wasn't just you."

"Thanks, that helps."

"I'll make sure he remembers that," Ekström said, with a parting smile.

Krister had had enough. He wanted to get Avril home, back to the guesthouse, so she could rest. Her words were still slightly slurred, and he could tell by the way she squinted her eyes that she had a headache.

Avril got dressed, pulling on her clothes and sitting down to fasten her shoes.

"Let's go," he said, once she was ready, putting a protective arm around her shoulders.

For once, she didn't argue. She even smiled at him as he led her to the elevator. "Thanks, Krister," she said softly. "I can't believe you drove all the way here. Again."

He snorted. "I wouldn't have to if you didn't keep getting into trouble."

She gave a soft chuckle. "I'll try to remember that, although I quite like having you around."

A warmth flooded through him, and he lowered his head and kissed her softly on the forehead.

chapter
forty-seven

AVRIL STOOD IN SUNDSTRÖM'S OFFICE IN THE SERIOUS Crimes Division, facing his desk. She'd just given him a full run-down of the events of the last few days. He'd read her report but had wanted to hear it in her own words—and, as he'd said, find out how she was doing.

She and Krister hadn't lingered in Norrdal longer than necessary. After she'd been discharged from the hospital, they'd spent one more night at the guesthouse during which she'd slept for eight solid hours, before driving back to Stockholm the very next day.

Avril had never been so pleased to get home in her life.

Home.

It was a strange concept. She'd never felt at home anywhere before, not since her mother had died when she was little. But this time it was different—like she was meant to be here. For now, anyway.

"There is going to be an investigation," Sundström said, his expression grim. "The Special Investigations Division are looking into how Bergqvist could be allowed to get away with this for so long."

"People trust those in authority," she said simply. "Maybe they shouldn't, but in a small town like that, they do." She thought about Pastor Henrik, a controlling, abusive husband. Ingrid should leave him, but she probably wouldn't. Bergqvist was able to prey on young women all over the north of the country, unchecked, because he was the

Kommissarie. "We like to believe that people who hold those positions are who they claim to be."

He grunted. "Except in this case, it was the perfect cover. Bergqvist was anything but trustworthy."

Avril nodded. "It helped that he knew how the system worked and was able to manipulate it. He pointed the finger at his brother, planted evidence, directed us to the cabin." She shook her head. "It was diabolical, really."

"He got what he deserved," Sundström said, gruffly.

He'd died like so many of his victims. In the ice. Still, she couldn't dredge up much sympathy for Bergqvist. He'd have killed her and disposed of her body, just like he'd done to Lara, given the chance. She shuddered at the thought.

"You okay to come back to work?" Sundström asked her.

She nodded. "Yes, I want to." The last thing she needed was to be sitting around at home doing nothing. It helped to keep busy.

"You can take some time, if you need it." He frowned at her. "You went straight into this case after dealing with those eco-terrorists, and Odin is still out there. Are you sure—"

"I'm fine," she insisted, cutting him off. Odin was no threat to her at present. One day he might try to get revenge, but it wouldn't be now. The heat was still on him, the trial of his disciples ongoing.

"Okay, good, because we've got this gangland case that's escalating. Two rival gangs, highly organized, causing havoc on our streets."

"I heard," she said.

He smoothed a hand over his thinning hair. "As it stands, I don't know if we've got capacity to handle it. I might have to hand it over to the National Task Force, and I really don't want to do that. Not after the work Krister and his team have put in."

The NTF would sweep in, and at the end of it, they'd take all the credit. It had happened before. Not to her, but in the department.

"If you're looking for more detectives, I do happen to know someone," she said, slowly.

He glanced up. "Oh, yeah? Who?"

"Polisassistent Maja Ekström."

"Ekström? From Norrdal?"

Avril nodded. "She's a good police officer. A genius at research and digging into suspects. We could really use someone like her in the department."

"And she'd relocate?"

"You could ask her. I don't think she has anything keeping her there." Lundgren had a young family, and with Bergqvist gone, he'd be in charge of Norrdal Polisstation until they found a replacement. Ekström would remain a polisassistent, however, unless she transferred out.

"She's the one who came after you when Bergqvist—"

Avril nodded. She didn't want to revisit that. "She did. It was a brave thing to do. She showed a great deal of courage."

He grunted. "Okay, I'll make a call."

Avril smiled. It would be a great career move for Ekström. She hoped she would consider it.

"Thank you, sir."

He nodded. "Okay, then. I'm assigning you to this gangland case. Krister needs all the help he can get. From today, you're back on official duties."

Avril left his office and returned to the squad room. Krister looked up as she walked over to where he was standing. She met his gaze and gave a pleased nod.

He broke into a wide grin. "Good to have you back on the team, Kriminalinspektör."

A warm feeling spread over her. "It's good to be back."

Avril Dahl's story continues soon in *Cold Witness*... Grab your copy here: Cold Witness
https://a.co/d/4iy5Q2I

Join the L.T. Ryan reader family & receive a free copy of the Rachel Hatch story, *Fractured*. Click the link below to get started:
https://ltryan.com/rachel-hatch-newsletter-signup-1

also by l.t. ryan

Find All of L.T. Ryan's Books on Amazon Today!

The Jack Noble Series
The Recruit (free)
The First Deception (Prequel 1)
Noble Beginnings
A Deadly Distance
Ripple Effect (Bear Logan)
Thin Line
Noble Intentions
When Dead in Greece
Noble Retribution
Noble Betrayal
Never Go Home
Beyond Betrayal (Clarissa Abbot)
Noble Judgment
Never Cry Mercy

Deadline

End Game

Noble Ultimatum

Noble Legend

Noble Revenge

Never Look Back

Bear Logan Series

Ripple Effect

Blowback

Take Down

Deep State

Bear & Mandy Logan Series

Close to Home

Under the Surface

The Last Stop

Over the Edge

Between the Lies

Caught in the Web

The Marked Daughter

Beneath the Frozen Sky

Rachel Hatch Series

Drift

Downburst

Fever Burn

Smoke Signal

Firewalk

Whitewater

Aftershock

Whirlwind

Tsunami

Fastrope

Sidewinder

Redaction

Mirage

Faultline

Switchback

Mitch Tanner Series

The Depth of Darkness

Into The Darkness

Deliver Us From Darkness

Cassie Quinn Series

Path of Bones

Whisper of Bones

Symphony of Bones

Etched in Shadow

Concealed in Shadow

Betrayed in Shadow

Born from Ashes

Return to Ashes

Risen from Ashes

Into the Light

Blake Brier Series

Unmasked

Unleashed

Uncharted

Drawpoint

Contrail

Detachment

Clear

Quarry

Dalton Savage Series

Savage Grounds

Scorched Earth

Cold Sky

The Frost Killer

Crimson Moon

Dust Devil

Savage Season

Maddie Castle Series

The Handler

Tracking Justice

Hunting Grounds

Vanished Trails

Smoldering Lies

Field of Bones

Beneath the Grove

Disappearing Act

Affliction Z Series

Affliction Z: Patient Zero

Affliction Z: Abandoned Hope

Affliction Z: Descended in Blood

Affliction Z : Fractured Part 1

Affliction Z: Fractured Part 2 (Coming Soon)

Alex Hayes Series

Trial By Fire (Prequel)

Fractured Verdict

11th Hour Witness

Buried Testimony

The Bishop's Recusal

The Silent Gavel

Stella LaRosa Series

Black Rose

Red Ink

Black Gold

White Lies

Silver Bullet

Avril Dahl Series

Cold Reckoning

Cold Legacy

Cold Mercy

Cold Witness

Savannah Shadows Series

Echoes of Guilt

The Silence Before

Dead Air

Receive a free copy of The Recruit. Visit:

https://ltryan.com/jack-noble-newsletter-signup-1

avril dahl series

Cold Reckoning
Cold Legacy
Cold Mercy
Cold Witness

about the author

L.T. Ryan is a *USA Today* and international bestselling author. The new age of publishing offered L.T. the opportunity to blend his passions for creating, marketing, and technology to reach audiences with his popular Jack Noble series.

Living in central Virginia with his wife, the youngest of his three daughters, and their three dogs, L.T. enjoys staring out his window at the trees and mountains while he should be writing, as well as reading, hiking, running, and playing with gadgets. See what he's up to at http://ltryan.com.

Social Medial Links:

- Facebook (L.T. Ryan): https://www.facebook.com/LTRyanAuthor
- Facebook (Jack Noble Page): https://www.facebook.com/JackNobleBooks/
- Twitter: https://twitter.com/LTRyanWrites
- Goodreads: http://www.goodreads.com/author/show/6151659.L_T_Ryan

---

Biba Pearce is a crime writer and author of the Kenzie Gilmore, Dalton Savage and DCI Rob Miller series. Her books have been shortlisted for the Feathered Quill and the CWA Debut Dagger awards, and The Marlow Murders was voted best crime fiction book in the Indie Excellence Book Awards.

Biba lives in leafy Surrey with her family and when she isn't writing, can be found walking along the Thames River path - near to where many of her books are set - or rambling through the countryside.

Download a FREE Kenzie Gilmore prequel novella at her website bibapearce.com.

Made in the USA
Middletown, DE
22 October 2025